PRAISE FOR
BODY MASTER

"I devoured *Body Master* like really good chocolate: in big, happy chomps. A tough yet sympathetic heroine locks horns with a mysterious, sexy hero—oooh, yum! Barry's skillfully structured story delivers all kinds of delicious pleasures—and zero calories. What more could a girl want?"   —Angela Knight, *New York Times* bestselling author

"In this novel, the action is nonstop and the sexual tension between Max and Seneca sizzles. Barry has created a butt-kicking yet vulnerable heroine and a story that keeps readers going until the last page."
—*Publishers Weekly*

"Barry returns with a near-future, action-packed tale of extraterrestrials that also explores troubling social unrest. Through her protagonists, Barry explores the gritty reality of a reluctant alien invasion and the resulting fallout. These star-crossed lovers have sparks aplenty and baggage galore. Barry's world just begs for future exploration, so readers can expect to take this thrill ride once again."   —*RT Book Reviews*

"Action, adventure, and romance abound in *Body Master*. C. J. Barry weaves together an intriguing tale that captures the reader's imagination from the first page. Pick up your copy and see for yourself."
—*Romance Reviews Today*

"The high-stakes story line is full of action and danger. The world she has created has plenty of intricacy, and enough hidden agendas and fully realized characters to fuel the series for some time to come."
—*Fresh Fiction*

PRAISE FOR THE NOVELS OF C. J. BARRY

"Sexy, intriguing, and a pure delight to read."
—Catherine Spangler, national bestselling author

BODY THIEF

C. J. BARRY

BERKLEY SENSATION, NEW YORK

THE BERKLEY PUBLISHING GROUP
Published by the Penguin Group
Penguin Group (USA) Inc.
375 Hudson Street, New York, New York 10014, USA
Penguin Group (Canada), 90 Eglinton Avenue East, Suite 700, Toronto, Ontario M4P 2Y3, Canada
(a division of Pearson Penguin Canada Inc.)
Penguin Books Ltd., 80 Strand, London WC2R 0RL, England
Penguin Group Ireland, 25 St. Stephen's Green, Dublin 2, Ireland (a division of Penguin Books Ltd.)
Penguin Group (Australia), 250 Camberwell Road, Camberwell, Victoria 3124, Australia
(a division of Pearson Australia Group Pty. Ltd.)
Penguin Books India Pvt. Ltd., 11 Community Centre, Panchsheel Park, New Delhi—110 017, India
Penguin Group (NZ), 67 Apollo Drive, Rosedale, Auckland 0632, New Zealand
(a division of Pearson New Zealand Ltd.)
Penguin Books (South Africa) (Pty.) Ltd., 24 Sturdee Avenue, Rosebank, Johannesburg 2196,
South Africa

Penguin Books Ltd., Registered Offices: 80 Strand, London WC2R 0RL, England

This book is an original publication of The Berkley Publishing Group.

Copyright © 2011 by C. J. Barry.
Cover illustration by Phil Heffernan.
Cover design by George Long.
Interior text design by Tiffany Estreicher.

PRINTING HISTORY
Berkley Sensation trade paperback edition / November 2011

Library of Congress Cataloging-in-Publication Data

Barry, C. J.
    Body thief / C.J. Barry.—Berkley sensation trade paperback ed.
        p.   cm.
    ISBN: 978-0-425-24331-2
    1. Shapeshifting—Fiction. 2. New York (N.Y.)—Fiction. I. Title.
    PS3602.A777549B63   2011
    813'.6—dc22   2011030539

PRINTED IN THE UNITED STATES OF AMERICA

10 9 8 7 6 5 4 3 2 1

This book is dedicated to my grandfather, Elwood Dishaw, who taught me the power of quiet wisdom.

ACKNOWLEDGMENTS

I'd like to thank the many fine people who made this book possible. My terrific agent, Robert Brown, for believing in me no matter how crazy the pitch sounds. My awesome editor, Kate Seaver, and the good folks at Berkley Sensation for pulling it all together. My beta-readers, Patti and Jill, who get the first ugly cut and still talk to me. My family, siblings, and parents who support me without question. And of course, every reader who takes my book to heart. Thank you.

Please visit me online at www.cjbarry.com. I'd love to hear from you.

CHAPTER
ONE

"Next time I use the valet service," Cam muttered to herself as she dragged her suitcase to her car on the fourth level of the self-parking garage. The Atlantic City morning sun gleamed across car hoods and the smooth concrete in the open garage. It was bright and quiet, and a long frickin' way from the hotel and casino.

It was her own fault. She should have opted for valet parking, but then again, she *was* trying to be a normal human being. Blending in with the locals was an important part of her modus operandi. Swoop in, make tons of money off the casinos, and sneak out. It'd worked for the past year, and unless proven otherwise, she was sticking with it.

She finally reached her Honda Accord and popped the trunk. As she threw her suitcase in the back, a prickle of foreboding spread across her body. In a split second, her senses heightened. Heavy footsteps shuffled behind her. She concentrated on the movements. Pants legs brushed together; three, maybe four of them, quiet by human standards and moving fast. Her nose picked up aftershave and sweat, definitely human males.

Maybe they were here for her, maybe not. She wasn't taking any chances. Slowly, she bent over her suitcase and reached inside the outer pocket for her Glock 17 9mm. It was small, but a gun was a gun in close quarters. She pretended to look for something in the trunk and tilted her head just enough to pick them up in her peripheral vision.

Three men, one in front wearing a gray suit, two behind in military clothes and carrying assault rifles. Yup, they were definitely here for her.

She had about one second to weigh her options—make a run for it, or stand and fight. Cam smiled; she'd never been one to run. After all, there were only three of them. She'd bet on those odds any day.

She stood up, slipping the Glock into the back of her jeans as she turned around to face them. Then she tried to appear as innocent and naïve as possible for her.

The gray suit stopped ten feet away, and she inhaled a quick breath when she met his eyes for the first time in bright daylight. Deep brown, confident, and serious. Nice, aside from the predatory gleam. He appeared to be about thirty. Just from the way he moved, she could tell he could handle himself well in a fight. Military-trained, perhaps. The two other men regarded her with dutiful intensity. She could take them, but the suit was different from your run-of-the-mill human, which intrigued her. Could be an exciting day after all.

He said, "I'm Special Agent Griffin Mercer working for the local extraterrestrial law enforcement agency."

Her pulse quickened. XCEL agents. Shapeshifter hunters. That explained all the guns. "Exciting" just jumped to "dangerous."

"You're under arrest," he added firmly.

"I'm sorry, I think you have the wrong person," she blurted, her eyes widening in horror. It was a damn fine acting job, if she did say so herself.

While Cam talked, she glanced around the parking garage for casino security or guests that could provide an easy diversion. She noticed the black van parked two spots down. That's how they'd snuck up on her. Her hopes for any diversions faded. They'd planned this, and probably shut down the entire garage. Plus she was alone, and it was daylight. Daylight was a problem for a shapeshifter.

Agent Mercer said, "Today, you're Camille Solomon. Alien shapeshifter, twenty-eight years old, five feet five inches tall, no permanent residence, fake identity, you make your money by cheating casinos, and there's a gun tucked in the small of your back." Then he smiled like the devil. "How am I doing?"

Not bad, she conceded. "I'm five-six."

"I'll note that in your file," he said, and his smile vanished. "Throw the gun in the trunk please."

Behind him, the van had pulled up, and every molecule in her body aligned for battle. She could see a driver and a passenger who got out and opened the back doors. That made five. The odds were stacking against her fast.

"What am I under arrest for?" she said, dropping the innocent act. "Being different?"

A hint of irritation crossed his features, ever so slightly, but she saw it. Ugh, he was one of *those* XCEL agents. The ones who hated shapeshifters with a vengeance and noble intent. She despised noble intent. It was highly overrated.

He replied, "Cheating the casino. Federal offense."

She laughed at the irony. "Right, like the casino doesn't cheat anyone."

"They report the odds. It's all legal and everything," he said. "Gun in the trunk."

Now she was getting pissed. Damn, how had she tipped them off? She was very good at cheating. Like, *the best*. On the other hand, it didn't matter how they knew, and she really needed to focus. It was time to get this show on the road. She had a dinner date with her father in SOHO tonight.

"Of course," she said. "Anything for XCEL."

Mercer's eyebrows raised a fraction, but he didn't respond to her acknowledgment of his agency. She knew all about XCEL and their weapons against Shifters—disrupters for localized paralysis, UVC grenades that mimicked the sun's rays to prevent shapeshifter transformations, and tranquilizers that no one ever woke up from.

Fortunately, she didn't see any of those weapons, just assault rifles. And that was because they thought those would be enough to capture her. A human form was a human form, and she'd suffer the same damage as any human would. Shifters couldn't shift to their native, dangerous forms in daylight.

Boy, were they ever in for a surprise.

Every rifle pointed at her as she reached around and tugged the Glock out of her jeans. She held it out in front of her with two fingers on the gun butt.

"You want it," she said to Mercer. "Come and get it."

His eyes narrowed dangerously. "Trunk. Please."

"Here," she said. *"Please."*

"Trunk," he repeated, more tightly this time. "We don't want to hurt you."

She smiled. As if that could happen. "Have it your way."

Cam hurled the gun against the open trunk top with all her might, which, considering she was a shapeshifter, was pretty mighty. It bounced hard off the metal and fired indiscriminately.

Every man ducked, which gave her the split second she needed to shift into Primary form. A collective gasp arose once she'd transformed.

Surprise, she thought, reveling in the look of disbelief on their faces.

And then everything moved really fast. Someone shot at her. She thinned her molecular structure, and the bullets passed through harmlessly. Her form remained vaporous but whole, prepared for anything else they might throw at her.

"Don't shoot!" Mercer yelled. "We want her alive!"

His orders made her only more determined. She thinned her structure even more and "popped" through the thick air, re-forming in front of the men with the rifles. She grabbed both their rifles and jammed the butts to their heads, knocking them out in tandem.

Someone screamed, "Get the disrupter!"

She popped to the van and wrenched an agent out of the back by his belt, tossing him across the garage concrete floor. He rolled a few times, struck a support column, and didn't move. The driver came around the corner with a disrupter, and she kicked it out of his hands. It hit the ceiling and shattered into pieces.

Then he had the nerve to get all pissy and reach into his jacket for a gun. She grabbed his forearm and broke it with a loud snap.

He yelled, dropped to his knees, and cradled his arm, and she dropkicked him in the face. He flipped backward and landed ten feet away.

Then Cam spun around to find Mercer standing behind her, holding the disrupter, looking stoic and dark. Everyone else was down, and she didn't see or hear reinforcements. Too bad for them.

"That's quite a trick you have," he said. "Shifting in daylight."

She took a step toward him, wary of the disrupter. It wouldn't slow her down for long, but it *would* hurt like hell. "I find it comes in handy when someone tries to kill me."

"We just want to talk to you."

She laughed. "Right. And the rifles and disrupter are, what, conversation pieces?"

He stared her down, which was pretty unusual. A normal, sane human would have been afraid. He definitely wasn't, and it worried her just a little.

He said, "I know you don't trust us—"

"Why would I?" she snapped. "XCEL has spent the last two years hunting us, freezing us, killing us, and moving the lucky ones to prisons."

"They aren't prisons," he said. "They're safe zones."

That did it. The disrupter would hurt for a moment, but it would totally be worth it to kick his ass. "When you lock someone up and don't let them leave, that's a prison. Even for humans."

"You're not human," he said, challenge in his eyes.

Her temper flared. Cam popped a split second before he dropped the rifle. When she re-formed beside him, he gripped her arm. Shocked by his speed and strength, she froze. How did he know where she was going to re-form?

She tried to strike him, but her arms wouldn't move. In fact, nothing would move. She stared at him in disbelief and panic. What was happening to her?

"I have a few surprises of my own," he said softly.

Then he jabbed a tranquilizer dart into her shoulder. The tranquilizer swamped her senses, and she couldn't do anything to fight it. Her body simply wouldn't respond, and it occurred to her that he was the reason.

Just before she blacked out, she heard him say, "So sorry."

◆◆◆

Griffin stood on the safe side of a bulletproof, shatterproof, Shifter-proof glass wall and watched his captive sleep off the tranquilizer. She hadn't moved since they dumped her on the bed in the holding cell two hours ago.

Her Primary form was a charcoal black humanoid-like body that was just female enough to be interesting. Her skin was smooth and tough, like a formfitting bodysuit. Her face was more delicately featured than the male Shifters he'd seen, her body leaner, and her frame tall and leggy. In Primary form, shapeshifters were like blank canvases. All they needed was a little bit of DNA to replicate any human they wanted, and they didn't care what they did as that human. Who they hurt. Who or what they ruined. They were opportunists. Like vultures, only bigger.

The door behind him flung open.

"For Christ's sake, what were you thinking?" Griffin's boss yelled loud enough to shake the long glass. "You think tranquilizing her is going to help our cause? Did you not understand your orders?"

Griffin didn't look at Director Roger Harding. His miserable mug was forever etched in Griffin's mind as it was. "I understood them."

His boss stood next to him, his cologne sucking up all the good oxygen. He wore a black suit, as always, along with a black tie and black shoes to go with his black personality.

"Those orders came from the president. Do you want to be the one who tells him that our one chance of protecting this city was blown because you couldn't apprehend a lone shapeshifter without incident?"

Technically, the orders came from a special senate committee, but Harding liked to think he was bigger than that. Griffin responded calmly, "No, sir, I wouldn't."

"Then what was the problem?" Harding said, his voice getting higher by the minute.

If Griffin were at all lucky, Harding would have a heart attack right then and there. He waited, but it didn't happen. Maybe next time. Griffin was, after all, a very patient man. It had been a hard lesson to learn, but he'd learned it very well.

"We didn't have a choice. She shifted."

Harding frowned. "You were supposed to prevent that from happening. You blew the operation—"

"She shifted in broad daylight," Griffin amended.

Then Harding put his hands on his hips. "That's crap. Shifters can't do that."

"*She* can. Ask the team. I don't know how, but she converted completely in a millisecond. All her abilities were full strength. It didn't slow her down at all."

"Christ, what next with these damn things?" Harding said,

running his hand through his hair. He stared at her through the glass. "Has anyone else reported that ability?"

"No," Griffin said. "Obviously, she's more special than we originally thought."

Harding frowned deeply. "Well, that's just ducky. But we can't force her to work with us, and this was not a good takedown."

Griffin took offense to that but didn't say so. The fact was, the takedown had gone as well as it could have. Everyone survived. Camille Solomon had been captured unharmed and was recovering nicely. And no one outside of XCEL even knew it had happened. It couldn't have gone better. Except the part where he tranquilized her.

Details.

Harding asked, "How do you intend to guarantee her cooperation *now*?"

"We have plenty of motivation for her."

"Those motivations better be bulletproof, Mercer," Harding muttered.

They were. Griffin hadn't spent the last two months tracking her for nothing. He'd memorized her file, watched her on video, tailed her movements, and documented every single one of her identities. He knew more about her than she probably knew about herself.

Harding asked, "You're positive that you can handle her? If she gets off your leash and does something stupid, it's my head that will roll."

Griffin could always count on Harding to cover his own ass. "I'm positive."

"What, are you going to use your Indian voodoo to track her?"

Griffin felt the rush of anger through his bones. Harding hated him because he was special, and would use anything to attack Griffin's self-confidence, including his half-Navajo heritage. Tough shit for Harding. Griffin had never put much faith in his heritage. "If I have to."

For a moment, Harding just stood there staring at him, and Griffin knew he was considering putting another agent on this case. Someone who didn't drink too much, who followed orders to the letter, and who would kiss his uptight ass. Well, screw that. Griffin wasn't the perfect agent, but he was for this case. Besides, his assignment had come from the above Harding's big head, and that's really why Harding hated him.

"Let me know when she wakes up," Harding said as he turned to leave.

Right after I talk to her. Griffin replied, "Yes, sir."

Cam awoke with a start.

I'm alive. It surprised her to the core.

Then she registered white lights, white square room, two doors, and wall made of dark glass. She was lying on a bed in Shifter form. It was silent, except for her heartbeat, which was now pounding at a rapidly growing clip. Alive, yes, but in what kind of trouble?

She felt the UVC light emanating from the sealed lights in the ceiling. Shifter prison, the UVC lights intended to prevent transformations. So much for "talking." Humans were so full of crap. It was same everywhere she went on this frickin' planet— you couldn't trust any of them.

She sat up and winced at the crushing headache that accompanied the move. Damn tranquilizer. Damn XCEL agent. What was his name? Mercer? Agent Mercer. He was at the top of her hit list.

Then she remembered how he had grabbed her arm and locked up all her shifting abilities. Hell, all her human abilities too. She hadn't been able to move, and that had never happened to her before. There weren't weapons here, or on the last planet Shifters had settled, that could do what he did. God, what if XCEL had managed to develop some kind of agent that actually affected Shifters?

"Terrific," she murmured. Just when she thought it was safe to beat up humans.

Now to test if the immobilization was permanent or temporary. She groaned as she got to her feet and made a controlled shift to her last human form. Her mind and body seemed alright, aside from the throbbing headache that stayed with the transformation. All systems go.

Now it was time to find out just how much trouble she was in.

Cam circled the room and checked both doors—one was locked and the other led to a small bathroom where everything was built into the walls. A tiny mirror over the sink, a toilet, and a shower. None of it could be used to break out of here. She splashed cool water on her face and gazed in the mirror. Her blue eyes were still a little puffy from the tranquilizer. The red in her long auburn hair glowed in the artificial light. Her ivory skin was unharmed.

They had wanted her alive, but why? XCEL wasn't exactly known for their compassion or mercy toward her kind. Hundreds of Shifters had simply vanished after being captured by them. Why hadn't she?

Although, maybe she *was* vanished, and she just didn't know it yet.

"Hell," her reflection said back to her.

Cam exited the bathroom and walked over to the dark mirrored wall. The glass was thick and damn strong, no doubt. They would certainly have her under surveillance twenty-four/seven in here. She flipped them the bird and smiled. Two seconds later, a light went on on the other side of the glass.

Mercer stood right in front of her. He was still wearing the same clothes, so she hadn't been unconscious that long. Short black hair brushed his white shirt. He was a good six feet tall, broad and solidly built. He seemed older under the fluorescent lights, but his skin was smooth and tanned, his forehead wide, nose straight, jaw angled. He had mean, rugged, almost exotic good looks. Average, really. Except for his eyes. They were dark brown, nearly black, and it felt like they could see right into her. Hard, seasoned, and cynical. She expected no less.

And his hands, of course, which housed the ability to freeze Shifters.

"That's not very ladylike," he said, putting his hands in his pockets.

"Well, you're no gentleman either," she snapped as she studied the shallow room behind him. The back wall was lined with a wide flat screen, electronic equipment, and cameras. Some pretty high-tech cell she had here. She was beginning to think she should have run.

Cam crossed her arms. "What do you want with me?"

He hesitated for a moment before saying, "We need your help. There is a national security issue that requires your . . . skills."

She felt her mouth drop open. *Unreal.* Not only were humans full of crap, they were unbelievably arrogant. "You grabbed me, knocked me out, and locked me in here because you need my help?"

He shrugged casually. "I said I was sorry."

It wouldn't do to try to break the glass to kill him. She'd just hurt herself. "Apology accepted. No, I won't help you. Now let me go."

He nodded a few times, absorbing her rejection with little expression. "There is the small matter of you cheating casinos."

She wouldn't bite. "I'm lucky at craps, what can I say?"

"We have you on tape over the past few months. At The Venetian, Golden Nugget, the Bellagio, Harrah's, Tropicana, Foxwoods." He paused, knowingly. "Should I continue?"

She was stunned. That was *impossible.* They couldn't have caught her at all those places. She hadn't *been* Camille Solomon in all those places. She'd played those casinos in other human forms with different names. He couldn't know she was the same person. He was lying; he had to be.

"Prove it," she said, calling his bluff.

Without a word, Mercer walked over to the big screen and picked up a remote control. Seconds later, there she was at the Bellagio craps table, as a blond-haired woman. Then The Venetian as a brunette. Each casino and each security camera showed her standing at the tables. She shook her head. *How?*

"That's you," he said walking back to her. "In every shot."

She eyed him, and dread filled her.

He could see shapeshifters.

She'd heard of them, feared them. They called them Scouts, the few humans who were capable of identifying Shifters while in human form. Of course, Shifters could do that, but humans who could were few and far between. Even fewer worked for XCEL.

"I can get a second opinion if you'd like," he added, looking far too smug. "It might take a few months though."

Bastard. "I want a lawyer."

He shook his head. "National security trumps lawyer."

Of course it did. "I'll worry about national security as soon as your government recognizes Shifters as legal citizens with legal rights. No lawyer, no cooperation."

Emotion flashed in his eyes, and his expression turned harder. "And what have you done to earn that right?"

She blinked. "Since when do sanctioned beings *not* have that right? Hell, all you have to do is be born here. What the hell kind of initiation fee is that?"

He didn't answer that, but it was clear by his expression that she'd struck some kind of nerve. She was getting a really bad feeling this would not go well for her.

Then he turned and pointed the remote at the TV again. The image changed to another white room much like hers. An older man sat on a bed, resting his head in his hands, but she still recognized him. Shock turned to dismay, and then to fury. It took every ounce of self-control not to throw herself at the glass to get to Mercer.

So much for dinner reservations in SOHO. Neither she nor her father was going to make it. Cam fought to keep her voice even. "Is he here? Is he okay?"

Mercer replied, "Yes, and yes."

Thank God. "Why?" she asked, gritting her teeth.

"He's your accomplice. We found him in every security shot with you at the casinos. You worked as a team. You handled the dice, and he collected the winnings. That's a solid three to five years of prison time for each of you."

She clenched her fists as she kept her eyes glued to the only person she cared about. Dewey Solomon didn't *have* three to five years. He might not even have three to five months. It was time to throw in the towel and whatever pride she had left. "It was my fault, my idea. I forced him to go along with me. I threatened to hurt him if he didn't. Lock me up forever, I don't care. Just let him go."

Mercer seemed to take his time replying. "You work with us, with me, and we'll clear all charges against both of you."

She turned to glare at him. That explained a lot. She'd been set up; she should have figured it out sooner. They were using her, blackmailing her, and she had no choice. Her father was sick. Maybe they knew that, maybe they didn't. She couldn't be sure. Either way, it didn't matter. She needed to get her father out of here as soon as possible.

It took a lot more effort to formulate a plan that didn't include kicking someone's ass, but she finally settled on cooperation. As much as she hated being used, she'd give them what they wanted. But she was going to make damn sure that she got something in return.

Somewhere during the plotting, it occurred to her just how big this was. The time and effort they'd put in this whole capture wasn't normal. They'd targeted her specially, and she knew why. She could do things other Shifters couldn't.

First off, she was female, which was highly prized. There were literally a handful of surviving female Shifters. She could hold myriad human forms, which was also unusual. Most Shifters could only handle one or two additional forms. And to top it all off, she'd shown them firsthand that she was capable of shifting in daylight, which she now regretted. All of those characteristics made her valuable to XCEL. She wasn't afraid of much, but that scared her.

"We'll discuss the details of the operation first thing tomorrow morning," he said. "Get some sleep."

Cam glared into his dark eyes with every bit of animosity she felt. He didn't ask her if she was in. He knew she was trapped, and he was the trapper. *Bastard.* "Whatever happened to justice for all?"

"If you're looking for justice, you came to the wrong planet," he replied calmly, and he shut off the lights, turning the glass to black.

◆ ◆ ◆

That could have gone better, Griffin admitted to himself. She was willful and intelligent, and the only reason she'd stayed in control was to save her accomplice. Which was good for Griffin, because otherwise, he'd have bigger problems.

"You want a refill?" Lyle, the bartender, asked him over the Celtic music playing in the background.

It was ten P.M., and the bar was sprinkled with an odd assortment of executives and lovers and diners tucked into the corners. It was Lyle's place, and Griffin liked it. The walls were covered with everything Irish—flags, banners, signs, you name it. It wasn't really an Irish pub any longer. Lyle just never bothered to redecorate when he bought it.

"Sure," Griffin told his friend, and Lyle reached for the scotch. He poured Griffin a double and put the bottle back on the shelf. Lyle was tall and rail thin, with a long face and short red hair. His eyes were a little too close together, and a scruff of a beard hugged his chin. He leaned both his boney elbows on the bar in front of Griffin.

"Rough day?" Lyle asked.

Griffin wanted to laugh. Every day was a rough day. The best parts were when he was in danger or otherwise occupied by his work. The worst parts were when he came home to a quiet, cold, dark apartment. Probably explained why he spent so much time here.

"Got my Shifter," he told Lyle, keeping his voice low.

Lyle's eyes widened. "No." He checked to see if anyone was listening. "The female?"

Griffin nodded, and Lyle blew out a long breath that smelled of cigarettes. "I gotta say, I haven't ever seen a female Shifter."

"They look like the males, only smaller," Griffin said. "And they smell better."

Lyle laughed, a familiar sound. Lyle laughed at everything, even when it wasn't that funny. It made Lyle a good bartender, and one of Griffin's few friends. The fact that Lyle could also see Shifters, and bore that curse along with Griffin, made them even closer. They were isolated in a way that most people couldn't understand, because being able to see shapeshifters was not a good thing.

On the other hand, Griffin's ability to see Shifters was going to clear his reputation and his name. It wouldn't bring his wife back though, clear up his finances, or fix the past that his bastard shapeshifter ex-partner John Parker wrecked when he'd taken over Griffin's home and life. It wouldn't give Griffin back the four months he'd spent in XCEL's detention center as a prisoner, trying to clear himself of the murder Parker committed disguised as Griffin. But it would be something, and if he had to use Camille Solomon to get that, then he would.

A server motioned from the end of the bar, and Lyle headed down to handle the order, leaving Griffin alone with his scotch and his thoughts.

The accomplice was related to Camille somehow; he was sure of it now. Their Shifter shadows were very similar, and he suspected that meant relatives. Whoever the old man was, she'd laid down quickly. He meant a lot to her. That alone confirmed Griffin's theory, because he couldn't imagine anything else moving that woman when she didn't want to be moved.

He flexed his fingers around the warm glass. And his Shifter grip had worked once again. He didn't know how it worked, had never questioned why. Just one more curse to add to the list, but at least this one froze Shifters in their tracks. It would be enough to keep Camille in line. He hoped.

The TV over the bar was showing yet another demonstration on the local news station. There was no sound, but it didn't take much to see that the protesters were anti-aliens. They were your average Americans, wearing sneakers, jeans, and baseball caps and shaking signs of big-eyed alien faces with red lines through them.

They'd come out of the woodwork after alien Shifters had been discovered in America—so-called refugees fleeing from another planet that didn't want them there. Too bad Earth didn't have the space technology to hurtle them back.

Griffin watched the protesters with tired amusement. They didn't even *know* what Shifters actually looked like. They couldn't see the shadows that hovered within their "borrowed" human bodies. Bodies that shapeshifters had stolen human DNA for and replicated. It was wrong. Everyone should have the right to be unique, not be clone fodder.

A patron came up and stood at the bar next to Griffin. He watched the TV for a few moments before saying, "Fucking aliens, here in America. Makes me sick."

Griffin wondered if the guy knew that his waiter was one of them. "Yeah."

The guy yelled to Lyle, "Gimme two Mic Lights."

Then he leaned on the bar and watched the next footage of a

pro-alien march. He said, "Unbelievable. Look at those bleeding hearts. I bet half of them are the aliens."

Nope, just stupid humans that think aliens aren't here to ruin them. "Right."

Lyle set two beers on the counter and took the man's money to make change. Lyle handed the guy his change and said, "Thanks."

The guy nodded at Griffin and left.

Lyle grabbed a rag and wiped the bar. "People like him are just scared of what they don't understand."

"They'd be more scared if they knew the truth," Griffin told him.

Lyle put his hands on the bar. "I never had any problem with Shifters. They're hard workers, and most just want to stay to themselves. Live a normal life."

Griffin shook his head. Spoken like a man who'd never been DNA fodder. "Our lives. They want to live *our lives*, Lyle. The ones we worked our asses off to build."

Lyle shrugged. "You just got screwed. Probably never happen again."

"Why? Because I already had my turn?" he said. "Nothing's even in this world. You should know that by now."

Lyle cleaned a glass and frowned at him. "When you start talking like that, I know you've had enough."

Only Lyle could get away with cutting him off. Which was just as well, because Griffin was getting worked up about something he couldn't change. Shifters were here, and short of blowing them into little bits, they were here to stay. Here to destroy human lives. Here to divide humanity into sides . . . Hell, Lyle was right. He had had enough. He pushed back from the bar. "I got an early morning tomorrow anyway."

"Hot date with your female captive?"

"Hot" was one word to describe her. "Lethal" was another. "I'm giving her the night to cool off."

Lyle's eyebrows rose. "You think that'll help?"

"No, I don't," he admitted.

"Better bring your A game," Lyle said, grinning from ear to ear.

And a gun, Griffin thought.

Lyle reached under the bar and handed Griffin a stack of letters. "Your mail. All bills. Sorry."

Of course. Bills that weren't even his to begin with. He was still paying for a life that Parker had charged while living as Griffin. How do you prove to a creditor that a shapeshifter stole your DNA and ran up the bills? You don't. Just another reason to drink.

Griffin gave Lyle a wave good night and walked through the kitchen to the back of bar. He pushed open a heavy door and climbed the stairs to the small apartment Lyle sublet him.

His cell phone rang, and he checked the incoming number before taking the call. "Hey, little brother, what's up?"

"I got you by one inch," Tommy Mercer replied. "When are you gonna stop calling me 'little'?"

Griffin smiled. "When you can kick my ass on the basketball court."

"Bring it on, shorty." Tommy laughed.

"You just calling to check on me again?" Griffin asked, partly serious. Everyone in his family thought he had a drinking problem, and he swore that they were taking shifts calling him to make sure he wasn't lying in a gutter somewhere.

"Please," Tommy said. "If anyone deserves to get loaded every night, you do." Then he sighed. "Listen. I screwed up, and now Jen won't talk to me."

Jennifer was the sweetest woman on the face of the Earth. How she'd managed to stay married to Griffin's brother for a year was still a miracle in his mind. "Why are you calling me?"

"'Cause you were married once, a lot longer than me. You know how to handle these things."

Griffin slowed his steps. "I'm not the best person to ask about married life."

"Well, you're gonna have to do. Listen, I told Jen I'd watch the baby so she could go out Friday night for dinner or whatever with her friends. But then I found out it's my turn to host the poker game. So I asked her if she could, you know, move her girls' night out? And she freaked out on me. What did I do wrong? I mean, they can do it anytime."

Griffin shook his head. His brother was an idiot. He reached his apartment and unlocked the door. "Give her the night."

"What? No way. I got five buddies planning on this. There's even a game on."

"You made a promise. Keep it."

Tommy swore. "This sucks. I never used to have to rearrange my life for anyone."

"And you didn't have anyone who loved you as much as Jen does either or a baby with your name. Take your pick." Griffin stepped inside. It was dark, and he left the lights off as he tossed the mail on the coffee table.

It took a few seconds, but Tommy finally came around. "Okay, okay. I'm a jerk."

"Truer words were never spoken," Griffin said and turned on the TV. He muted the sound.

"Fuck you. You're uninvited to the poker games."

Griffin grinned. Tommy lived in Arizona. "I'm working over-time this week anyway."

"See? That's what I'm talking about," his brother said. "You don't have to clear your schedule with anyone. I bet you don't miss being married at all."

Griffin stood in the middle of his empty apartment. The only sign of life came from the TV. The only sounds came from the city below and through the walls. No one made dinner for him. No one greeted him.

"Have fun babysitting."

"Thanks for nothing." Tommy hung up.

Griffin set his cell phone next to the blinking answering machine. He pressed the Play button and slipped off his jacket.

"Mr. Mercer, this is the Fairwell Collections Agency calling about an outstanding debt—"

He loosened his tie and hit the Skip button.

"Hello, Mr. Mercer. We have called several times about a bill you owe—"

Skip button. He tugged off the tie as he listened to two more collections calls. Damn vultures. He no sooner got one off his back than two more popped up. He threw his tie on the back of the chair, sat down, and rubbed his eyes.

He skipped through the messages until he heard his grandfather's voice.

"Hello, Griffin. This is your grandfather, Sani, calling from the reservation."

Griffin gave a quiet laugh. Every day, it was the same. His grandfather called and introduced himself. Like Griffin might actually get a chance to forget who he was.

"I hope this message finds you well."

His grandfather's voice was even, strong, and patient. His Navajo Indian accent warm and proud. Griffin had worked hard to shake the unique way his people spoke. It only made him more different from everyone else here.

"I had a vision about you last night."

Griffin frowned at the phone. His grandfather rarely shared his visions. He preferred for Griffin to make every mistake in the book. When he *did* share his visions, they were so cryptic that Griffin rarely figured them out—until the bullets started flying.

"I saw a Skinwalker standing over your still body on the ground. The Skinwalker wore a woman's face."

Camille's face came to mind immediately. He was tempted to stop the message right then and there, but that would disrespect his grandfather.

"Her hair was the color of the red fox. Her body was as a wolf. Her eyes were like an eagle's. The Skinwalker was covered in blood. Her hands were bloody."

That would be the flying bullets.

"Rain came down and turned the ground to winding rivers. Lightning set the trees on fire. Great thunder shook the ground."

And all hell breaking loose.

"The Eagle cried."

Griffin closed his eyes and laid his head back. As he expected. Weird, and cryptic, because there was no way in hell she would cry for him.

"Heed this, Grandson," Grandfather said. *"Hágoónee."*

Then he hung up, the answering machine gave a long beep, and silence swallowed the living room again.

CHAPTER
THREE

Cam had woken from a restless sleep in a lousy mood, and it didn't get any better after that. They wouldn't let her talk to her father. They wouldn't answer any of her questions. They were assholes, every one of them. By the time Mercer and his boss made their appearance in the interrogation room, she was ready to tell them all to shove it.

She sat across the table from them, glaring at Director Harding or Hard-ass or whatever his name was standing in front of a map of the tristate area on the wall monitor and rambling along as if she wasn't even there. Three armed guards stood inside the room, and there were more outside—lots of security. XCEL was afraid of her. That was the best part of her day so far.

"These are the locations we believe the Shifters targeted and attacked." Director Harding tapped his fingers on the map. "Your job is to visit every site and catalog each Shifter scent you find."

"Catalog?" she asked.

He glanced at her as if she was a pesky fly. "Yes, catalog. By scent. *Shifter* smell."

He emphasized "Shifter" as if it was a dirty word. And on this world, it was. She'd gotten used to it in the short time she'd been here. Still, the hatred of her kind ran deep and to human base fears.

Cam cut a glance at Mercer. He met her eyes but said nothing. His dark stare gave him away though. He hated Harding. It didn't make her feel better that she agreed with him on that.

She frowned back at Harding. "You want me to play bloodhound for you?"

He nodded, completely blowing off her comment. "Yes. Only a Shifter can identify another Shifter by scent."

Cam addressed Mercer. "There are plenty of other Shifters who could do this. Why me?"

Mercer shrugged. "You got caught."

She glared at him with all her might.

Harding continued. "That's only half the mission. After you and Agent Mercer investigate those areas, we have several suspects we want you to check out. We think they are part of a larger group bent on terrorizing this region. We need to infiltrate their ring so we can bring them down."

She raised her hands. "Again, why me?"

"All the Shifters we have working in XCEL have been exposed already. We need someone new who can go undercover, blend in, and talk their language," Harding replied, sounding annoyed by her questions. "Someone who can gain their trust and get Mercer inside without suspicion. Someone who won't be seen as a threat."

Cam felt her irritation rising. She wasn't even sure which part of that logic to attack first. "Because I'm a woman? You think I'm no threat."

Harding smirked. "You're captive in a detention center. What does that tell you?"

It told her that Mercer was the one she needed to be worried about, and Harding was a dick.

The director planted his hands on the table and leaned forward menacingly. "Look, it's just a couple of weeks, and you and your accomplice will be free of all criminal charges. We'll take care of everything you need. And you'll have Mercer as your handler."

None of those things made her feel any better, especially Mercer handling her. She'd already had enough of that. In fact, she had a bad feeling she knew exactly why they wanted her. "I'm a woman."

"As far as we know," Harding retorted.

"And Mercer's a man."

Mercer raised an eyebrow. "Thank you."

She flipped him the finger and kept her eyes on Harding. "So by 'get Mercer inside,' you mean . . . what?"

"Girlfriend. Wife. Whatever it takes," Harding said, "to make sure he finds their operation so we can take it down."

She crossed her arms. "Forget it. Mercer here can have a boyfriend just as easily."

"Female Shifters have a more acute sense of smell," Mercer said evenly.

She knew that, but who the hell told him? "Says who?"

"Jesus," Harding barked, pushing back from the table. "It's not like we're asking you to do anything that you don't do every day. Sniff each other."

Harding had officially moved up ahead of Mercer on her I-hate-you scale. "Like dogs?"

Harding expelled a disgusted huff and turned his assholeness

on Mercer. "We agreed that you would secure her full cooperation. I trusted you to do that much right."

Mercer gave his boss a benevolent look, but Cam noted the
subtle vibration under the suit. Mercer was pissed. If she had
Harding for a boss, she'd be too. On second thought, she'd just
kill him. It'd be easier.

"I will," Mercer said simply.

Cam glared at him. She might have to kill him first, after all.

Harding snapped. "I don't call this cooperation."

"Hello, right here," she said. "Sorry if I don't jump at the opportunity to be manhandled by your agents. I've seen them in
action. I won't be your sacrificial Shifter."

Harding sneered at her like she was just that. "You don't get a
lot of say-so here. It's not my fault that you chose to ignore the
laws of this great country for your own criminal gains."

She could slit his throat in two seconds. She wouldn't even
break a sweat. Her father was the only reason she didn't.

"The laws of your country only apply to us when it's convenient for you," she hissed.

Mercer finally stood up next to Harding. "Why don't I take it
from here, Director Harding? I'm sure you have more important
business to deal with today."

Cam gave Mercer an "Oh please" look that he ignored.

Harding seemed appeased by Mercer's ass kissing and pointed
a finger at her. "Just remember, you could be here forever."

"And you could be dead," Cam murmured.

One corner of Mercer's mouth curled just a bit. Harding was
too busy turning red to notice. "Make this work, Mercer." And
then he walked out.

Most of the tension in the small room left with him. Not all of it, because Mercer was still there. Buttoned up in a dark brown suit, crisp white shirt, and tie, he'd spent the conversation studying her. Like a lab rat. She wasn't taking too kindly to it.

"Harding's a douche bag," she said. "Why hasn't anyone killed him yet?"

Mercer cast a quick glance to the one-way mirror on the wall. *So careful,* she thought. So patient, controlled. And so controlling. She hated being in this position. When she gambled, she knew the odds and chose whether to accept them. This was different and not at all appealing.

"Let's go for a walk," he said when he finally answered.

She blinked a few times and said, "You're letting me out?"

He nodded at the guards and held the door open for her. "Unfortunately, it's going to happen sooner or later."

As she followed him out the door, past the guards outside, and down a nondescript white hallway, she started ticking off the security setup. Three sets of men, four card swipes, two handprint units, and a chemical sniffing unit. Nothing she couldn't handle. Hell, if she had twenty minutes, she could get her father out of here . . .

Then it dawned on her why Mercer wasn't afraid of her doing anything stupid. He knew the odds too. He held her "accomplice" as collateral. He knew she wouldn't do anything to jeopardize his safety, and she wouldn't. Getting *to* her father would be easy. Getting him out alive—almost impossible. Besides, Mercer could use his freeze ray on her if he needed to easily manage the situation. Manage her. Use her.

Crap. Were there more like him? Was XCEL now recruiting Shifter hunters with specialized skills? She didn't want to think about that for long. One thing was clear though—she'd make damn sure she kept her distance from him.

They walked out into the warm sunshine. The building was big, gray, and low, surrounded by parking lots and a few trees. The sign at the entrance read White Enterprises, a generic and equally nondescript name.

"Jersey City?" she asked.

Mercer nodded. "Good guess."

It was just another survival skill on this planet. Know the lay of the land. "Does XCEL know you can see Shifters?"

"Yes. That won't work as blackmail."

He was catching on fast. "So you work in the local field office and they use to you locate Shifters and let the troops do the dirty work of catching them."

"Nothing new there either," he said. "You can keep trying though."

Fine, she would. "Your shirt was professionally laundered and pressed. You wear boxers. And you stopped at Starbucks on the way into work this morning." She glanced at him walking next to her. "How am I doing?"

He stared straight ahead. "I make my own coffee."

"I'll note that in your file," she said, enjoying her small victory. The underwear was a total guess, but it'd worked. Now he could worry if she had X-ray vision.

They walked across the building lot and into a private park that connected to the compound via a narrow bridge. The empty path meandered through cherry trees that wrapped a large pond. Ducks floated lazily on the smooth water. Cam inhaled floral fragrances, felt the warmth of the sun, and pretended she was alone.

"What will it take?"

Mercer's question broke her small moment of peace. "For what?"

They stopped at the edge of the pond, surrounded by over-hanging shrubs. "What will it take for you to buy into this? Money? A new car? Fresh DNA? What?"

Cam crossed her arms. He was negotiating. Interesting. They must really, really need her. "You're desperate."

Mercer's cool gaze didn't flinch. "I don't want to have to worry about you killing me in my sleep."

"I don't know, that's pretty tempting. Could take quite a bit," she countered.

Mercer eyed her. "Give it your best shot, Camille."

Was he talking about killing him or negotiating? "Call me Cam. My father—" She stopped. She was going to say that her father was the only one who called her Camille.

"Your father?"

She winced. Damn. That was stupid on her part. She licked her lips and noticed Mercer's gaze drop to her mouth. Then he looked away, at the pond. Too late. She'd seen it, she could use it, and she would. That went into the mental file as well.

Cam said, "If I go along with you, I want a *guarantee* that you will let us both go. In writing that any court would uphold."

"That's the deal on the table," he answered smoothly.

She added, "Regardless of whether this little gig succeeds or fails."

By the way he tensed, she knew he didn't like that part. As she suspected, this wasn't as simple as Harding explained. There was something more they didn't want to share. Call it instinct, but that was the part that she knew she needed.

He said, "You're an integral part of that success or failure."

True, but still negotiable. Cam tried a different tack. "In that case, I want to know everything. A full partner. Full disclosure."

"Impossible," Mercer said.

That was bullshit. Anything was possible. Look at Shifters.

She stepped in front of him, blocking his view of the pond and forcing him to look at her. "Then I can't be responsible for the outcome, and whether or not you like what I lead you to. I'm a full partner, or this doesn't happen."

Their eyes locked, and Cam could feel the undercurrent of tension that held him together. Ah, not tension. Anger. Determination. His eyes betrayed him, and the suit barely contained the man. Keeping it all under tight wrap. It was at the same time intriguing and disconcerting. She'd met angry humans before. Ones that hated Shifters because they feared them. Mercer didn't fear them. He just hated them.

"If I give you full disclosure, you'll do your very best to make sure this mission is successful?" he asked. "You'll follow my orders. You'll trust me—"

"Don't push it," she interrupted. The deal was probably as good as she would get. "Yes, I'll behave."

Suspicion clouded his eyes. "I doubt that."

You have no idea, she thought. "You'll answer all my questions."

He hesitated. "Agreed."

That settled the free-floating anxiety she'd been feeling since talking to Harding. Now for the bonus round. There was something else that had occurred to her last night while she stared at her cell ceiling. "And I want you to locate my brother."

Mercer narrowed his eyes. It took him a few moments to reply. "Brother?"

Huh. They didn't know about Thaniel. Obviously, her brother was better at keeping a low profile than she was, which made sense since *she* hadn't been able to locate him in the last year. "Yes."

Mercer continued to stare at her. "Family reunion?"

She put on a currish smile. "What else?"

Mercer's expression darkened. "Now see, that worries me."

She shrugged. "Deal breaker, Mercer. Take it, and I'm all yours."

He seemed to ponder that for a minute. "When was the last time you saw him?"

"Last year."

His eyebrows rose slightly. "He could be out of the country—"

"He's not," Cam interrupted sharply.

Then she drew a breath to calm herself. No point in giving Mercer any more ammo than he already had. Besides, her lack of emotional control was what got her into this situation in the first place. So stopping and thinking was good. Thinking avoided a lot of problems. But fighting was so much more rewarding.

She added, "Look, XCEL has resources that I don't and won't ever have. I can give you the last name he used and all the information I have on him."

Mercer nodded. "Agreed. Once this mission is over, we'll hand over what we've uncovered."

She was half surprised that he acquiesced so easily. Hell, at this rate she could get herself a nice rental car and a sweet loft in Brooklyn—

Mercer leaned forward suddenly and drew her full attention. He was close enough for her to see the streaks of gold in his dark brown eyes. His voice was low but firm. And all that hate rushed her senses. "But I'm in charge. That means you do what I say, when I say. I want you in, *all the way*."

This job would be dangerous, and she'd be working for them on a mission they'd gone to a damn lot of trouble to put together.

This negotiation meant little once the shooting started, and she was sure they would.

So far, she had secured her freedom, her brother's location, and with any luck at all, her father's salvation. That was as good as it was going to get. All it would cost her was every bit of her dignity.

"I'm in," she said, and made a deal with the devil. "All the way."

◆◆◆

Griffin needed a drink, but since he was still in the office at seven P.M., he doubted he'd get it anytime soon. He paced the small office that belonged to his technical analyst and scanned the printout of attacked locations to visit along with the list of suspects and possible places to find them.

He summarized, "All in the worst neighborhoods in the city. Sure you don't want to do some fieldwork?"

Ernest let out a rather unflattering raspberry. "No thanks. I'll stick to my computers and my numbers."

And he did just that. Six side-by-side monitors were lined across three disheveled and mismatched desks, there was enough cable to rewire the entire building, and a stack of blinking boxes threatened to topple any minute. It also made him the best technical field analyst Griffin had ever met.

"What are you worried about?" Ernest asked. "Just say the word; I'll hook you up with whatever you need. The agency has your back."

Griffin laughed. Right. "Like always."

Ernest's crazy tapping fingers stopped. He was thin and pale, and his eyes were a bit too big for his head. "You got a second chance here," he said. "That's more than most people get at this place."

"That's because they didn't have anyone else who can see Shifters," Griffin corrected. "Otherwise, I'd still be locked up."

Ernest checked the glass windows that lined one side of his office, and he leaned toward Griffin. "You just gotta come through on this one mission, and you're back to where you were. Good as new."

Griffin liked Ernest, even if he was totally oblivious to the real world sometimes. "All I want is to clear my name. After that, I don't give a damn what happens to Harding or this agency."

Ernest grimaced. "You need to be careful saying stuff like that around here. Never know who's listening." He leaned back. "Granted, my detectors would be beeping like crazy if there was a bug in here, but hey, even I don't know everything."

Griffin folded up the papers and tucked them in his pocket. "You're close enough for me. I figure we can cover the list of attacks in a few nights. Then we'll check out the suspects."

Ernest grinned suddenly at him. "Do I get to meet her?"

"I'll bring her by in the morning before we leave," Griffin said. The thought of escorting Cam around made him *really* want a drink.

"I hear she's wicked hot," Ernest said.

Yes, she was. And dangerous and absolutely untrustworthy. He considered their "deal" and wished he'd had more leverage. "She's okay."

"Man, what happened to you? Are you dead inside or something?" Ernest asked.

Griffin noticed his reflection in the windows. A man in a suit stared back at him. Dead inside. That was close. That's what hap-

pened when your life was devastated by a Shifter. You lost everything you loved and cared about, all that you worked for. There
was nothing left except one chance.

He considered his deal with Cam and brushed aside the guilt.
He'd given her everything he could that didn't involve Harding.
But her brother? He wasn't giving her that, because then he'd
have to explain it to Harding. Griffin was on thin ice as it was. If
Harding found out they were supposed to find her brother—
another Shifter, no less—he'd fire Griffin on the spot. This was
not going to end that way. Not this time. This time, the Shifters
were going to get the short end of the stick.

He reached out and slapped Ernest's shoulder. "Get some
sleep, bud. Because you'll need it to deal with Cam. I promise you
that."

◆◆◆

"Please don't do this for me, Camille," her father whispered. They
had their heads together in his cell to keep their conversation as
quiet as possible, but Cam knew that XCEL was listening to
every word.

She clasped his cool hands in hers. Dewey appeared tired and
worried. His human body was failing him, and there was nothing
he could do about it. He'd lost the ability to revert to Primary
Shifter form months ago. It was his Shifter DNA that was killing
him from the inside out—slowly, painfully, and without mercy.

"It's our only hope," she insisted. *His* only hope. "Their resources to find Thaniel are much better than ours."

He shook his head. "I'm going to die someday, Camille. You
have to let go. I don't want to take you with me."

Right, and leave him here? With them? XCEL had more respect for a bug than they did for Shifters. Cam pursed her lips and glanced at the mirrored wall of his cell.

"You won't," she said, patting his hand.

"I'm not worth it," he insisted.

Cam blinked away the tears that threatened. He had no idea how much she needed him. But there were so many ifs. If XCEL found Thaniel. If Cam could convince Thaniel to come here. If she could get the three of them together in one place to perform the blood transfusion. If the transfusion saved her father's life.

And every single one of those ifs was worth it to save her father from the disease that was eating away at him. She gave him a hug, all the while savoring the bit of warmth he had left. "I'll call you every day. If they don't treat you well, let me know."

He stood with her and nodded. "I have a nice place to stay, free food, and drink. What more could I want?"

To live. "I'll call every day."

He nodded, looking even frailer in this sterile environment. Cam stared at him for a long moment, fearful it might be the last time she saw him. He'd survived so much, suffered, and lost. He didn't deserve to die this way. Then she turned to leave before her emotions got the better of her. She walked out of his room and into the hallway to find Mercer waiting. Cam avoided his curious stare and followed him to an office on the other end of the building.

There were no windows, and monitors lined most of the walls. Computer cables crisscrossed the floor, the trash can was overflowing, and it smelled like coffee was burning somewhere close by.

A tall, lanky man jumped to his feet, knocking over a pile of papers on his desk. He had super-short brown hair and a pale complexion. He scanned down her body and let out a long, drawn-out, heartfelt "Wow."

Mercer cleared his throat, and the man's eyes flicked back to hers. "Sorry. I heard about you, but—" He shot out a boney hand to her. "Agent Vincent, but you can call me Ernest. Everyone does. Nice to meet you."

"Cam." She gave him a man-killer smile as he continued to pump her hand. Cam watched the red rise up from his white collar and cover his face.

Cam grinned. "I know. Nice, huh?"

What did she care? It wasn't like this body was really hers.

"Have a seat, Ernest," Mercer said loud enough to make Ernest nearly jump out of his skin. She took a chair in front of a big monitor as he moved to his keyboard and starting tapping out instructions.

Mercer stood behind her, leaned over, and whispered, "That's not behaving, Cam."

"Trust me," she whispered back. "That's behaving."

Then she watched the monitor. A map of the tristate area appeared first, then dots started to pop up across it.

"So the locations," Ernest began. "We got strikes everywhere. I uploaded everything you need into your phone, Griff." He handed Mercer a phone, but Cam was only half paying attention.

"Strikes?" she asked.

Ernest shrugged. "Bombs, mostly. Sometimes fires, and an occasional gas explosion. We also have lesser strikes, more like sabotage. Or outright theft of shipping vessels, train car contents, delivery trucks, that sort of thing. All strikes occur at night and when the places are empty."

"What kind of places?" Cam asked.

Mercer leaned forward and answered, "Transportation companies, train stations, business offices, laboratories, chemical plants, even private residences."

Cam glanced over her shoulder at him. "That doesn't make sense. Despite what you've heard, Shifters don't generally do anything unless it suits them."

Mercer replied, "That's why you're here."

"And me," Ernest said. "If you need anything while you are scouting the locations, I'm your man. I got connections everywhere, stats, intel, whatever you need."

"At least I know I can count on one person," she said and smiled a smile that made Ernest blush to his toes. She reached over and laid her hand on his arm, which made his eyes light up in a very sweet way. "Can you do me a favor?"

"Be careful, Ernest," Mercer warned.

She wrinkled her nose at him and turned back to her geek. "Can you check on my father once in a while? He's alone."

Ernest grinned. "Sure."

"Daily?" she said, her voice low.

Ernest's grin stayed. "Yes. Daily."

He was telling the truth, she could see it in his eyes. He didn't carry the anger or heaviness that Mercer did. She squeezed his lean arm. "Thank you."

Mercer said, "And thanks for the briefing. We'll contact you later tonight."

Cam stood up and faced him. "Tonight?"

He smiled. "Tonight."

CHAPTER
FOUR

Washington Heights at midnight, and Cam's carefully crafted deal wasn't looking so good. They were standing on a corner in front of a one-story building surrounded by makeshift chain-link fencing, no trespassing signs, and yellow crime scene tape. Graffiti decorated surrounding buildings, and in the distance, the hills on the other side of the Hudson etched the night sky.

The exterior of the building was scorched and warped. The roof sagged. Half the building was down to the bare infrastructure of beams and brick. Inside, all was dark. The smell of the recent fire overshadowed all other scents. This wasn't going to be as easy as she, or XCEL, thought.

Mercer read from his phone. "Neotech Supplies. Torched three days ago. They distributed biotech equipment and supplies. Our investigators found traces of an accelerant. Definitely arson."

And it was up to her to tell them who'd torched the place. She scanned their immediate surroundings. They were on a busy intersection that never slept. Buildings were packed closely together in this area, and foot traffic was moderate, even at this time of the night.

A pang of doubt prompted her to ask, "Are you sure this is the place?"

Mercer glanced at her. "Do you see any other buildings that look crispy?"

She didn't, even with her superior long-distance vision. Still, this was wide open and heavily traveled. Not a prime location for Shifters to be scavenging. What were they after? What would make them risk getting caught? And why torch the place afterward? It would only draw unwanted attention.

"Started inside?" she asked.

He pocketed the phone in his jacket. "Yes. No grenade launchers, if that's what you're thinking. They definitely got up close and personal with the building. Fire was reported by a passing motorist at 2:35 A.M."

"Which means it could have been started at any time before then. I doubt the neighborhood watch is real active around here."

He nodded in agreement under the streetlight. This was the first time she'd seen him in something other than a suit. He wore nicely fitted jeans, a black T-shirt under a black jacket, and boots. Somehow, they made him look bigger and more dangerous. Like the animal had been released.

"What was taken?" she asked.

Mercer narrowed his gaze. "You ask a lot of questions."

She arched an eyebrow at him. "Call me naturally curious."

"Or paranoid." He crossed his arms. "It's not your job to investigate. We have investigators."

She gave a quick laugh. "All biased against Shifters. Besides, we had a deal, remember?"

Mercer said, "Which I regret more every minute."

Cam smiled. "What did the owners of this fine establishment report missing?"

He replied, "They couldn't tell if anything was stolen. There was too much damage."

She rolled her eyes. All that grief for nothing. Good thing she was born stubborn or this little hide-and-seek game could get frustrating.

"Now let's see what *you've* got," Mercer said as he walked over to unlock the gate of the chain-link fence. His tone caught her attention. It was soft but firm, with just a little edge that made her shiver. There was much more to Mercer than he let her see, and she was determined to uncover it all. Because it could mean the difference between getting what she wanted and not.

When she passed him, she caught a quick whiff of his scent, which, despite everything, was welcomed next to the stench of burnt building.

Mercer locked the gate behind them while Cam circled the exterior of the building, stepping through puddles of water left-over from the fire hoses. Footprints dotted the ground, clogged with soot and mud. A lot of people had been through here. It would make her job tougher.

Cam stopped in front of the building and closed her eyes to concentrate on the slurry of scents. The air was still, breezeless on this warm summer night. Having extraordinary senses in a city like New York was difficult for Shifters. She'd had to learn to turn them down so as not to overload.

When she thought she had her senses retuned to enhance her

olfactory nerves, she started sorting through the smells. Burnt materials, one by one, she noted and excluded. Sooty runoff, mud, city odors, she eliminated from her mind. Slowly, the other smells rose, more pronounced.

Mercer moved up behind her, jarring her concentration. Suddenly, she focused on his movements—the rub of the jacket against his jeans, the way he moved so as to not jostle the gun holstered over his T-shirt, the soft footfall of his step. Then his scent wafted over her, full-bore and unhindered by her normal filters. It was nice, clean, and musky. He must have showered before coming out tonight. Her mind wandered there, following an intangible trail before she could stop herself. She dawdled awhile in a fantasy world until she remembered that he was her sworn enemy.

She opened her eyes, breaking all the concentration she'd worked so hard to gather, and glared at him over her shoulder. "You need to give me some space. This isn't as easy as you might think."

He hesitated only a moment before taking a step back. "Far enough?"

No, but she wasn't going to ask again. Instead, she closed her eyes and retraced her mental steps until all the inanimate smells were identified. That left the humans. Mercer, she had on permanent file. Then there were others. They could be investigators, firefighters, owners, or arsonists.

"I'm getting seven strong human scents. Any one of them could be your arsonist," she told him.

"Any Shifter scents?" he asked.

Cam blew out a long, slow breath and then inhaled. Traces of Shifters filtered into her mind, each with their own distinctive fingerprint. Every Shifter could do this. They'd developed their unique tool kit of abilities over thousands of years in order to survive. It was always safer to smell your enemy before they tried to kill you.

"Cam?"

Speaking of enemies.

"Yes." She found each distinctive scent and fought the disappointment. Mercer was going to love this. "Three Shifters, all male."

She opened her eyes and turned to face him. "But that doesn't mean they set the fire. They could have come here as customers or in some other capacity."

He gave her a dubious look. "Do you really think that?"

His face was shadowed under streetlights, but she could see his irritation perfectly. "Innocent until proven guilty? Isn't that what Americans are all about?"

He didn't move for a moment, matching her glare for glare. She could almost read his mind. *If you're looking for justice . . .*

Instead, he said, "Let's go inside."

Why did she even try? The man didn't believe in any of it. She wondered why. Seriously, he lived in the greatest country on the planet by most standards. He had a job, even if it *was* killing her people, and he lived without fear of certain death on sight. What more could he want?

Mercer turned on a flashlight, and she followed him through the empty frame of a metal door into the reception area. Water dripped from steel trusses overhead. Charred ceiling tiles littered the floors and furniture. The fire seemed to have scorched every surface.

"They believe the fire started in several places, including here," Mercer said.

Shifter scents were strong, but she still wasn't convinced. It didn't add up. Shifters only went to this kind of trouble if they wanted something badly. "Where else?"

He led her through the building, room by room. They were all the same. And they all smelled like Shifters.

"Well?" Mercer finally asked once they were back outside.

"Shifters set the blaze," she said, disappointed and not really knowing why. After all, she wasn't in charge of all the Shifters. She couldn't care less what the rest of them did. But her twisted gut and the headache that had formed across her forehead said differently. They were all linked by association. Check that. All *guilty* by association.

Then again, she'd bought into this knowing that. Use, or be used. Right now, she was using Shifters. She was no better than XCEL, and that really made her head hurt.

She turned to find Mercer grinning. It was the first time she'd seen him smile. It was very sexy, riveting even, and not in the kind of way she wanted to think about with a man who owned her for the foreseeable future.

"That'll make Harding happy," he said, the smile vanishing in a flash.

She huffed. "I can't believe you put up with his crap. Desperate for a job or something?"

Mercer reached for the lock on the gate and froze. She'd readjusted her senses, but even she could feel the tension emanating from him. His breathing deepened, and his pulse sped up. That was one big-ass nerve she'd just jumped on.

"Or something," he said and yanked the lock open.

Cam eyed him. "Must be a *really* big something."

He held the gate open for her, and their eyes met. His were

dark, almost blending into the night. "It is, and that's all you're getting out of me on that subject."

She'd never been one to back down from an opening. Cam walked up to him. He had rugged good looks. Not smooth, not polished. Just all male. Or in his case, all male human. She'd met a few of them that were interesting and fun for a night. Mercer would be fun for a lot longer than that.

"Afraid I might get too close, Mercer?" she asked softly, moving near.

He watched her with singular intensity. "You won't."

Cam felt her smile grow. "You'd be surprised what I can do."

He grinned back, challenging her. "I have a few tricks of my own, remember."

She did. She was also ready to move out of his reach in a heartbeat. But for right now, this was fun and risky, and frankly, she hadn't had enough of that lately. "That's what they all say."

Then he leaned in, his expression turning serious and his breath warm on her face. His hair brushed his forehead. She forgot about keeping her distance. "They might, but I'm the real deal."

He said it like he meant it, and she believed him. One thing was clear: He'd do what he had to to keep her under control. Under his control. He may smell good, he might even look good, but he was still her adversary.

"So am I, Mercer," she whispered back and moved through the gate.

◆ ◆ ◆

It was nearly daybreak when Griffin unlocked his apartment door and held it open for Cam. She walked in, still looking fresh and wide awake even after six hours of trudging from site to site across New York City in the wee hours.

"You live here alone?" she asked, walking through his apartment without waiting for an invitation.

He was really regretting the whole full-disclosure deal. "Yes."

Cam stopped and faced him. Neither one of them had turned on the lights. He could see her by the Shifter glow that hugged her human frame. She could see him in pitch-dark with her super Shifter vision. It made them equal for a brief moment.

"What, no goldfish?"

"I killed them." He closed the door, locked it, and flipped on the lights. "Thirsty?"

Cam eyed him warily. "Depends. How'd you kill the gold-fish?"

"Too much excitement," he said as he went to the kitchen. The cupboard above the sink contained scotch, vodka, whiskey, and tequila. He opted for the tequila and two glasses. If he was at all lucky, Cam would be a cheap date and crash before he did. She might have agreed not to kill him in his sleep, but it wasn't like it really counted for anything.

Cam took a seat on a stool across the ceramic tile island from him as he poured a shot into each glass. She raised hers to no one in particular and swallowed it in one gulp. She gave a shudder and slammed the glass on the island. "Hit me."

Griffin readily refilled her glass. He took a sip of his, felt the liquor burn down his throat, and tried to ignore the fact that a Shifter had invaded the one place he'd manage to keep Shifter-free. "So you're certain we've only identified six Shifters?"

Cam raised her glass and held it to her lips. "*I* identified. *You* were a distraction."

He wasn't sure if that was a complaint or compliment. "I stand corrected."

She gave a *humph* and downed her drink.

"All working in teams of two or three at a time," he continued and filled her up again. She showed no signs of getting sleepy. "But with the same base scents?"

"They all came from the same place, or at least the same environment. I can't tell you where though unless I can find that exact combination of smells." She leaned over the island to retrieve her shot glass.

He was torn between the surprise show of cleavage and the line of questioning he was working on. "Do you think the teams know each other?"

She swiped the refilled glass off the island and walked into the living room with it. "I can't tell."

It was a start, at least. He might not have all the answers yet, but he was relieved that this may actually work. Cam was better at isolating scents than he thought possible. Unless she was lying. Which was also possible.

Cam ran a finger across the top of his flat-screen television as she walked around his place. "So, exactly what are we supposed to do with these guys once we catch them?"

"We're not catching them. We're just identifying them."

She inspected the Bowflex exercise system set up in the corner of his living room. "Right. Can't step over that line, can we?"

Griffin eyed her. Where was she heading with this? "I have orders."

Cam turned to him and gave a mock salute. "Orders. Yes. So if we find something that isn't quite right?"

"We report it to Harding," he said, feeling like he was being ambushed in some way. "He'll decide whether or not to investigate."

She smiled benignly. "Of course he will."

Griffin placed his hands on the edge of the island. "Why don't you just come out and tell me exactly what is going on here?"

Cam wandered over to his mail and started sorting through it. "Maybe *you* should tell *me* what exactly is going on here."

That covered a lot of territory. Most of it he had no intention of stepping into. "You'll need to be a little more specific."

She trained her eyes on him. "Don't lie to me, Mercer. Do you know that I can hear your pulse quicken when you lie?"

He eyed her. She was bluffing. Probably.

"This is bigger than you and me finding some bad guys." She cast him a pointed look. "At least for you. This is *personal*."

Hell. When had she figured that out? He was going to have to watch himself. He set down his tequila.

Griffin shrugged off his jacket and tossed it on the island. "Nothing personal about it. We can't allow these Shifters to continue to bomb places."

Cam walked back to him slowly, the breaking sun setting her aglow for a moment. They'd spent most of the night in the dark, so he hadn't had a chance to appreciate her sleek red hair and big blue eyes. The shirt she wore was unbuttoned down as far as it could go without being illegal. Jeans hugged her hips and legs.

He caught himself and stopped. At least Ernest would be proud of him. Griffin took a big swig of tequila and refocused on the Shifter shadow around her body. It wafted with every movement, sometimes preceding her actions, sometimes trailing, but always there as a reminder that she wasn't human.

Cam slid one knee up on the stool and leaned far over the island, her expression serious and intense. "You can't allow Shifters, period. Sooner or later, XCEL is going to figure out how to get rid of us. Permanently."

Griffin eyed her. That was a leap. "That's not part of the plan."

"No?" she said. "Then what are you going to do with us?"

"I'm not cleared on Shifter policy," he said simply. It was true. No one in XCEL trusted him right now. He'd have to earn that, with this mission. And right now, she was way, way too far ahead of it.

A flash of disbelief crossed her face. "If you were, you wouldn't tell me anyway."

And that was true too. "Full disclosure, remember?"

She surprised him with the heaviness in her voice. "Not on everything. Who's the woman you used to live with?"

He stared at her for a full minute, debating his response to her acute insight and even more acute senses. He thought he'd purged everything that remained of Deirdre. Not so.

"Ex-wife," he said, careful to control any emotion in his voice that Cam could use against him.

She raised her eyebrows. "Ah."

Bringing Cam here was necessary to shed the scent of the XCEL detention center, but now he was seriously reconsidering that decision. Working with her was one thing, but he didn't need anyone looking into his soul. And every time he saw her Shifter shadow, it reminded him that he couldn't trust her. He couldn't trust any of them. They had one goal: to beg, borrow, and steal any life they wanted.

She shot down the tequila. "Where do I sleep?"

Griffin noted with some satisfaction that she appeared tired. "My bed. I'll take the couch."

"Good night, Mercer." Then she disappeared into his bedroom and shut the door behind her. His apartment returned to silence.

Griffin glanced at the flashing light on the answering machine and decided to save anything Sani had to say for later. His grandfather always knew what he was doing, even though they were thousands of miles apart. Sani wouldn't approve of him using a shapeshifter to clear his own name. His grandfather cherished all living things, including aliens. It was one of the reasons they didn't talk anymore. Well, Sani talked. Griffin listened and then deleted the messages.

Griffin gazed into the bottom of his glass, fighting the feeling of disgrace and guilt he experienced when he thought of Sani. He'd fought for this chance to clear his name and get some semblance of normalcy back. It was the hell he had to pay to make his life right again after it had been blown to hell, much like the buildings they'd visited tonight. Shifters were very good at that.

Anger resurged. He deserved to feel the way he did. And he deserved to deal with it the way he wanted to. He was using a Shifter to get back his life that was destroyed by a Shifter. It was justice. His way.

Then he reached for the bottle and poured himself another drink.

◆◆◆

Harding leaned back in his chair at his desk and regarded his right-hand man, Agent Roberts. "Everything is proceeding on schedule?"

"Yes, sir," Roberts replied, standing at the ready. "They covered three places on the list last night. We'll let them do another five or six, and then send them out to track down the suspects."

"Good," Harding said and pushed a folder on his desk over to Roberts. "These are the latest hits."

Roberts picked up the folder and flipped through it. "I'll send them to Agent Mercer today."

Harding smiled. Roberts was a good soldier. It was so much easier working with Roberts than with Mercer. No questions, no discussion, no ego involved. Just full, blind cooperation. Harding liked it that way. That was the way it should be. "Who is the technical analyst assigned to them?"

Roberts tucked the folder under his arm. "Ernest Vincent. He's our best man."

That could be a problem, Harding pondered. Vincent also happened to be one of Mercer's few friends in the organization. "I'd like Ernest watched twenty-four/seven. I want his communications and access monitored."

Roberts' eyebrows arose. "Would you like me to assign someone else to them?"

It would look too suspicious if Harding did that. He'd played this game a long time. He splayed his fingers across his stomach as he leaned into the chair. "No. I simply want to make sure that everything is fully reported. This is a major case for us. The biggest, possibly, we will ever get. No mistakes."

"No, sir," Roberts said. "Anything else?"

"That'll be all," Harding replied, and waited until Roberts had left his office before pulling out his phone. He dialed a number that would never be kept in his contact list. It picked up on the third ring.

"Hello?"

Harding stood up and closed the door. "When is the next test scheduled for?"

"The latest batch is brewing now. We can try it as soon as we can get a test subject."

Harding smiled. "I'll take care of that."

"We'll be ready." The line went dead.

❖ ❖ ❖

Cam awoke from a dream about being naked and serving XCEL agents their dinners. She checked under the covers. She wasn't naked. A long sigh slipped her lips, and she rolled over to see the clock next to Mercer's bed. It read one P.M.

She rolled back and put her arm over her eyes. Mercer's scent radiated from everywhere. The bed, the closet of clothes, the dresser drawers. The reminder hurt, because he was using her and she was letting him. And to that end, she would ultimately betray Shifters everywhere. As if they hadn't been betrayed enough before on the last place they'd tried to settle.

Govan was a peaceful planet when Shifters arrived as refugees. That changed fast enough once the government tired of dealing with them. The subsequent genocide of her people had been nearly complete. Escape had been the only way to save the rest. She, her brother, and her father had been the lucky ones to escape, or so she'd thought. And now they were here. It was only a matter of time before it happened all over again, except this time there was no escape. They had nowhere to go and no way to get there. Earth was their last hope.

Maybe that was why she hated discovering that Shifters set

the fires. It was proof, a crime against them. A reason to hate them.

She could see the headlines now: "Shifters Attack New York City!"

And they'd be wrong.

Well, mostly wrong.

It had dawned on her at the third site last night that these Shifters were executing the attacks with pinpoint accuracy. They weren't sloppy, didn't leave anything behind except their scent. They were pros, and they weren't in it for the money. And that was just plain wrong.

The same teams of Shifters had burned and destroyed a series of buildings. Buildings. Not banks or ATMs, and not the typical places Shifters went for easy cash. She prided herself on how she could adapt to any culture, identify what was needed to survive, and find the ways to fill those needs.

But these buildings? A chemical lab, a medical equipment seller, and a business office. They made no sense. She wouldn't need anything from those places to survive. No Shifter would. So why hit them?

It was a mystery. One that Mercer showed no inkling to investigate further. As far as she could tell, he was just her chauffeur and followed whatever orders Harding gave him to the letter. The big question was, why? Mercer clearly wasn't happy about being ordered around, but he did it. Unless Harding had something on him, or he needed the paycheck. The stacks of overdue bills would attest to that. You'd think that someone who could see Shifters would be well paid in an organization like XCEL.

Regardless, Mercer wasn't going to step outside the tiny box of guidelines he had. He didn't care. No one would care, the least of all XCEL. All they wanted to do was find the Shifters and do God knew what with them.

Cam ran her fingers through her hair and then stretched her long body to ease the tension. She smelled like smoke and ash. What she needed was a shower and clean clothes. That's when she noticed her suitcase by the bedroom door. Mercer must have brought it in. Next time, she was going to lock the door.

She picked up her cell phone to call her father. A text message was waiting. It was from Ernest and it said, "Your father is okay."

Cam smiled. Her little geek was a man of his word. She dialed the number to reach her father. After a few transfers, he answered weakly. "Hello?"

"Hey," she said, and feigned attitude. "You didn't call me."

He laughed softly. "First off, you were going to call me. Secondly, you're working nights. Didn't want to wake you."

Cam frowned. "How did you know I was working nights?"

"That young man. I can't remember his name."

"Ernest?" she said, hiding the worry in her voice. Her father remembered less and less these days.

"Yes. Ernest. He seems very nice. And he sure likes you."

"Really?" she said with a smile. "I'm almost afraid to hear what you two are talking about."

Her father chuckled. "No worries. We have started playing chess though. He stops in a few times a day and makes a move."

Cam smiled. "That's good. Don't beat him too badly, or he won't play with you anymore."

"Naw," he said dismissively. "He's sharp. He'll make a game of it for me."

"Good," she said. "Everything else alright?"

"Fine here. I'm more worried about you."

Cam glanced at Mercer's bedroom door. "You know I can handle myself."

"I do know, but you are still my daughter and I love you."

Cam pursed her lips. If her father only knew precisely what she was doing, he'd be very disappointed. He didn't abide by her use-or-be-used motto. But if she didn't do it, he'd die.

"I love you too. Talk to you tomorrow."

"Tomorrow." And he hung up.

Cam ended the call and grabbed her suitcase. After selecting her clothes and toiletries for the day, she opened the bedroom door to the living room. The television was on, but there was no sound. She peered over the back of the couch and found Mercer sprawled out on his stomach, mostly naked. No shirt, no pants, just a pair of shorts and blanket haphazardly draped over him.

He was a big man. Long legs, broad back, strong shoulders, evenly bronzed skin. Very nice. Too bad he was also an XCEL agent.

"Sleep well?" he murmured into the small pillow his head rested on.

"Great," she replied, hiding her surprise. And he had very good hearing for a human. "You?"

He twisted around on the couch, which was about six inches too short for him, and gave a groan as he lay on his back.

Also nice, Cam thought. Deep chest, thick biceps, lean muscle structure. Such a waste.

"I slept great," he said with a slow drawl. "Can't wait to do this every night for the next few weeks."

She quipped, "I'll bet you say that to all the ladies."

He got to his feet and rolled his shoulders, gritting his teeth as he stretched. She watched every movement, every flex, with reluctant admiration. He walked around the couch and paused in front of her. "Usually, if there's a woman here, I'm sleeping in my bed."

Cam caught the sudden light in his eyes, and then it was gone as he focused on her. Seriousness and distrust returned, hardening his features. As if he just remembered that he hated her and her kind. She knew it. This *was* personal.

"Too bad you're stuck with a Shifter," she said.

He didn't answer for a long time, a little too long, and she felt the anger settle into his body. The curiosity was killing her, but whatever it was, he wasn't going to share it with her anytime soon.

"Too bad," he repeated, and walked past her to the bathroom.

FIVE

The sun was just setting over the Brooklyn Navy Yard as they stood in front of their first location of the day. Sounds of machinery and chugging air conditioners filled the air. Cars snaked around the few roads that meandered through the renovated yards. Workers and tourists wandered the historic and newer buildings. Cranes and smokestacks crisscrossed the sky.

Griffin would have preferred to work later when there were fewer distractions and less people around, but he'd decided last night that he really wanted this mission to end as soon as possible. His tiny apartment simply was not big enough for him and Camille Solomon. Between the too-small couch and the knowledge that she was in his bed, he'd gotten maybe two hours' sleep.

Cam turned to look at him, and the red glow of the afternoon sun caught her hair. It was long, wavy, and just a little wild. Of course, it wasn't really hers. Neither was the tight body or alabaster skin. The only things that really belonged to her were the jeans and a blue tank top that pretty much left nothing to his imagination.

"You're sure about this location?" she asked, a quizzical look on her face.

Griffin checked his smartphone again. "PSI Distributors, LLC. Building twelve, first floor. Hit night before last. I think the blown-out windows and yellow police tape give it away, don't you?"

She blinked at him. "You care what I think?"

Griffin eyed her. He wasn't ready for twenty questions today. "What?"

One corner of her mouth curled. "You're starting to like me."

"Christ," he muttered. He lifted the Do Not Enter tape to let her under. "Move it."

She made a little face at him and ducked under the tape. They walked through the first-floor entryway. Marble floors and walls were smeared and dusty. Aside from that and the muddy footprints of firefighters and law enforcement, nothing appeared out of place until they reached the back of the building, where PSI used to do business.

The main door into the suite was off its hinges, singed around the edges, and ajar. The smell of smoke swept over him as he ripped through the yellow tape across it and shoved the door open. Inside, the place was blackened by fire. Scorched steel beams supported what was left of the ceiling. The concrete floor was layered with burnt wood and furniture. Skeletons of metal storage racks stood stark against the charred walls.

The Shifters made sure that these places wouldn't be doing business anytime soon. It pissed him off to think of them pouring gasoline all over everything these people had worked for and sending it up in smoke. They didn't have the right.

Cam walked ahead of him, stepping through the destruction. She seemed to be muttering something, but he couldn't make it out. He'd learned not to bother her when she was concentrating, or risk dismemberment.

"Not the same Shifters," she whispered as if in a trance. "Not the same. Different, but . . ."

"But what?" Griffin asked, not sure he really wanted to know. He was hoping that this mission would identify only a few Shifters, making his job easy. But more suspects meant more nights on the couch, and that didn't make him happy.

Cam's eyes were closed as she answered him. "I'm picking up the same oily scent that the other two groups carried."

Damn. He hated that couch. "How many Shifters this time?"

"Two," she replied, sounding lost in her concentration. Griffin had more questions, but he knew better than to push her. She was doing her best, he could tell by the depth of focus. He wondered how she felt about betraying her own. Shifters didn't seem to stick together much. They were all out for themselves. So perhaps it wasn't even a factor.

She lifted her face, looking almost angelic in the sunlight. Wouldn't last.

"All males," she continued. "I definitely smell oil. Refined." She opened her eyes to look at him. "Where would they get petroleum oil?"

"Anywhere. This city uses a lot of oil."

She nodded, frowning, and stepped through the wreckage. "Still, rather interesting, don't you think? They must be around some kind of industry."

"Or underground."

Cam walked between the racks of supplies, moving them around and rummaging through the crispy supplies. She picked up a needle. "Syringes."

She asked Griffin, "What do they ship?"

"Did," he corrected. "Medical supplies."

Her frown deepened, and he was getting that feeling again that she was not sticking to the plan. Why was she so damn curious?

"But the products are still here," she said, peering into another box. "Disinfectant. Latex gloves. Sutures. They didn't take any of it."

The bad feeling that Griffin had in his gut grew. He was not biting at her challenge. "We aren't here to find out why."

"Maybe we should be," she said. Then her gaze met his, direct and stubborn. "We walked by a drug supplier business. Much easier pickings than these, and better money. So why torch medical supplies? Why not target the drugs? In fact, why not just steal the stuff? Why bother destroying it?"

Griffin had noticed the drug company. He'd hoped Cam missed it. "I don't know."

"And you don't care," she added.

Frustration seeped into his bones, replacing any doubts. "No, I don't. My job is to find whoever is doing this and identify them."

Cam moved toward him and stopped a foot away, fearless. "Don't you think it would help us find them if we knew *why* they were hitting these places? Like an MO?"

It would, but he was following orders this time, even if it killed him. He'd learned his lesson. Harding would take any opportunity to pull his deal. "Sometimes. In this case, no."

"Why not?" she asked, unfazed.

She was relentless. "These Shifters have hit dozens of targets. There's no pattern, no reasoning behind it. And why do you care?"

She narrowed her eyes. "Why *don't* you care? Afraid of what you'll find?"

Griffin replied, "Don't tell me you give a crap what happens to these guys. You're no saint. You and your father aren't robbing casinos blind for the good of Shifters everywhere."

A flash of something dangerous passed through her features, and then fire took hold. "At least I can think for myself. I'm not some puppet on a string."

"Aren't you? And I think I'm the puppeteer."

Cam glared at him for all she was worth. "And you have no qualms about using me, do you?"

"You use casinos," he countered.

"But you can't kill a casino. I've tried," she said. "Why do you hate us? Is it just general blanket paranoia or something special?"

Her question was unexpected. "I have my reasons." None of which he planned to share with her.

She didn't back down. "They better be damn good."

"They are."

Cam's voice lowered. "Good enough to blame an entire race?"

"Yes," he replied. "And you've reached your quota for questions for today."

A slow, smug smile stretched across her face. "Day's early, Mercer."

◆◆◆

"Aristotle!"

Aristotle recognized the boyish voice and stopped in the

middle of the underground tunnel below West Village. It was pitch-dark in the tunnels under New York City, but Shifters didn't have to worry about that. What he did have to worry about was running from someone. His old legs weren't as strong as they used to be.

"What is it, Red?"

The young Shifter slowed to a walk, barely breathing hard, and spread his arms out wide. "Where have you been? I've been all over these tunnels looking for you."

Aristotle showed him the rolled-up map in his hand. "Working, boy. Why?"

Red put his hands on the hips of his newest human skin in the form of an Asian male, roughly twenty years old. "We got trouble."

"We *are* trouble, Red. That's the whole point."

Red waved a hand at him. "No, no. XCEL has a new team hunting us down. Found out about them last night. Combing through all our hits. You know what this means?"

Aristotle turned and continued his lumbering walk. Red rushed up along his side. "This *means*," Red said, "they are onto us."

"They've been onto us for a while. They just don't know how to catch us."

"Well, they got help now," Red said. "Shifter help. And she's the daughter of a friend of yours."

There were only a few surviving female shapeshifters, and even fewer that were daughters of his friends. "Cala."

"She's going by Camille Solomon now, but yeah."

Disappointment filled his ancient bones. Aristotle slipped to a distant past for a brief moment. Long ago when life was good, or at least tolerable. Before fear of shapeshifters took everyone he loved and cared about on a planet far from here. Before this world became their new home, and these humans their reluctant hosts.

"Where is her father?" Aristotle asked.

"No idea. Only got an ID on her. She's working with an XCEL agent named Griffin Mercer. One of Harding's underlings."

Harding, of course. Harding was the enemy. *So it begins,* Aristotle thought. He knew this day would come. He'd counted on it. He hadn't counted on one of his own turning against him. That was unforgivable, but not unexpected. Every Shifter had to find their own way to survive in this world, and Cala had found hers.

Too bad she'd picked the wrong side.

Red ran up ahead and pushed open a heavy door that led to a concrete room, just like everything else down here. This was one of many such rooms his teams used for their meetings.

Twelve members of Aristotle's team had already gathered around or stood near the large table in the center of the room. To humans, it would look rather odd to meet in total darkness. To his people, it was a matter of secrecy. Because this world was about to launch a new genocide against shapeshifters, and Aristotle and these men were the only ones who stood in their way.

Aristotle greeted the members one by one. Each held hope for the future or hatred from the past. He really didn't care which, or why they were here, as long as they were. Then he unrolled the city map that nearly covered the entire six foot length of the table.

Red circles designated their targets. Xs marked those that had been completed. "We've been able to shut down the supply chain for operations at the shipyard. That should give us another few days while they search for new suppliers. Nice work, everyone."

A smattering of kudos rippled through the group. It was

short-lived because their work was never done. Or at least, it felt that way.

Aristotle tapped a red circle near Medford, Long Island. "New location, Burton Research. Test lab for skin grafting. Wilson, this one is yours. Pick your team and get there before the end of the week." He handed his oldest and most dedicated team member, Wilson, a blueprint of the building. "You can't just blow this one up. There's a clean room in the basement. That's your goal. A major shipment is scheduled out of there for Monday. We need to stop that."

Wilson scanned the blueprint and nodded once. "Got it."

Aristotle smoothed the White Plains area and pointed to a transportation center. "Mitchell, I want your team on a truck coming in from California. It's a very large superconducting magnetic energy storage system. Steel construction, practically impossible to damage, and it weighs a few tons. I figured you'd appreciate if it was already on wheels."

Michaels moved forward to get the transport documents from Aristotle and grinned. "Thanks, boss. What do you want me to do with it once I get it?"

"Dump it in the Hudson. That should ruin it for good." Then he addressed the group. "Those are our big targets this week. Anyone who's not on one of these teams is on surveillance duty."

Someone piped up. "Who are we surveilling?"

"XCEL."

A groan filled the small room, and Aristotle waved a hand. "We knew it would happen eventually. They aren't *all* stupid."

That got a few snickers.

"We have two XCEL agents snooping around our targets. One of them is a Shifter. You might know her as Cala. Came over with her father and brother."

Someone swore, and Aristotle concurred. "Exactly. For now, I just want them watched. See where they are going, what they are looking for. But don't get too close and don't engage. I don't want any wild car chases."

"Aw, man," Red said. "I thought you were going to let us have some fun for a change."

"What? Blowing up buildings isn't enough fun for you?" Aristotle asked.

Red shrugged. "It's okay, I guess."

"Good, then go blow up some buildings. We meet next Saturday at midnight. Greenwich room."

Everyone nodded and dispersed quietly. Red stopped in front of him as he collected his map. "Do you need anything?"

"No," Aristotle said. "Go have fun."

"Where's the fun for you?" Red asked.

Aristotle gazed at the young man. "This is fun."

"No," Red said. "This is work. You wanna come hang out with me and my friends for a while?"

Oh yes, an old Shifter and a bunch of kids. That would last long, but he loved Red for asking. "I think I'll get some sleep, but thank you for the offer."

"Suit yourself." And with that, Red was gone.

Aristotle shook his head and laughed at the kid. He reminded him so much of his son. He was about Red's age when he was slaughtered by the government on the last planet the Shifters had tried to build new lives on. They hadn't wanted Shifters. No one wanted Shifters. But that didn't mean that Shifters didn't deserve to live peacefully like other races.

It just meant that Shifters had to work harder at it.

CHAPTER
SIX

"How in the hell can you tell me that this is right?" Cam yelled at Mercer. He stood stoically in front of her in a warehouse where one corner had been blown to bits. The rest of the place was untouched. And he still wouldn't admit that she had a valid point.

He put his hands on his hips. "Not part of your job. And keep your voice down. We're trying to be quiet. Think, stealth."

"Think, *kiss my ass*. I know you're smarter than this. You can't tell me you don't see it."

She turned her back and kicked a metal can as hard as she could. It launched across the warehouse, trailing dust behind it before hitting an I-beam and ricocheting loudly. The clattering sound echoed from one end to the other of the football-sized warehouse. She yelled at the top her lungs, "Harding has us on some stupid wild-goose chase, Mercer, and you are too chicken-shit to find out why!"

"Don't kick—"

She nailed a paint can and it flew over a pile of crates, landing loudly on the other side. She didn't know what else to do to get through to him.

He put his hands on his hips. "Cam, this is a dangerous neighborhood."

"Do you recall the history of my people? Refugees escaping persecution on another planet and crash-landing here only to be hunted down by the likes of you? Do you really think a bad neighborhood scares me?" She picked up a chair and tossed it through a window. Glass shattered and rained to the floor. Then she turned to him and grinned in challenge.

Mercer raised his eyebrows. "Are you almost done?"

"No. And I'm not going to stop until you agree that something is very wrong here. There's a hundred thousand dollars' worth of supplies and equipment in this place, ripe for the picking. Just like the other places."

Cam grabbed a length of pipe and hurled it. It hit the steel siding and stuck, making a powerful vibration that reverberated through the rest of warehouse. "They aren't stealing stuff. And they could. So why aren't they?"

"Lazy?" he suggested. "Stupid?"

She rounded on him. "Have you reported this to Harding?"

Mercer's expression was blank, and that was her answer. He hadn't. They were all the same. Why would she think that he'd be any different?

Cam said, "You're good at following orders, aren't you?"

"I don't have a choice," he replied, his jaw clenched.

"Luckily, I do." She was about to throw another pipe when Mercer grabbed her arm. The shock jolted up her arm as she spun to face him. He was inches away from her, quiet and furious. "That's enough."

Cam glanced down at his hand around her arm. "Don't touch me."

Mercer's eyes narrowed, and then he released her. She stepped back, rubbing her arm where he left heat. The memory of the fear and futility she felt when he'd paralyzed her returned. He couldn't be trusted, not with her, not with finding answers.

He frowned. "I didn't hurt you."

"I know," she snapped. Damn him and his super-Shifter-whatever grip. "Just don't touch me."

"Then don't throw things," he came back.

"It relieves stress," she snapped. It was partly true. "You've had me locked up tight. I have to do something—"

Then her senses refocused swiftly and instinctively to danger. Every part of her being went on high alert. Something moved toward them. Her hearing focused on the creak of a door and footsteps on concrete. "Company."

She spun around to find a gang of young men approaching and blocking the main exit. They moved in with supreme self-importance and menace.

"What do we have here?" the one in the front said with the cocky attitude of a man holding a big gun. Tattoos marked every part of his body. A red bandana wrapped his head and closely cropped hair underneath. His dark features were surly and arrogant.

"Trespassers, looks like to me," another one said.

Griffin didn't move. In a few moments, he assessed the situation. The gang members had four guns and a few knives that he could see, and there'd be more tucked into pockets and waistbands. All of the men could handle themselves. Not a runner in the bunch, which left Cam and him against six. Or maybe just him against six. Who knew what Cam was going to do?

Either way, he was going to have a few words with her if they survived this. He replied, "This is private property, and I don't think it belongs to any of you."

Laughter rang through the structure. The leader stepped forward, eyeing Cam the whole time. "You don't know who you're talking to, do you? We *own* this territory and everything in it. Including you and the little lady here. So put your hands out where we can see them."

The other members gathered around them, looking more than ready to rumble. Must be a slow night in the neighborhood. Griffin raised his hands. "I'm warning you. Leave now while you can."

That got another round of laughs and shaking heads. He cast a glance at Cam. She was grinning like the Cheshire Cat. *Terrific.* He had a bad feeling this was one way Cam relieved stress.

The leader nodded at his minions, and they searched Mercer roughly, relieving him of his Glock and then throwing him a couple elbows as a warm-up. His gun was passed around like a trophy.

Cam scowled at the leader. "What about me? I could be carrying."

Griffin had just lost his gun, they were outnumbered and surrounded by armed thugs, and she was more worried about her rep.

The leader smiled at her, and gold teeth gleamed in the dim light. "Why don't you come over here, and I'll pat you down myself."

"Don't do it, Cam," Mercer warned.

She ignored him and walked up to the leader. He grinned wider and lowered his gun. "Well, well. You want to play?"

She smiled. "Oh yeah, I want to play."

"Christ," Griffin said. It was like watching a cat toy with a mouse. "How long are you going to let this go, Cam?"

"Don't ruin my fun, Mercer."

"Quit playing already," he said and eyed the three guys closest to him. "I'm getting tired of holding my hands up."

She slid him a glance over her shoulder, and he caught a glint of fluorescence in her eyes. That was his signal. Mercer tensed, mentally counting his targets and moves. When it happened, it'd have to be quick. Cam might be indestructible, but he wasn't, and he'd sure like to live long enough to enjoy the new life he was earning.

Adrenaline flooded his senses; time slowed as the leader reached out, grabbed her forearm hard, and yanked her toward him. Griffin fought the sudden urge to move. She hadn't sprung the trap yet.

"I wouldn't do that if I were you," Griffin said, flexing his hands. "She doesn't like to be touched."

Cam came nose to nose with the leader. "I really don't."

Then she grabbed him by the shoulders and gave him a brutal head butt. His skull cracked against hers, and the warehouse went dead silent. Then the leader stared at her in shock as blood gushed out of his nose and he dropped to the floor.

Cam shifted to her big bad Primary Shifter form and let out an inhuman growl. Griffin grabbed the two closest gang members and bounced their heads together. They went down in a heap. The other one attacked him from the back, and Mercer elbowed him in the face and threw a right to finish him off. From there, it was all instinct and training. He ducked, swung, and punched as the rest of them converged on him.

He glimpsed Cam tossing gang members around like they were rag dolls. Then someone fired a gun, and Mercer grabbed one of his guys with an arm tight around his neck and used him for a shield. Twenty feet away, one of the men was firing a revolver at Cam point-blank. Griffin marveled at the way the bullets passed right through her body.

She calmly walked up to the goon, yanked the pistol from his hand, and tossed it aside. Griffin was about to tell her not to kill the guy when he sensed movement behind him and saw the flash of metal.

The blade slashed his shoulder even as he tried to swing his human shield between them. Blood spattered, a strip of his flesh burned, and Griffin dropped the guy he'd been holding. A second attacker grabbed Griffin's throat from behind. Griffin wrenched around, trying to break the headlock as the other gang member drove the blade toward his gut. Then there was a puff of black and suddenly the knife attacker was flying across the warehouse, screaming.

Griffin spun, kneed the second attacker in the balls, and then in the face when he doubled over. He dropped like a rock.

When Griffin checked the scene, everyone was either down or gone. Cam stood next to him in Shifter form, looking like a meaner, leaner, far scarier version of Catwoman. The warehouse fell into a mix of moans and running feet.

Cam shifted back to human and assessed the carnage. "Not bad, Mercer."

"We could have avoided this," he said as he scouted the bodies for his Glock and found it in one of the pockets. "They'll be back with reinforcements. We can't stay long."

Cam rolled her shoulders. "I needed that. Kinda like Pilates."

"You and me are going to have a little talk about how we operate," he told her, trying to sound mad. The truth was, he'd just found out exactly how she'd operate when there was trouble. First, she'd play with her food, and then she'd kill it. She was getting to be more like Catwoman every minute.

"You're bleeding," she said suddenly. She was staring at his shoulder. The look of concern on her face surprised him.

"Is it serious?" she asked.

"It's nothing." Actually, it hurt like hell and would require a few stitches. He hated knives. He hated people who used knives. And more importantly, he hated people who used knives on him.

"So." Cam studied him. "I guess I just saved your life."

Hell, she was up to something. He said, "I could have handled them."

She leaned on one hip, looking more like a sexy gambler than a ruthless fighter. "Really? Because I could have sworn you were about to be filleted. But if you insist, next time I won't bother."

Sirens wailed in the distance. Time to move on. If he could get Cam to move. And he only knew one way. "What do you want?"

She slipped in front of him, and his eyes immediately focused on her. "We look for answers. For why the Shifters are operating this way."

Her voice was low and husky. *Borrowed voice*, Griffin reminded himself, even as he stared into her eyes. Gold highlights moved in her hair. He should say "Forget it," but those sirens were getting closer by the second. When she raised her chin in challenge, he followed the long line of her neck down to the T-shirt and the breasts that filled it out.

"Mercer?" she asked.

She wasn't going to let him off the hook.

"Two hours' worth of XCEL's resources," he said.

"Six," she countered. "And I want Ernest."

Damn, she was good. "Four. Not Ernest. He's a kid."

"Three, and we need Ernest," she said. "He's brilliant."

She was right about that. Ernest wasn't bleeding all over the floor at the moment. Griffin offered, "Three, and Ernest."

"Deal," she said as she turned and headed toward the exit. He shook his head, wondering why he'd given in. He was way out of line, and Harding would have his head. Then he noticed the sexy way her hips rolled when she walked, and he realized he needed a good night's sleep pretty damn soon.

◆◆◆

"I thought you said this was just a scratch," Cam said as she watched Lyle stitch Mercer's shoulder. It had to be painful, but Mercer was far tougher than she realized. He just sat there on the kitchen stool and didn't say a word. Like this happened every day.

"Do you do this a lot, Lyle?"

The bartender stood up and gave a loud sigh. "More than I care to. Used to be a medic in the army."

He cut the last of the threads and tossed the needle on the countertop behind him. "Griffin has a thing about doctors."

Mercer winced and pulled on a clean shirt. "Don't tell her anything. She'll use it against me."

"My kind of girl." Lyle winked at her and washed his hands in his kitchen sink. "Come downstairs when you're ready. It's last call. I'll buy you a drink."

Cam nodded at Lyle as he left. There was a pile of bloody paper towels in the sink. "You must really hate doctors, because this couldn't have been pleasant. There's a rumor that Novocain works wonders for humans."

Mercer stood up and rolled his arm. "I don't hate doctors."

Cam said, "No? So what's the deal? Childhood trauma? White coat phobia?"

He put his hands on his hips and squared off in front of her. "You ask a lot of questions."

"You don't ask enough." She smiled. "So why the aversion? Because I have a funny feeling that this won't be the last time we end up here."

Mercer turned serious. "Let's just say that I don't want any official medical records of my injuries."

Cam frowned. "Who would care?"

"XCEL would," he said, sounding surprisingly disgusted.

And she was confused. "You can't tell me that XCEL agents don't get hurt all the time. I know better."

Mercer held her gaze. "I'm not an XCEL agent."

Cam took a full step back. "Whoa. What? You're not an agent? What the hell are you, then?"

For a moment, he didn't reply and she wasn't sure he would. Getting information out of him was like pulling teeth. From a tiger. Cornered.

Finally, he seemed to come to some kind of decision. "I *was* an XCEL agent. And then a Shifter took my place."

Now *that* she hadn't expected. "And?"

He started to say something and then shook his head. "Let's just say that I've been trying to convince everyone that I'm really myself ever since. It's been a blast."

His tone turned bitter, and she understood why. Humans were really attached to their uniqueness, their *specialness*. Not that she'd ever personally agreed with that. Mostly, they were all identical assholes.

"That sucks," she said. "But what does that have to do with you refusing to investigate something you know is wrong?"

He eyed her. "You've met Harding."

She wrinkled her nose. "True. I don't suppose he handles surprises well."

Mercer grabbed his jacket off the chair and pulled it on. "He doesn't handle anything well, but I have to go through him."

To get what I want, he left unsaid, but Cam heard it loud and clear. That meant Mercer didn't give a damn why Shifters were blowing things up. He just wanted to give Harding his answers and get his job back. His identity back. She didn't care as long as she got what she wanted too.

"We had a deal," she reminded him. "Three hours."

"How could I forget?"

But he grinned in the shadows when he said it, and Cam realized he would keep his word. She didn't know how she knew it, but she did. Either that or she was getting soft.

◆◆◆

Griffin lay on the couch with an aching shoulder and a stiff neck. Midday sun tipped through his window blinds. He sat up gingerly and checked his apartment. No sign of Cam, and his bedroom door was shut. One less thing for him to worry about. She was too curious for his good.

He stood and felt every punch he threw and every stitch he'd earned last night. He was getting too old to be fighting punks. Once this mission was over, he could go back undercover, tracking down Shifters posing as humans, and at least one part of his life would be normal again.

Griffin reached for the answering machine and skipped all the collections calls. His grandfather's voice was a welcome change.

"Hello, Griffin. This is your grandfather, Sani."

Griffin went to the kitchen to make coffee while the message played. He briefly considered scotch, but it wasn't quite noon and he never drank before noon. At least not lately.

"You have been heavy in my thoughts this past day. I feel pain."

Griffin glanced at his shoulder wound. His grandfather always seemed to know what was going on, even when Griffin was a kid. He could tell when Griffin broke his arm or fell off his bike. These days, though, his falls were much bigger.

The message continued. "Today, I heard the Eagle cry. The wind had carried it far from home, and it was lonely."

Griffin turned on the coffeepot, listening carefully. It was a habit he'd learned long ago. Elders were respected. Family was all-important. And everything you did—good or bad—reflected upon them.

"The Eagle missed the familiar things. It missed the water and the earth. It missed its family," Sani continued in his slow cadence.

Griffin walked back into the living room to find Cam standing just outside her door. She frowned at him, listening to the message in rapt attention.

"It wanted to go home. But the wind would not go that way. The Eagle cannot get home. This is its home now."

Griffin walked to Cam, their eyes meeting. His grandfather said good-bye, and the message ended.

"Who was that?" Cam asked, her voice sleepy.

"My grandfather," Griffin replied.

Her expression softened into curiosity. "Does he always say weird stuff like that?"

"He's a Traditional Navajo." He amended, "He believes in a lot of legends."

A hint of humor lit in her eyes. "I see. So nothing hereditary?"

"No," he admitted. At least he hoped not. Although he didn't abide by the cultural part of his heritage, he knew it well. He'd had no choice. Sani had made sure of that.

"Does he live around here?"

"He lives on the Navajo reservation in Arizona."

"Who's the Eagle?"

He almost stopped her, because it was way too early for twenty questions. Then again, she asked nicely. He sighed. "I have no idea."

"He's a storyteller?"

Griffin eyed her. How did she know that? "Yes."

"Like my father," she said.

That surprised him. "Your people have storytellers?"

"We had many a long time ago," Cam said, and walked past him toward the coffeepot. "Very long. My father is probably the last one."

Griffin took out two mugs, and Cam poured coffee into both.

He hadn't really thought about Shifters having a culture of their own. "Do you know the stories?"

She nodded. "Most of them. Not all." She gave Griffin a little smile. "My father says I don't have enough patience to listen."

"There's a surprise," Griffin said over his coffee.

"Funny," she said. "Do you know your stories?"

He took a sip of coffee. "Most of them."

She grinned, knowingly.

"I've learned patience the hard way since then," he said.

She didn't reply, but he could almost see the wheels turning in her head. Which part of this conversation would she spring on him down the road? He was beginning to look forward to the challenge.

Griffin leaned against the counter across from her and noticed that she was wearing one of his T-shirts. A strange awkwardness stretched between them, and he found himself staring at her long legs under his shirt. Then he remembered that she was his ticket to normal. Or as normal as a shapeshifter hunter's life could get. He had no business looking at legs.

"When do I get my three hours?" she asked.

Griffin laughed despite himself and realized that it had been months since he found anything funny, maybe longer. "Today."

Cam gave him a brilliant smile. "Good."

"Quietly," Griffin amended.

"I can do quiet."

He highly doubted that. "Ernest is not like us."

"No, he's smarter," she said.

Griffin said firmly, "The only reason Harding tolerates him is because he is the best geek he has. I don't want that to change."

Cam set down her coffee and narrowed her eyes. "I'll be careful, I promise. I just need a little research."

They understood each other. It was getting a little scary, actually. Of course, by next week both of them would be on their merry ways. As it should be. Working on the same side with Shifters felt unnatural. Yes, there were one or two shapeshifters in XCEL, but no one ever really trusted them.

"By the way," she said as she headed toward the bathroom, "thanks for the shirt."

"No problem." Then Griffin breathed into his coffee. "Nice legs."

"Thank you," she called from the other room.

◆◆◆

Roberts told Harding, "They've identified three distinct teams so far."

Harding tapped his fingertips together while Roberts sat across his desk and gave his report.

"No problems?" Harding asked.

Roberts replied, "Just some local trouble last night. They handled it. We cleaned up the mess."

Harding checked his displeasure. He knew when he picked Mercer that there would be problems. "Any other issues?"

"Nothing. Camille Solomon appears to be cooperating, and Mercer has her under control."

For what that was worth. Mercer was the loose cannon. The only reason he was following orders was because this was his one chance to get back into the organization. "And Ernest?"

"No issues there either."

So far, everything was going exactly to plan. It was better than he could have hoped. "Excellent. Thank you for the update."

Roberts stood up, turned on his heel, and left.

Harding waited until the door closed behind him before dialing the phone number on his cell.

"Hello?"

He leaned back in his chair, feeling the smooth leather under his hands. "Report."

"The final locations will be addressed this week."

Harding smiled. "Make sure there is no trail left, nothing to follow. Understood?"

"Understood." The phone disconnected.

Harding hit the End Call button. For the next few minutes, he scrolled through communications, e-mails, faxes, and everything else that came into and out of this location. Even though Roberts had already given him the information, he didn't trust anyone to do their job right. That's how Shifters got a foothold in his organization. Sloppy work.

Which meant he'd had to step in to make things right, because otherwise, people became complacent. Their memories grew short and skewed. Before they knew it, Shifters would be walking around like they belonged, surrounded by ignorant sympathizers who called themselves Americans, letting anyone and everyone into this country. Well, it was high time this country went back into the hands of the rightful owners. The true Americans who took care of true Americans first.

And he was going to make damn sure that happened. Starting with his city.

CHAPTER
SEVEN

Cam sat in a booth at the back of Lyle's bar between Mercer and Ernest. It was late afternoon and the place was pretty dead except for the half dozen or so Shifters prepping the bar and tables for the night rush.

She wondered if Lyle knew he'd hired Shifters. Mercer must have told him already, but Lyle had hired them anyway. It must drive Mercer nuts. She smiled.

"So you want me to dig deeper into the locations you checked?" Ernest asked. "Why?"

Cam turned her attention to him. "I'm wondering if there is a connection between them."

Ernest sipped his Diet Coke. "Like what?"

She shook her head. "I don't know, but I can tell you that these hits are not random. There's a reason. A pattern. The Shifters destroy parts of a building but leave the rest. They ignore valuable inventory. They take risks for no apparent reason. Why?"

Ernest nodded his head slowly. "I didn't think about that before." Then he frowned. "But that's really not our job."

"Humor her," Mercer said over his scotch. "She's relentless."

She made a face at him and then addressed Ernest. "I just need a little information. Are these places connected somehow? Are the rest of the hits like this? Anything you can give me."

Ernest bit his lower lip. "The thing is, I think I'm being watched."

Mercer went very still. "How?"

Ernest glanced around the bar and leaned forward. "I discovered a tap on my office phone. My communications to you are being intercepted. I also located digital tracers throughout my systems. Poorly embedded, I might add. And I'm pretty sure they're monitoring my cell phone too."

Cam gave Mercer a victorious smile. "Still think I'm crazy?"

He didn't bite. "No offense, Ernest, but remember last year when you thought there was a conspiracy to plant a virus on your computer?"

Ernest pointed a finger at him. "They did. I was working too fast and showing up the other techs. I was sure then, and I'm sure about this now."

Mercer studied him for a moment. "You think it's Harding?"

Ernest winced. "I don't know who it is yet."

Mercer cut a glance to Cam and raised an eyebrow.

"*Because*," Ernest added, "I have to be careful not to tip them off. This is a delicate operation."

She said, "So big surprise, Harding doesn't trust us. Can we work around him?"

Mercer finished off his scotch. "Not easily."

"Not since last year's big mess—" Ernest began. Then he glanced at Mercer and stopped talking.

"What mess?" Cam asked, unable to conceal the shock in her voice. "Involving Mercer?"

Ernest stammered a little. "Just a breach in security."

Mercer thinned his lips. "I told her about the Shifter."

Cam put the pieces together. "He took your place in XCEL?"

"For a few weeks," Mercer said, his tone rough. "While I was undercover."

"Long enough to get his hands on some highly confidential stuff—XCEL missions, directives, and operatives. Then he tried to blackmail XCEL for money," Ernest said, shaking his head. "And here he was Griffin's partner and everything."

Partner? She closed her eyes for a second. Crap. When she opened them, Mercer was staring at his drink but radiating enough anger to torch the booth.

Ernest kept talking. "He really screwed the whole organization. We lost an agent—" He stopped and eyed Mercer. "Sorry. I'll shut up now."

Mercer frowned deeply. "Don't worry about it."

"What happened to your partner?" she asked, hoping for a happy ending.

Mercer stared at his empty glass. "XCEL killed him."

Ernest added, "After Griffin spent months trying to track him down. XCEL still didn't trust him to do the job. I'm surprised they even let Griff out of the detention center to look for him." He winced. "Damn. Didn't mean to say that."

"Wait. XCEL put you in jail?" she gasped. And here she thought being a Shifter was bad. Who would have guessed that XCEL agents were only one rung above her?

He lifted his glass and gazed at her. "End of discussion."

"Why the hell would you want to work for them?" she pressed. "You don't need them."

He took a swig and set the glass down hard. "Because it's the only thing I'm good at."

"I don't believe that," she said.

He cut her a quick glance and then spun the glass on the table. And that was the end of it, because he wasn't saying anything else and Ernest was busy sucking the life out of his Diet Coke.

She sat back in the bench. No wonder Mercer could give a damn about Shifters. No wonder he followed orders to the letter. Mercer had been locked up for the crimes committed by an imposter who stole Mercer's DNA and life. His partner had done a lot of damage—personally, professionally, and obviously, emotionally. She was surprised Mercer had even agreed to have Ernest look deeper. She must be better than she thought.

She broke the silence. "Don't you think Harding monitoring Ernest here is overkill? I mean, look at him."

Ernest appeared mortally wounded. "Hey."

"You don't look dangerous to me," she added, placating him. "How could Harding not trust you?"

"Because he's working with us," Mercer replied. "Are we being watched too?"

Cam hadn't even thought about that, but of course, they would be. Harding wouldn't trust an agent who'd already been compromised once, and a Shifter who was a bona fide criminal.

Ernest shrugged. "Probably. But we *can* get around this."

"How?" Cam asked.

He grinned boyishly. "I have a special network set up outside of XCEL. Same system access, but with bogus accounts."

She smiled back. "I knew I liked you for a reason."

Ernest blushed. He reached into his pocket and handed Mercer a smartphone. "Use this when you don't want to be monitored. The number to my secure cell phone is programmed in."

Cam glanced between the two of them. "Wait, I don't get a phone?"

"Sorry," Ernest said. "I only got one. I didn't want to draw suspicion."

Cam turned to Mercer. "And you were worried about our boy."

Mercer held her gaze as he said to Ernest, "Can you access information about the targets without getting caught?"

"I'll find a way," Ernest said. "I'll forward what I have to your phone in a few hours."

Cam slapped her palms on the table in victory. "Now see, that wasn't so hard, was it?"

Mercer eyed her. "Haven't gotten it yet."

She ignored him. "How's my father doing?" she asked Ernest.

He nodded. "He's good. I guess. I'm not sure I'd know if he wasn't."

I'd know, she thought, feeling the guilt to her bones. "He's moving around okay?"

"Sure. Although, I did kick his butt in chess."

Cam inhaled sharply. "For real?"

"Oh yeah. It wasn't easy. He's pretty sharp for an old guy."

Her heart sunk. "He lost at chess."

Ernest turned from her to Mercer. "That's what I said. It's not a big deal."

It was a big deal. Her father knew every move there was to play. He'd memorized thousands of strategies. He was a virtual superhuman when it came to chess, to any game. He never lost, not even to the best computers. It made him a hell of a gambling partner.

Maybe he was just tired, she told herself. Maybe it meant nothing. Or perhaps it was another sign that time was running out.

◆◆◆

Griffin drained spaghetti in the sink with his bugged cell phone cradled on his shoulder and pretended to be paying attention to his boss. "Our preliminary findings indicate that there are three separate teams. We plan to contact suspects tonight."

"How many suspects?" Harding asked. His condescending tone irked Griffin to no end. He couldn't wait for this check-in to end.

"Two," he answered curtly. Hell, he had no idea, but it would shut Harding up.

"That's the best you can do?"

Griffin set the pasta in the sink to finish draining and wiped his hands on a towel. A noise behind him brought his head around. Cam walked in, fresh from a shower and carrying three hours' worth of Ernest's printed dossiers on the sites.

"It takes time to track down suspects," Griffin responded flatly.

Cam eyed him with curiosity. He mouthed, "Harding," and she rolled her eyes in disgust.

"We have informants. Find a way to move faster," Harding said.

Griffin watched the way Cam's hair separated into thick, red ringlets when it was wet and nearly forgot his train of thought.

"We are finding some inconsistencies with the sites. Have the investigators noted anything unusual about the Shifters' MO?"

Cam's eyes widened as she stared at him. Big, blue, and beautiful. He had to admit, she was the best-looking thing his dismal apartment had seen in a long time.

"What the hell are you talking about? Since when do you *think*?" Harding barked loud enough for Cam to hear. She gave Griffin a commiserating look.

Harding continued, "You focus on your mission. I don't need to remind you what is on the line for you and for our country."

Cam flipped Harding the finger.

It was all Griffin could do not to laugh in Harding's ear. And then, just because Harding was being such a prick, he said, "It could help our interrogation of the suspects."

"The only thing you need to worry about is getting that woman close enough to smell them."

"That woman" was glaring at the phone with murderous intent.

"Concentrate on your own job. Remember, you can be replaced," Harding said.

Griffin felt the surge of humiliation flood over him. Heartbeat by heartbeat, he pushed the anger and resentment down beneath what was left of his pride. Blood thrummed in his head, burning away at his soul. "Yes, sir."

"Damn right," Harding said and hung up.

Cam was watching him as he set the phone down, carefully. Otherwise, he'd throw it across the room. Griffin braced himself on the counter for a moment to put his emotions back in check.

"I should have killed him when I had the chance," Cam said.

Griffin raised his head to look at her. Blue eyes peered back at him. "I need him."

She set the printouts on the counter. "I know. I'll just have to wait until you don't."

He'd pay to see that.

"You really need to let that anger out," she said.

He regarded her with surprise. "Excuse me?"

She sat on the stool across from him and leaned forward. The front of her bathrobe opened just enough for him to see silky skin. To his dismay, he felt himself getting hard. He moved closer to the island to hide his indiscretion. What was he thinking?

"If you don't, it'll eat you alive," she said and smiled wickedly. "Want to arm wrestle?"

Wrestle. That could possibly be the one thing that would re-lease the tension he was carrying. It would also be a very bad idea. "You'd go down."

Challenge flashed in her eyes. "You could try."

For a moment, he forgot that she was a Shifter. That her peo-ple were the reason for all his misery. For a moment, he imagined wrestling. And then he remembered all his sleepless nights and merciless collectors. He reached out and tapped the papers. "Let's save our strength for the bad guys. Find anything?"

"Not yet. On the surface, the companies that were hit don't appear to have anything in common."

"Told you," Griffin said, and turned back to the sink to dish out the pasta.

"On the surface, I said."

He grinned out of her line of sight.

"It's a little like doing a puzzle and finding the edge pieces," she continued. "You know there's a pattern, but there are big gaps that don't make sense. One thing is for certain; they all deliver a service or product to someone else."

"That's called business, Cam. Everyone does it."

She wasn't giving up. "What I need is a list of their customers, particularly any that they have in common."

Griffin spooned sauce on the pasta and sprinkled on grated cheese. "Maybe Ernest can figure it out."

Cam was staring at him in shock when he turned around with the plates. He held them for a moment. "What?"

"Well, number one, you cook. I didn't see that coming."

He slid her a plate. "It's not cooking. It's pasta. Any moron can make it."

She shrugged. "I can't."

Griffin pulled up the stool on his side of the island. "And?"

"You are giving me Ernest—free of charge. He already used his three hours," she said warily. "Why?"

Griffin loaded spaghetti on his fork, not wanting to admit that something felt wrong. The way Harding reacted to his questions. The way Ernest was being watched. The big rush to get this job done. And as much as he didn't want to look for trouble, he also didn't want to have this end badly. Right now, it had that feeling. Besides, Harding had pissed him off.

"You might be onto something," he finally said.

Cam raised her hands. "Halle-frickin'-luiah!"

A fork full of pasta was poised at his mouth. "Don't get used to it."

She laughed. "Are you kidding? Dinner and a confession? Doesn't get any better than that. Happy here."

He swallowed his pasta. "I'm not confessing anything. I'm just covering my ass. I don't trust Harding."

Cam sucked a long string of spaghetti between her lips and licked off the sauce. "Right."

Griffin finished his meal thinking of wrestling.

◆◆◆

The sad truth was all bars were the same. Whether they catered to humans or Shifters, male or female, the games were all the same.

Cam led the way through the third bar they'd visited tonight, her nose on alert. She was getting pretty tired of sucking cigar smoke and bad cologne into her lungs. She had a headache from trying to sort through the other scents and was getting meaner with every jostle. Jumbled music thrummed through the walls, floors, and patrons, making for a slurry of chaos. It wasn't helping her mood.

Their suspect had been spotted here thirty minutes ago by an XCEL informant. She tried to squeeze between two humans who didn't feel like moving until they noticed Mercer behind her and let her through. She glanced behind her and caught her breath. Mercer's face was intense and fierce as he stared down the men who blocked her way.

She turned around before he saw her, surprised by the possessiveness he radiated. No man had ever looked like that for her. Maybe he was just doing his job, protecting his mission. It was no secret how much he wanted this and what he'd give up to get it. She was simply a vehicle. The thought didn't bother her. Any pride she had had been lost years ago. It was a Shifter thing.

She moved from the front of the bar to the back and spotted their man sitting at a booth with three other Shifters. He wore a gray hooded sweatshirt that he had pulled down over his head. His skin was brown, and he had distinctly Latino features. The name they had on him was John Smith. Not exactly original.

Mercer stopped her about fifteen feet away from the booth, which was the best position they could get in the crowded joint. Cam was trying to figure out how to move close enough to check the suspect's scent when Mercer slipped his arm comfortably around her waist to pull her against him. He nestled his mouth against her hair and whispered, "You see him?"

"What are you doing?" she asked, stunned by his sudden and totally unexpected touch.

"Trying to be quiet. I know that's difficult for you."

Her senses were taking a serious turn toward Mercer, absorbing every part of him. She could play along too. "Yes, I see him. But I need to get closer to identify him. This place smells like urine."

Mercer turned them a bit so he could get a better look at the suspect. The movement sent a whole new set of sensations across her skin. Cam realized that no one was even paying any attention to him or her. They were embraced like any other couple in love. They belonged here. She'd never belonged anywhere before. It felt nice, and yet, terrifying.

Mercer said, "This is not a good place to approach him. We'll wait him out."

He was right about that. The suspect wouldn't be happy when they tried to talk to him. And in a tight place like this, that'd be trouble. Mercer stepped back and took her by the hand as he led them to a quiet spot in the back where they could watch their man. The lamp over a pool table was the only tangible light in the vicinity, so it was dark, at least by human standards.

Mercer eased her against his chest. Cam put her hands out instinctively and then rested them on his jacket.

"Easy," he said low.

"What are you *doing*?" she asked in no uncertain terms.

He kept his gaze on the bar area. "If we order a drink, I won't be able to handle him. Especially if he brings his friends along."

He'd had only one drink tonight, but she was getting the feeling that he drank a lot. Of course, if she worked for Harding, she would too.

"And if we drink soda, we'll get beat up," he added with a rare smile.

Cam burst out laughing. "So that leaves groping me?"

He finally looked down at her. She was a few inches shorter than he was, but it still felt too close. His mouth curled. "Think of it as being handled."

She raised an eyebrow. "Really? Is this how you handle everyone?"

His focus intensified, and her belly fluttered a little.

"That's dangerous territory, Cam," he said softly.

She moved a fraction of an inch closer. "Chicken."

Time ticked by one heartbeat at a time as she waited. She shouldn't provoke him, but he was buttoned up so tight by XCEL, Harding, and this job that she couldn't resist finding out what was really underneath.

A moment later, she had her answer when he leaned back against the wall, taking her with him to his chest. He kept his eyes on the bar scene over her shoulder, but the rest of him belonged to her. The flutter grew to a tremble as his fingers flexed on her waist, and she felt the heat spread out across her body. His breath was warm on her face. His thumbs traced a circular pattern through her shirt and ignited little circles of flames.

Oh, this is so wrong, she told herself. He was hot and getting hotter. She should back down now, but her body wasn't responding to threats, and she decided to hell with it. Playing with fire had always been one of her favorite pastimes. Besides, she was in full control and held all the cards.

She closed her eyes as steam built between their bodies, and every super sense she possessed heightened to the just-bearable range. Her fingers pushed into his chest between them, feeling the smooth skin over steely muscle. Griffin's hands slid up under her jacket, fingers splayed, dragging fire across her skin.

Her breathing turned faster, and deeper. She leaned into him and let his thigh wedge between her legs. A low sigh escaped her lips at the wondrous sensation it drew from her core. His heart pounded under her hands, and his breathing deepened. The brush of his lips grazed her temple, every movement building on the last.

She was burning up inside, her senses reeling. His cheek pressed to hers, rough with shadow. His breath was warm and deep in her ear. And her control was slipping by the second.

She pressed her hip against his erection and heard him swear. Thick. Hard. In fact, all of him was hard and lean. Mean. Dangerous. Fire. She growled a little as he lowered his head, his mouth right next to hers. She turned her head toward him—

Then someone dropped a bottle on the floor behind her, jerking her back to the present. She opened her eyes, and her gaze met Mercer's. Too late, she realized her mouth was open in a very obvious way.

She closed her lips and donned a forced smile as she leaned back. Mercer released her, and she took a step back. Her heart was thumping away, and her body hummed with unfettered lust with nowhere to go. She pulled in a deep breath and let it out slowly, trying to douse the fire that had gotten away from her.

So much for having the upper hand. This wasn't her first rodeo. There was no excuse for acting like this was any different, even if it was. The only variable was Mercer, and that was going to be a problem. At least she knew what it'd be like now.

For his part, Mercer was dead serious. In fact, he looked angry. What did he expect?

"You started it," she reminded him.

"You liked it," he noted.

"So did you." She grinned knowingly.

Mercer's gaze focused over her shoulder toward the front of the bar. "Our man's leaving with his buddies. Time to move."

She nodded, thankful for the promise of a good fight.

◆◆◆

They exited the bar onto the street, and Griffin spied their foursome heading north. A warm rain cast a mirror of lights across the streets. Cars and taxis splashed through puddles and across wet asphalt.

The rain felt cool on his face and body after holding Cam. It had been a stupid move on his part, letting her seduce him into a place he knew better than to go.

A pedestrian ran into him, and he forced his attention back to the mission at hand. Together, they followed the suspect and the other three Shifters across intersections and blocks. Griffin kept far enough behind so they wouldn't be spotted. He didn't want to spook the Shifters. Then again, that was one of the reasons he had Cam with him. She gave him some credibility with other Shifters. At least so he could get close enough to talk to them. After that, all bets were off.

At the end of the block, the four Shifters halted on the corner and parted ways—three heading east and one continuing north—their man. It was about damn time they got lucky.

He turned to Cam, and she nodded. "Let's get him."

Griffin hoped his luck held out as they followed John Smith and closed in on him in the middle of the next block. They were right behind him when he ducked into a narrow alley between two stores.

Now things would get interesting.

Griffin pulled his gun, ran to the alley, and peered around the corner. Cardboard boxes lined the sides of the alley. Random spotlights gave the alleyway an orange glow as their suspect walked down the center.

Cam whispered, "He's not going to like the gun."

Griffin replied, "I like the gun."

"Suit yourself. I'm impervious."

When John Smith disappeared around the end of the alley, they ran to catch up. They turned the corner and came face-to-face with John Smith—in full Primary Shifter form.

Their luck just ran out.

John Smith took the first swing at him, knocking the Glock out of his hand and against the cinder block wall. Griffin avoided the second blow, but not the third. It caught him in the side of the head, sending stars across the dark alley.

That's when he decided that he'd had enough. When the next punch entered his line of vision, he twisted and grabbed Smith's arm with his bare hand. Energy pumped through his hand, and

Smith froze. All fight went out of him as he stumbled back against a building, slid down the wall, and stared at Griffin.

Cam walked up beside Griffin to stand in front of the Shifter. "Sucks, doesn't it?"

"Thanks for the help," Griffin said to her. She hadn't even shifted.

She crossed her arms and eyed him. "I know how sensitive you are about me fighting your battles."

He was still seeing stars, and his head hurt like hell. "Okay, fine. You can help whenever you want."

Cam smiled. "I don't know. It's kinda fun watching you get knocked around."

Jesus. "We're partners."

"We are?" she said, feigning surprise. She was loving this.

"Heeeyyy!" John Smith said, his words slurred heavily. "What-dafuck?"

Griffin stood in front of the Shifter. "Sorry. We just want to ask you a few questions. Not looking for trouble."

Smith spat. "Widagun?"

Cam said, "I told you."

Smith's head banged against the building as he tried to focus on her. "Wh-youhere?"

"I won't hurt you. Just need your scent signature." She kneeled in front of him and then turned to Griffin and shook her head. "No match."

All that for nothing. "You can go."

The Shifter blinked. "Gowhaw? Whadda dodo me?"

Griffin retrieved his Glock and slid it into his underarm holster. "The effects will wear off in a few hours. Sorry."

Smith blinked a few times. "Sowy? Sowy?"

Griffin took Cam's arm. "Let's go before he can kill me."

He led her back to where he'd parked the car. They were done for the night. Screw Harding. These were his leads, and they all sucked.

Griffin tried to find some consolation about wasting the entire night. They could have checked a few more sites. Maybe confirm Cam's list so far. Or even pick up a few new ones. But no. Now he had to go back to his small apartment with a woman he shouldn't touch and couldn't get out of his head.

Griffin was lost in thought when Cam said, "Does it hurt when you do that?"

He eyed her. "Do what?"

"Use your freeze ray?" she asked.

"No," he said. "I don't feel a thing. Did it hurt you?"

Cam shook her head. "No. I just felt numb all over."

He nodded. "That's good."

She turned to him. "I'm surprised you care what we feel."

Maybe he did. Or maybe it was just her he cared about. He was still feeling the aftershocks of "handling" her in the bar, and he doubted he'd ever shake her easily. "Wouldn't want an injured partner."

Out of the corner of his eye, he saw her smile.

CHAPTER EIGHT

Griffin stuck his head under the showerhead again, turned the lever to cold, and let the water pound away. When he came up for air, she was still there in his mind. The hard workout on the Bowflex, a few hours of restless sleep, and the spray of the shower did nothing to relieve the tension in his body this morning.

He had Cam to blame for that.

Her smell, her heat, the way her lips parted when he caressed her. He knew she was hot from the beginning. He knew that she was perfect from head to toe. But he never could have guessed how that would affect him. She was a Shifter, for Christ's sake.

So how could he have fallen under her spell so easily and so quickly? He'd already been burned once.

Sleep deprivation was also to blame, and as soon as this mission was over with, he was buying a more comfortable couch. He shut off the water and grabbed a towel to dry down. On the other side of the bathroom door, he heard the answering machine click to accept a new message.

Probably another collection agency. They were vultures. Then his grandfather's voice came on. Griffin tied the towel around his hips and walked out to listen.

"Grandson, this is your grandfather, Sani."

Griffin walked over to pull open the drapes. The day beamed brightly, flooding the room with light. The street was lined with parked cars and an occasional tree. But mostly it was all concrete.

"I had a dream last night about you and the Eagle."

Griffin turned to look at the answering machine while Sani continued.

"The Eagle called out to her people in the sky. They circled the sun, looking for food. They did not want to listen to her."

His bedroom door opened, and Cam stood just inside. Her expression was curious. Her hair was wild and fiery in the sunlight. Legs, long and lean under his T-shirt. She was perfect to his sleep-deprived brain. He needed to rent a hotel room or something.

"The Eagle asked you to help tell her story to the others. She spread her wings to show her true colors. She danced. She sang."

Both of them stared at each other, listening, caught up in Sani's story.

"But you would not listen. You did not see her tears. Without your help, she knew she would fail."

Cam's eyes held a certain sadness, a weariness that belied her toughness. What would she be sad about? Her father?

Sani said, "I cannot tell you what this dream means. Or what you should do."

Griffin watched Cam walk toward him, slowly and deliberately. With every step closer, he remembered last night. He shouldn't have touched her, shouldn't have crossed that line.

"But seek the truth with your heart. Do not let your mind stand in your way."

Cam stopped in front of him, the answering machine sitting between them.

"*Hágoónee.*" The call ended, and the answering machine made a loud click that broke the spell.

Cam's expression turned to accusation. "He was just on the phone. Why didn't you pick it up?"

And last night vanished in a flash. He didn't want to explain himself to her, not about this. His relationship with his grandfather was hard to explain. He wasn't even sure he understood it. "We have an understanding."

"He calls, and you ignore him?" she said, sounding more upset by the moment. "How can you do that to him? He loves you."

Griffin felt her disappointment, and his guilt. Neither of which he needed this morning. He stepped around her toward the kitchen. "It's complicated."

Cam followed on his heels. "Love is not complicated."

He poured cold water into the coffeepot, debating what he could say to get her off his scent. She wouldn't be happy unless he told her something that she could understand. "I can't talk to him until I fix things."

She planted herself on the stool on the other side of the island. So much for getting her off his trail.

"Fix what? Your credit? Your job? I doubt he cares about any of that."

Griffin shoved the carafe in the coffeemaker and punched the

On button, feeling trapped. She didn't know him, didn't understand what he'd been through. "It's more than that."

"I don't—"

"Stop!" He rounded on her, and all his self-control evaporated. The words rushed out. "It's none of your goddamned business. Just because we're partners doesn't mean you get to know everything about me." He pointed to the answering machine. "You can't have that. You can't steal it. That's mine."

Cam's initial shock quickly turned to anger. She slid off the stool and tapped her chest. "I didn't ask to be born this way. I didn't ask to be dumped here on your pithy little planet with its pithy little people. You all think you're so special. Well, let me tell you, you're not. You're not even average."

Her words bounced off him. He wasn't backing down. The floodgate had opened, and he had no idea how to close it. "Then why the hell do you steal our identities? Our lives? Why can't you just be who you're supposed to be?"

Cam's eyes glowed iridescent, and the color rose in her face. "We tried that on the last world. And they came after us. Into our homes and into our schools. They murdered our children in their beds. They tracked down our men and enslaved them. And they killed my mother."

Her voice broke on the last word, and her body shook. Beads of sweat covered her forehead, and her hands were white from being clenched so hard. And in her eyes, he saw it—not sadness. Grief and pain. And now he knew why. Gone was his wisecracking partner. Gone was the human whose form she'd taken. This was Cam, right to her raw, tortured core.

His anger dissipated as quickly as it had overcome him. Shit. He braced himself on the island. "Look—"

"Shut up, Mercer. You said what you had to," she snapped, and glared at him with eyes that shone with tears. "We're not partners. We'll never be partners. So stop using it when it's convenient for you. As far as I'm concerned, you can take your self-righteous bullshit and shove it."

Then she turned, walked into his bedroom, and slammed the door. Griffin ran his hands through his hair. He'd managed to piss off the one person who could help him get his life back. It was beginning to occur to him that maybe all his problems were his own damn fault.

They'd killed her mother. Hell, it never crossed his mind to ask Cam anything about herself. He only cared about the parts that could help him. He glanced at the answering machine and could almost see Sani shaking his head at him.

The cell phone that Ernest gave him rang on the counter, and Griffin picked it up. "Yeah."

"We got a live one," Ernest said on the other end. "You and Cam should come into the Maplewood detention center. Right now."

Griffin glanced at his bedroom door and marveled at his shitty timing. "Will do."

"Oh, and you didn't find out from me," Ernest added before he hung up.

◆ ◆ ◆

"We caught him trying to steal a truck from a transportation center in White Plains," one of the XCEL agents said as he took them to an interrogation room in yet another highly secure facility. Cam wondered how many more of these XCEL owned and operated. And how many Shifters were locked up inside them.

"Was he alone?" Mercer asked.

The agent said, "No, but the other two got away. He was the only one we could catch."

"That's because he let you," she said.

The agent punched a panel on the wall, and a door slid open. He glanced at her. "What makes you say that?"

"Why do you think the others got away?" she replied and entered the room. The captive Shifter's clothing was piled on the table, and she went straight for it. A few sniffs and she confirmed that his scent matched one of the groups she'd discovered. The oily mix was there as well, the common link between all of them. She nodded at Mercer. He dismissed the XCEL agent.

The captured Shifter sat in human form on a cot as she stopped in front of the thick glass between them. Mercer moved up beside her. It felt weird as hell being on the other side of the glass, and not in a good way.

The Shifter wore a pair of orange cotton pants and a matching V-neck T-shirt. His head was in his hands, his shoulders hunched.

She tapped on the glass, and he gazed up. For a moment, he was surprised, probably because she was a Shifter. Then he turned red. His face twisted in anger.

"Are you shittin' me?" the Shifter said, disgust thick in his voice. He got to his feet and walked directly to Cam. "How can you do this to us?"

She stared at him, a bad feeling growing in her gut. Did he know her or was he just pissed because she was a Shifter? That had to be it. Her paranoia was getting the best of her. She blamed it on Harding.

"Why were you stealing the truck?" Mercer asked.

The Shifter ignored him and narrowed his eyes at Cam. "You know what they are trying to do. Or did you forget what happened on Govan?"

"I didn't forget and this isn't Govan," she said carefully. She was still raw from her argument with Mercer this morning, and this was not the place to lose control. In fact, no place was the right place to lose sight of her goal. This was about her father, and if she wanted to save him, she'd keep her focus on that. "Why the truck?"

"Go to hell," he said to her. And then he turned to Mercer. "And you too. I want a lawyer." Then he stopped. "Oh, wait. I'm not allowed a lawyer. That right is only given to humans. We don't qualify."

She ignored his valid point for the sake of finishing this job and getting as far away from Mercer as possible. "Spare me the crap. We know what you and your teams are up to."

She caught Mercer's eyebrows go up in her peripheral vision. They didn't know anything, but she was a hell of an actor.

The Shifter put his hands on hips and leaned toward her arrogantly. "You don't know anything."

Mercer coughed into his hand beside her.

Okay, maybe she wasn't as good as she thought. Cam leaned forward too. "The question is, why are you doing it?"

The Shifter laughed and turned his back on her. "Like I'm going to tell you anything." He dropped back on the cot. "Does your father know what you're doing, Camille?"

And with that, she froze, unable to frame a response. He did know who she was. Granted there were very few surviving female Shifters, but he knew her and her father. How? What did this mean for her father? For this entire mission? If they knew she was working with XCEL—

"That better not be a threat," Mercer said, interrupting her spiraling line of thought. "Because I'd take it very personally."

The Shifter laughed. "You and what army."

Mercer eyed her. "He hasn't seen you in action, has he?"

Despite the jumble of thoughts and fears vying for attention, she smiled at his respect for her skills. "Apparently not."

Then the door behind them flung open, and Harding came charging in. He glanced at the Shifter prisoner and shut down the open communication between them. The glass went opaque, the speakers muted, and Harding turned a nice shade of crimson.

"What the hell is going on here?" he said to Mercer through clenched teeth.

"This is one of our attackers. We were asking him a few questions," Mercer said, staying surprisingly calm in the face of Harding's wrath. Cam realized that his outburst this morning was the first time he'd let go of that steely self-control. That put her in a category worse than Harding. She wasn't sure if that was good or bad.

Harding pointed his finger at Mercer. "You don't ask questions. You do your job, and let us do ours."

Mercer didn't back down. In fact, he seemed to get stiller and more focused. Her skin prickled from the wave of intensity that shadowed him. She heard his heartbeat rise, blood rush through his veins. Instinctively, Cam took a step back.

"You don't want to know if he's one of our Shifters?" Mercer asked.

"We figured that out ourselves," Harding snapped. "No thanks to you two."

"How did you know?" Mercer pressed.

Harding looked as if his head was going to explode. Sadly, it didn't. He responded, "There are other agents out there with your *affliction*."

Cam narrowed her eyes at him. Right now, she'd give anything for laser vision.

"I can replace you," Harding added. Then he turned on her, and all her senses sharpened, ready for battle. She was in no mood for his crap.

Harding said, "But they know you."

Sonofabitch. He might not want them interrogating the captive, but he'd heard the conversation; he was probably listening the whole time.

"Gee, I'm not sure I like the sound of that," she said, donning Mercer's super-calm tone.

"You want your father back?" he said, menacingly. "Then you'll make contact with them. You'll offer to come in, talk to them, whatever it takes to find their location."

She could barely hold the words together, she was so furious.

Then he pointed at her and Mercer in turn. "Do not tip them off. You pass along the location, and we will take it from there."

Mercer said, "Yes, sir."

Cam heard the softness in his voice, the dangerous edge that it teetered on. Harding, of course, missed it completely.

Satisfied with being the biggest asshole in the room, Harding hitched his head at the Shifter. "And you make it fast, because if we get their location of operations out of this Martian—"

Cam felt a growl rumble in her throat.

"Then both of your deals are off," he finished.

She was about to tell him to shove it when Mercer stepped between her and Harding. She didn't need to see his face to know he was livid. His soft tone said it all.

"We all agreed to the deal," Mercer said evenly.

"The deal was *if* you succeeded."

Cam felt the tension increase in the small room with every passing second. Male testosterone thickened as Mercer moved deep into Harding's personal space.

Harding backed up under Mercer's advance, all the while trying to keep hold of his dominance. But Cam could smell him beginning to sweat under his suit. Amid the face-off, she realized that Mercer made Harding look like a scrawny weakling, overshadowing Harding by inches.

"And what about Cam? What about her deal?" Mercer said, his voice rough.

She held her breath for Harding's answer. The director's face was flushed, but he smiled through it. "Of course, we'll honor her deal."

Cam leaned around Mercer. "I want that in writing."

Harding cut her a glare. "You're lucky—"

"Don't start with her," Mercer said, and took another step forward, driving Harding's back to the door. "This is between you and me."

The challenge was not lost on Harding, but he was wise enough not to take it. Instead, he raised his chin and donned a haughty frown. "Your behavior is bordering on insubordination."

Mercer didn't say a word as he started taking off his jacket in a slow, deliberate way. She couldn't see his expression, but she could see the fear grow on Harding's face. God, it was priceless.

Then Harding wrenched the door open and stepped outside. He stared back at them from the relative safety of the hallway, his arrogance back. "Now get out there and do your fucking job."

The door slammed shut in their faces.

"Prick," she said under her breath. "He deserves to die in some horrible way that involves castration and torture."

"He will," Mercer said.

Cam eyed him. He was lost in a deep, dark thought that was more than a little scary. "He's probably listening to us now," she noted.

Mercer's gaze cut to the camera mounted in the corner. "I hope so."

◆◆◆

Aristotle rocked on his feet as Red delivered the bad news.

"They were waiting for us at the transportation center," Red said. "They knew we were coming."

Aristotle absorbed the information and what it meant. XCEL was either very lucky or they had a line on his activities. A spy perhaps in his operation? He'd chosen each member of his team himself and trusted them to follow him to the grave. He couldn't imagine any of them betraying him.

"They got Mitchell. He held off XCEL so the rest of the team could get away," Red added. "He won't talk, but we need to move our meetings. Just to be safe."

Further disappointment settled over his old body, taking its toll as it always did. Aristotle held no hope for fairness, or anything close to it. He'd abandoned that long ago. Still, he'd hoped for better than this. He drew a deep breath, and then once more, he accepted what he couldn't change.

Mitchell had sacrificed himself. He was a good man, and there were so few of them left. Not only had he lost a leader, the shipment would be delivered and bring Harding one step closer to destroying all of them.

Not one of his best of days.

"Was Camille there?" he asked.

Red shook his head, his long black hair floating around his head. Today, he was a Latino male, well built and strong. "No, but I'll bet she's involved somewhere. That could be how they knew."

It was possible, and he'd prefer that scenario over a traitor in his midst. Aristotle braced himself against the railing that ran the length of the underground tunnel they stood in. Cold, damp steel made his hands ache. This underground world was harsh on his body. If he could acquire a new, younger form, he would. But those days were over.

"We have to kill Harding," Red said. "There's no other way."

Aristotle shook his head. "Then we become exactly what they think we are."

"What difference does it make?" Red replied, throwing his hands up in frustration. "They hate us anyway. We'll never change that."

"Killing him won't stop this," Aristotle persisted. "There will be another Harding. And another. Until they perfect a way to kill us all."

Red gave a sigh. "It's hopeless."

Aristotle put his hand on the young man's shoulder. "The truth will come out. Trust me on that. It always does." Sooner or later, he added silently. Hopefully, sooner.

"Relocate the meetings," Aristotle said. "Tell the teams to move their plans along faster, if at all possible. Only the team leaders should know the details. We need to keep XCEL guessing."

Red nodded. "I'll pass it along. Anything else?"

The end of the tunnel was pitch-black, at least to a human. But he could see the end perfectly. "Find out where Camille's father is."

Red squinted at him. "Why?"

"It's personal."

"Suit yourself," Red replied. Then he said good-bye and left. His footsteps echoed, each one getting fainter.

Soon, silence descended over the tunnel, broken by an occasional rattle of a pipe or random thump from somewhere unseen. Aristotle felt the dampness overtake his skin and seep into his human bones. He closed his eyes and meditated on his existence as he had so many times before. His life was coming to its end; he'd known that for years and kept it hidden from those closest to him. He could feel his cells weaken and fragment, one by one. The process was slow, and not without pain.

However, he'd lived his life, and far longer than he'd wanted or planned to. That made him fearless and bold enough to take on a task that no one thought possible—stop the total annihilation of the Shifter race.

Yes, he'd lived his life, but the others, the teams he'd assembled, the Shifters who shared his vision and his will, they hadn't. They deserved better, and he couldn't promise them that.

CHAPTER NINE

Griffin watched Cam methodically pacing the trucking company parking lot, concentrating on the scents. He wished he could do more than just stand and watch her, although it wasn't a bad view.

He rolled his shoulders. He desperately needed a workout or a battle or something equally destructive, because he'd come very close to killing Harding with his bare hands. And that wouldn't do much to help his climb out of the trenches. If that was indeed still possible.

He didn't trust Harding to keep his end of their deal, even if they succeeded. Harding would do whatever was necessary to make himself look good to the higher-ups, regardless of who he stepped on. Griffin had seen him do just that firsthand.

So he'd spent much of the drive between the detention center and here trying to figure out how to make sure Harding followed through. So far, he'd come up blank.

Cam had stopped in the middle of the parking lot with her hands on her hips looking discouraged, and Griffin joined her.

"It's the second group. The ones who hit the navy yard location," Cam said, her tone low and serious.

Mercer liked the husky quality, her certainty.

"So definitely not a random hit," he said.

She shook her head and scanned the parking lot. "No. They knew exactly what they wanted."

A big rig passed nearby along the road that ran the perimeter of the transportation center. Dust arose, turning the late day sky a light shade of pink. The smell of diesel fuel and trash wafted indiscriminately across acres of asphalt and stone. According to Ernest's research, the warehouse was over sixty thousand square feet, with rows of docks around three sides. The day the tractor trailer was hit, there were over two hundred trucks in and out of this facility.

"How did they know where to look?" he asked out loud. "They couldn't have checked every truck."

"That's an excellent question," Cam said and smiled at him. "I'm so proud of you."

"Funny," he said and headed for the truck that the Shifters had tried to steal. It was still parked in the far back corner of the ten acres that comprised the property. He and Cam circled the truck together. They peered into the empty trailer. There was no cargo.

"Why steal an empty truck?" he said.

Cam frowned. "More importantly, how did XCEL know they were coming here and when?"

That had crossed his mind as well. Who called them in? Because no one could tell that this was a Shifter heist, and it wasn't like everyone had XCEL's phone number. They didn't operate that way.

Griffin put all the pieces together and decided that Harding was a lying son of a bitch.

"You look pissed," Cam said, eyeing him. "Anyone I know?"

"Give you one guess."

She stopped next to him at the front of the rig, and his anger melted away just a little. Her hair caught the sun, shimmering gold and red as it fluttered in the breeze. The loose, sheer blouse pressed against her breasts. His mind went to wrestling.

A bad place to go.

"Too many questions. No answers," he said.

Cam scanned the tractor trailer front to back. "Like who hooked the cab up to this empty trailer before we got here."

Griffin turned to her in surprise. "What?"

She walked past him toward the back of the truck. "This is definitely the cab. Reeks of Shifters. But this isn't the trailer. It's clean."

"You're sure."

"Positive. That's what you pay me the big bucks for."

That explained the empty trailer but also raised more questions. Like why switch trailers? And what had been inside the original trailer? That's the question that really worried him.

Cam kicked the pavement with the toe of her boot. "And this isn't the place the heist happened either. It was over there."

He followed her to a vacant corner of a parking spot on the other side of the lot. He noted the scuffmarks and blood on the pavement when they reached the spot. Now this looked more like a crime scene.

Griffin asked her, "You didn't find the original trailer, did you?"

She shook her head. "Not yet. But someone sure went to a lot of trouble to hide it from us."

"We know the Shifters didn't take it," Griffin added.

"So who hid it?"

Damn good question. Griffin pulled out his cell phone and called Ernest. He picked up on the second ring. "Agent Vincent here."

"Ernest, we're at the transportation center. I need to know what that tractor trailer was hauling," Griffin told him. "In fact, I want originating company and location, and who it was going to and where."

Ernest replied, "Yes, sir, that should be possible."

Griffin stilled at Ernest's formal tone and response. Ernest was being watched. "Thank you. Would it be possible to get that information delivered to our location tonight?"

"I'll work on it as soon as I can."

"Thank you," Griffin said.

"You're welcome," Ernest said, and hung up.

There was trouble. "We have a problem."

"Really? Just one?" Cam said. She'd been watching him the whole time he'd been on the phone. He already knew she'd heard the exchange.

He pocketed the phone. "Ernest is definitely being watched."

"But your phone's secure," she said, turning her attention to the empty field that bordered the facility.

"Mine is. Not sure about his end. We need to meet him to-night at Lyle's." Griffin stood next to her and followed her line of sight. "What have you got?"

She nodded toward the field. "I found the trail they took."

❖❖❖

In her mind's eye, Cam saw them running for their lives through the field. Over sturdy tufts of grass, shape shifting into their faster, Primary Shifter forms to escape XCEL agents and dodge bullets. The captive dropped behind and was hit with anti-Shifter ammo and a tranquilizer.

She found the spot where he went down, but not without a fight. There was human blood in the grass. XCEL blood. Good.

The other two had leaped over the chain-link fence that ran next to the highway, crossed the lanes, and jumped down into a narrow culvert on the other side. She scrambled down to where a thin ribbon of water flowed along the culvert floor. Tree branches and shrubs crowded the edges and fought for sunlight.

She was so focused on the Shifter scents and the scenario, she barely noticed Mercer behind her as she pushed her way between the branches and sloshed through water. After two hundred yards or so, the scent of human ended where the culvert disappeared into darkness under a highway.

"The XCEL agent stopped here," she said.

Mercer seemed surprised. "Just one?"

"There were only two agents. One followed these two Shifters. The other one took down the captive." She noted his shock. "That's not normal?"

"For three Shifters, there would have been more agents," Mercer said, frowning. "At least a half a dozen."

Cam blinked. "So what does that mean?"

Mercer turned to her. His eyes settled on her for a moment before he spoke. In the sunlight, they were dark brown, not the black, menacing shade they donned in the shadows. He was looking damn good in a navy T-shirt, leather jacket, and jeans. Her acute senses smelled his scent, and her belly fluttered just a bit. She was sweating, and really, it wasn't *that* hot. Just when Mercer was around.

"Maybe they didn't know how many Shifters there were," he said.

It didn't make sense, although so far, nothing about this entire mission made sense. "Or maybe they were riding shotgun."

Mercer's expression turned thoughtful. "If they were, why didn't they tell us that?"

She stated the obvious. "Because they didn't want us to know they were here all along."

"Why?" he added.

Jesus, once she got him asking questions, he didn't stop. Was she this annoying? "Because then we'd know that they weren't just protecting an empty trailer."

He nodded. "Exactly."

Oh, crap. "Is it me, or is it one hell of a coincidence that XCEL was protecting a shipment that Shifters had targeted?"

"It's not just you," he said, sounding bitter.

She eyed him. "It makes me nervous when we agree."

"Scares the shit out of me," he replied with a slight smile. "Let's see where our Shifters went."

They walked through the culvert tunnel under the highway and emerged on the other side. Cam followed the trail up a steep embankment to a gravel pullover off the exit ramp.

Then it went cold. Cars whizzed around the exit ramp.

She said, "Trail ends here. This is where they were picked up."

Mercer nodded quietly, taking in all the details. "No surveillance equipment. Not sure we'll be able to find witnesses."

She rubbed her forehead where a killer headache was forming. "How are we going to do this, Mercer? How are we going to find these guys?" She dropped her hand. "And what if the prisoner talks? Tells Harding everything he needs to know?"

Mercer met her eyes. "He won't talk."

She laughed. "You're sure about that?"

"He knew what he was doing when he gave himself up."

Cam considered that. "He must have had a good reason for stealing the truck and whatever was in it. For taking that risk."

They walked back more slowly, and this time Mercer was in the lead. She watched him move easily through the tree branches and trash in the culvert. He was quiet and efficient in everything he did. Sure about his body. Sure about his movements. It made her feel safe, and she hadn't felt like that in a very long time. Usually, she was the one who kept others safe. The only other time she'd felt this was when her brother was with her.

Mercer helped her out of the culvert, and she stopped in front of him, catching his gaze. "I didn't thank you."

He narrowed his eyes warily. "For what?"

"For sticking up for me to Harding."

"Harding might screw me, but I deserve it. You don't."

Cam frowned. "How do you deserve it?"

Mercer turned and started across the field back to the warehouse. Cam walked beside him. He stared into the distance for a long time before he started talking again.

"My Shifter ex-partner killed one of our agents. As me."

"Bastard." Cam closed her eyes for a moment. And that's why they put him in prison. "I still don't understand why that's your fault."

Mercer stared straight ahead. "XCEL doesn't quite see it the way you do."

"No, Harding wouldn't see it that way," she corrected. "But he's a dickhead."

That got a quick smile out of Mercer.

"What about you?" she asked. "How do you see it?"

"Happened on my watch," he said, looking at her then.

She blinked a few times. He blamed himself for something that clearly wasn't his fault, that he'd had no control over. It made her wonder what else he carried.

◆◆◆

Lyle's place was hopping at eleven P.M. Canned Irish music ebbed and flowed between the booths and tables. Griffin sipped his second scotch and listened patiently to Ernest try to explain how he got the information he was eventually going to share with them. Cam sat next to him, paying far better attention than he was. Of course, it didn't help that he could feel the heat of her thigh beside his. He was going to work out tomorrow, or he'd never sleep again.

"So," Ernest said for the fifth time. "*That's* when I found them."

"What?" Cam asked.

Ernest leaned forward in the booth. "More attacks. In this vicinity, same MOs, same types of hits. Except none of these are on our list."

That got Griffin's attention. He was supposed to have everything on this case. And he did, as far as he knew.

"Why wouldn't they be on our list?" Cam asked.

Ernest nodded over his Diet Coke. "Exactly. I was told that our list was complete. It's not."

Griffin asked, "How many more are there?"

"Got eight so far," Ernest said. "But the program is still running. Could be a lot more."

Harding was holding out on him; that was the only explanation. Griffin knew Harding didn't trust him, but why would he have left those locations off their list? What possible reason would he have?

"Give us whatever you have so far," Griffin said. "Did you find any connections between the attacks?"

Ernest shook his head. "Not yet, but that's only because I haven't been able to get everything into my computer. They keep checking on me. Harding sicced Roberts on me, and he's in my office all the time. Asking me questions, watching my monitors. It's a royal pain."

Cam asked, "Do you think they suspect something or are they just paranoid about this case?"

Ernest shrugged. "I don't know, but my ass is under a microscope, and I don't like it."

Griffin studied the amber liquor in his glass. They did suspect, which meant they had something to hide. He had a bad feeling that he was being played. There were holes the size of Buicks in this case. Missing information, XCEL agents where they didn't belong, and Harding blocking him every time he asked too many questions.

"Anything on the contents of the trailer?" Cam asked.

"Haven't started that yet," Ernest conceded. He put his hands up to defend himself. "I'm doing the best I can. We aren't supposed to be poking around. We aren't supposed to be asking questions. That's not our job."

Griffin said, "You don't have to do this. If you feel threatened—"

Ernest huffed. "Are you kidding? They're morons. I can dance circles around them."

Cam glanced at Griffin, concern in her eyes. "What about the other suspects they want us to check out?"

"Yeah, I got four more for you," Ernest said. He pulled a sheet out of his jacket. "Some of these even have home addresses."

Cam took the list and scanned it. "Thanks. We'll do these tomorrow night."

"Wow, all of them?" Ernest asked.

She gave him a pointed look. "We have to. If Harding gets anything out of the Shifter that was captured, the deal is off for both of us."

"Seriously? Did he say that?" Ernest said in disbelief.

"Succinctly," she replied.

CHAPTER
TEN

Harding sat in the comfort of his home office with a clear view of the medical laboratory arena displayed on his smartphone. In the background, he could hear his partner, Nick Braxton, giving the orders to begin the small-scale experiment.

Check that. A small-scale experiment would be performed on rats. These were much bigger subjects—a human and a Shifter. Harding didn't have time to waste on rats.

The Shifter that XCEL had captured at the transportation center lay strapped to a gurney in a room flooded with UVC rays to prevent him from shifting. He alternately yelled and swore at his captors as he fought the restraints.

The human prisoner was a Shifter sympathizer they'd "borrowed" from one of their detention centers, who lay on a gurney right next to him. Either way, no great loss, but he was unconscious so he wouldn't suffer. He was, after all, still a human.

Long leads were attached to monitoring equipment on both subjects. Computers would capture every vital sign and every change at each stage of the experiment. Results would be analyzed by his head scientist. This was the fourth test of the formula that Harding's researchers had been developing, and, he hoped, the last.

Braxton dismissed the highly trained guards that provided protection to Braxton and the chemical facility, leaving only himself and the head scientist to operate the controls in the viewing room.

Harding trusted few with his plan. Even fewer were allowed to witness the experiments. The many scientists who helped to develop the formula weren't present. Although they had contributed knowledge and time to the final product, only the head scientist knew exactly what they'd created.

The gas worked on Shifters; they already knew that from the previous experiments. Shifters were only required as control subjects. Today, though, they'd find out what it did to humans.

Braxton turned to camera and said, "We're ready."

Harding nodded. "Begin."

The head scientist worked the panel, opening valves that flooded the sealed room below them. Hissing sounds came through the speakers, and for a few moments, the captive Shifter was quiet. Green, heavy mist poured from the vents, cascading down the walls and pooling on the floor.

Harding waited, knowing what the next few minutes held. He'd seen it before, and it always gave him great pleasure knowing that he was ridding this world, *his* world, of one more alien being.

The captive's eyes widened as the toxin began attacking his

lungs and cells. A look of terror spread across his features, and he tried to compensate for the poison by shifting his form. It wouldn't work, of course. It never did.

And then the screaming started. Shrieking, actually, as his body began to disintegrate. DNA twisted and snapped. Molecules shuddered and split. The formula continued to work its magic on the Shifter, but Harding concentrated on the human prisoner.

The man remained unconscious, but his vital signs began to drop. His heart rate turned erratic, and his pulse raced out of control. Moments later, his chest started to convulse. Blood spurted from his mouth, spraying over his face and chest. Within two minutes, he flatlined completely.

Harding pursed his lips. Failure was simply not an option this late in the game.

The Shifter bucked a few times, and the screaming ended. His body swelled and bloated. His skin thinned and stretched. The straps that held him down created indents in his chest and legs. Foam poured out of his mouth, eyes, and ears. The test was complete.

Braxton stepped in front of the camera, frowning. "The human subject didn't make it."

"Obviously. Find out why and fix it," he told Braxton. "You have one week."

Braxton put his hands on his hips. "You know damn well that a week is impossible. We've already spent a year to get this far."

"Then you have a week and a half," Harding said.

"Don't treat me like one of your dogs," Braxton replied. "We're partners, remember? We got into this together."

Yes, they had at that. Both had been part of the first committee that ran XCEL into the ground. Both had seen what a mess a group of lazy, politically correct, yellow-bellied bureaucrats could make of a perfectly good military force like XCEL. As a result, they'd almost lost New York City to the Shifters in an underground coup last year.

Harding wasn't going to let that happen again. Not to his city, not to his country. That's why he'd worked his way to director. And Braxton was the man who would make the operations work. There was no one else Harding could use. No one else who understood.

"My apologies," Harding said. "You still have a week and a half."

◆◆◆

Cam and Mercer stood in the middle of a burnt office building on the edge of the Hudson in Yonkers. A building that wasn't on their list but that followed the identical MO. There wasn't much left after the blast and ensuing fire aside from steel girders and doorways. Every surface was charred and black.

Cam surveyed the interior, stepping through the utter devastation, each step triggering a small poof of ash. Through the structural remains of the building, the Hudson shore gleamed with lights. The city churned with cars, horns, and sirens.

This had been one hot fire, burning everything in its path. Blackened metal desks now held melted computers and phones. Chairs were stripped of their fabric. The moon peeked through empty roof sections. She walked through the first floor, checking each office one by one.

A single office had survived the firestorm better than the others, and she stepped inside. File cabinets lined the walls. Their drawers had been pulled out before the blaze, and their contents were now incinerated. She stopped in front of a floor safe, four feet high and two feet wide. The door was wide open, and the interior scorched clean.

"There's nothing left," she told Mercer.

He bent down to check the contents of the safe in the beam of his flashlight. After he poked around a bit, he said, "I'm wondering why they opened all the cabinets, the drawers, and the safe before the fire."

"Crossed my mind as well," she said. They both stood up, and Griffin turned off his flashlight. In the darkness, he probably didn't realize how well she could see him as he focused on her. In the absence of harsh daylight, his features were strong but less menacing. The intensity he wore like a glove lost its firm grip. The real man emerged, which was good, because he wasn't going to like what she found here.

"So was it our Shifters?" he asked.

"No," she replied.

He cocked his head slightly. "Different Shifters?"

She shook her head and took a breath. "No Shifters have ever walked this building. Only humans."

"Sonofabitch," he said, and the intensity returned.

In one way, it was good, because her Shifters had already been blamed for enough damage. However, it also left a big problem. Because if the Shifters didn't do this, then who did?

She added, "But someone sure tried to make it look like it was Shifters. Why?"

Mercer pursed his lips. "So it would look like they hit it. Everything resembles the other strikes, aside from opening the file cabinets and safe. They really wanted to put these people out of business permanently."

She couldn't wrap her head around anything that made sense. "But why attack this place at all? What is the significance of this office versus the office next door?"

Mercer stood in the darkness. "I don't know."

She raised an eyebrow. "Say it."

"Say what?"

"Say, 'Cam, you were right.'"

He grinned, albeit grudgingly. "You're going to be a pain in the ass about this, aren't you?"

The man was impossible. "Does anyone ever win an argument with you?"

"All the time," he said. "Look at Harding."

Ah. That was true. And it must kill Mercer to bow to that asshole. But he was so determined to fix the past, he'd give his soul to do it. Which in turn pissed him off more. It must be hell living like that. *Was it worth it?* she wondered.

"We have time to check one more site on Ernest's list before sunrise," he said and led her out. "I want to be sure."

"Before what?" she finished, almost holding her breath. Because they wouldn't get any answers unless Mercer believed her.

"Before everything goes right to hell."

◆ ◆ ◆

It was after four A.M. when they got back to his apartment. Tomorrow would be a busy day, and Griffin wanted to get as much sleep as he could on that uncomfortable couch.

Because, tomorrow he was going to ask Ernest to break every

protocol XCEL had to find out why they lied to him. Those other attacks followed the MO exactly, and they should have been on his list. They should have been investigated just like all the others, but he wasn't supposed to investigate those.

And the only reason they wouldn't be on his list was if XCEL already knew they weren't Shifter hits.

The niggling suspicions he'd carried through this entire mission parked front and center in his mind. XCEL was hiding something big, and he was about to go into dangerous territory. If he was wrong and there was a good reason that the human hits weren't included, he'd be in the clear. If not . . . if not, this whole situation was a setup from the beginning.

Cam headed to the bathroom, and Griffin punched the flashing answering machine button before walking into his bedroom.

"Mr. Mercer, this is the Greenville Recovery Agency. We are calling about an unpaid debt you owe. Please return our call as soon as possible." The woman left a number and hung up.

He pulled off his shirt and grabbed a pair of workout shorts.

The next call was from a company looking for two thousand dollars they weren't going to get out of him. And then the answering machine clicked to the end.

Only two collectors. Things were looking up.

He flung his shorts over his shoulder and walked out into the living room to find Cam standing next to the answering machine. She had already changed into her signature pajamas—one of his T-shirts. Long legs were smooth and sexy. Well, pretty much everything about her was sexy.

"How can you stand these calls? Why don't you just change your number?" she asked, confusion etched in her face.

And yet, she had a way of destroying fantasies with one sentence. He walked into the kitchen to get a glass of water. "Because that's the only number my grandfather knows."

"Are you serious?"

"Why wouldn't I be?" he said.

Cam came over to the other side of the island, a slow smile growing across her face. "I'm seeing a whole new sensitive side to you, Mercer."

"Don't get used to it," he warned her.

"Oh, I won't." She sat on the stool and leaned forward. "You work for a very powerful organization. Just have them deal with all these calls."

"No," he said quickly, and her eyebrows rose in question. He was so used to her prodding that he didn't even wait for her to ask. He put the glass in the sink. "They don't need to know."

Cam shook her head. "Your ex-partner is destroying your life, one call at a time. At the very least, your credit rating."

His credit rating was shot. Griffin put his hands on the island. "I'm aware of that, thank you."

"You think XCEL would hold this against you?"

Sure as shit. "That's part of it. Let's just say I don't want to remind them of past history."

She cocked her head. "You're doing all of this just to get your job back. This mission. Following Harding's rules."

"That's right."

She studied him. "Do you want it because you want it, or do you want it because a Shifter took it away from you?"

He wasn't expecting that question. "Does it matter?"

"Not to me," she said and stood up. "But it should to you."

She stared at him for a while, waiting for his response. He didn't have one. Then she frowned as she focused on his shoulder.

"What?" he asked as she walked around the island and stopped in front of him.

Griffin inhaled sharply when she ran her fingers along the knife wound on his shoulder. He'd pulled the stitches out this morning, and it was still tender. But that wasn't exactly why he was breathing heavy.

"You healed," she whispered, her fingers tracing the edge of the cut. "That was fast." Her eyes met his. "Too fast for a human."

"Not for me," he answered, hoping to fend off another interrogation. He hadn't recovered from that last one yet. "Runs in my family."

"Must be a very special family," she said, sounding skeptical.

He contemplated telling her about how Sani had taught him to heal his wounds quickly when he was young, but the words stuck in his throat because she was still touching him. He grabbed her fingers in his and pulled them away from his skin. "It is."

She didn't fight his grasp. "So you heal fast. What about Shifters? Can other members of your family see them? Can they freeze us like you can?"

The warmth of her fingers felt good. "I don't know. I've never talked to them about what I do."

"Never?" she asked.

He squeezed her fingers slightly. "Never. We both need to go to bed."

Finally, she tugged her hand out of his. For long moments, she didn't move, and then she turned for his bedroom. "'Night, Mercer."

He waited until the bedroom door had shut before exhaling. Then he grabbed a towel and hit his personal gym.

◆◆◆

Cam closed the bedroom door on Mercer and leaned back against it. He never told his family about his abilities? The man was an island. An impenetrable, dangerous, solitary island.

She sat down on the bed, the long night catching up with her in a yawn. She picked up her phone. It was far too early to wake her father, but she needed to hear his voice. Needed to know for herself that he was okay.

"Camille," her father answered. "Are you alright?"

She wasn't the one dying. "I'm great. Easy night."

"That's good," her father said, relief in his voice. "Then I can sleep too."

She smiled. "You do realize that I stopped being a child some years ago."

"Doesn't matter. You'll always be that squirming bundle of energy I held in my arms the morning you were born. One of the happiest days of my life was watching you enter the world."

Cam swallowed the lump in her throat, not knowing what to say. Thanks? That's nice? None of those worked. "How do you feel today?"

"Oh me," he said briskly. "I'm fine."

But he wasn't. Her hearing picked up his weak heartbeat and the shallow, quick breaths he took. "That's good. Did you see Ernest today?"

"Yes. He was here late last night," he said.

"That's good," she said. "Sorry to wake you."

There was a long pause before her father replied. "Do you

want to do this, Camille? Do you want to help XCEL stop these Shifters?"

Ernest must have told him. Guilt threatened, and she tamped it down. This wasn't about her. "They've blown up places and businesses. Destroyed property—"

"That's not what I'm asking," he said. "Do you *want* to do this?"

No was on the tip of her tongue. *I don't.* But if she told him that, he'd do something noble like up and die on her so she wouldn't have to follow through.

"Yes," she said. "If I don't do it, they'll find another Shifter who will."

"I see," her father said, sounding quiet. "I love you."

"I love you too." Tears broke down her face. "Good night."

"Good night, child."

◆◆◆

Harding paced his office. He never paced. He was the man in charge. People paced *for* him. "You're sure they canvassed the other sites?"

Roberts nodded. "We followed them to two sites, neither of which was on their list."

"So how did they find them?" Harding asked.

"We believe Agent Ernest Vincent may have provided them with the locations."

Harding stopped and faced Roberts. "Vincent? That geek?"

"I've been monitoring his activities, and I find them rather irregular. He is getting into systems he shouldn't need. Running an abnormally high volume of queries. Some queries are so short, they barely show up on the monitor reports. I think he may be digging deeper than necessary."

"He's not smart enough to do anything stupid," Harding said.

"Perhaps he's just following orders," Roberts replied.

Mercer. That man was going to be the death of him. Harding walked around and sat heavily in his chair. He couldn't pull Mercer from the case without raising suspicion. And he couldn't contain Mercer too much, or they wouldn't find their Shifter cells.

But he could pull the plug on Agent Vincent. "I want you to work with Agent Vincent more closely." Harding met his gaze. "Keep tabs on everything he does, every keystroke. All queries need to be approved before they are run."

Roberts nodded. "For how long?"

"Until this son of a bitchin' case is over."

"Yes, sir."

"Dismissed," Harding said. Roberts turned on his heel and left. Harding had his cell phone out before the door closed. Mercer wasn't the only bad news today. It had occurred to Harding last night that he had other problems.

He placed a call and waited for three rings, an interminable amount of time before Braxton picked up. "Yes?"

"We have a leak," Harding said, keeping his voice low. There were no listening devices in his office, but he didn't take any chances. "The Shifters knew the shipment was coming through the transport center. How?"

"I don't know, but I can find out."

"You do that. And you make damn sure that there is no trail left for anyone to follow. Not even a Shifter."

"In other words, no trail to you," Braxton said.

"Exactly," Harding said. "And don't forget it." Then he hung up.

CHAPTER
ELEVEN

Cam heard the phone ring and rolled over to look at the clock. It was only eleven A.M. She almost rolled back over until she heard Mercer's grandfather's voice. Then she threw off the covers and padded to the door, curiosity getting the best of her.

"Hello, Griffin. This is your grandfather, Sani."

Cam cracked the door open and peered out. The shower was running, and Mercer was nowhere to be seen. She opened the door and walked to the answering machine.

"I had a vision this morning," Sani said. "Under the harsh sun, the Skinwalker left a trail through the desert."

She listened to every word, every pause. The calm, gentle way he told his story. It reminded her of her father when he told his stories. Before he started to forget them.

"Her footprints left marks in the sand."

Her? Cam stared at the machine. The Skinwalker was a woman. She wasn't sure what a Skinwalker was, but it sounded a lot like a shapeshifter. A prickling sensation spread across her body. Was he talking about *her*?

"And where her tears landed, flowers grew. The Skinwalker mourned the loss of her family. She mourned the loss of her home."

His words spoke to her, and Cam sat on the couch. Somewhere deep in her mind, Cam saw the image. The lone woman walking through oppressive heat and unforgiving land. Unloved. Unwelcome.

"Father Sun did not show her mercy on her long walk. Mother Earth did not provide shade. The Skinwalker walked alone."

The stories her father told her rose from the images. Tales of hope and courage. Stories passed on from generation to generation. The wonderful and terrible legends of her people. Of their birth, life on their home planet—before it died, before the escape to other worlds. Before everything changed.

"I saw you standing on the mountain. Watching the Skinwalker. But you did not raise a hand to save her."

Cam felt the tears burn her eyes. Mercer. He wouldn't save her. He could barely save himself.

"The Skinwalker stumbled and fell to the ground. The sand burned her hands and feet. The wind raked her skin. The sun beat down."

Cam felt the warmth of her own tears.

"I know you, Grandson. You will not watch this happen. You will not stand by as she dies."

Cam closed her eyes and held on to hope for the Skinwalker.

"The day will come soon when you must act. The Skinwalker is not one of us. But she has nowhere else to go."

Her hands were shaking as it dawned on her: He was asking Mercer to help her. Telling Mercer what to do.

"These things I know." Then he said good-bye, and the answering machine clicked off.

She could hear the water in the shower turn off. She didn't want Mercer to help her because his grandfather; told him to. Griffin would do it for his grandfather, she knew that. Despite what he said about not talking to him, there was great respect. Maybe even shame. Would Mercer help her to avoid shame? She didn't want that. For once, she wanted someone to do something for Shifters with their heart and their mind.

Besides, she didn't need anyone to save her.

And before she could change her mind, she reached over and erased the message.

◆ ◆ ◆

"Our inside people tell us that the final testing is under way," Red told Aristotle. "And they got almost everything they need to make the toxin and make a lot of it."

Aristotle clasped his hands on the table that was the center of his meager home. Damp, concrete walls were covered with graffiti and moisture. A bed and a stove were the other luxuries he'd collected for this underground world.

Red leaned across the table. "Did you hear me?"

He nodded. "Yes. That is not good news."

"No kiddin'," Red said. Today, he had red hair and tattoos. "We tried sabotaging their supply lines. It didn't work. They found alternatives or slipped through our fingers. What do we do now?"

Aristotle had hoped that by cutting out their supplies, he could slow down the development of the toxin. A year ago, it seemed possible. Today, it was desperate. There simply were not enough

Shifters in his teams to stop them, and they'd succeeded where he'd hoped they'd fail. "Call everyone in. No sense in risking them now."

Red waited. "And what about the toxin facility?"

Aristotle flexed his hands and felt the pain of growing old. "We can't take the facility, Red. We don't have the manpower. We don't have humans to help us."

"We don't need humans," Red said brazenly. "We can do this."

Aristotle shook his head. *Youth.* "If they use the gas on us, we'll all be dead, and everything we've done will be for nothing. We need humans. They're not supposed to be affected."

Red slammed his hand on the table. "I can't believe this. Even when we try to save ourselves, we have to rely on them."

And so it was everywhere Shifters traveled. Always at the mercy of the natives. If Aristotle had more energy, he'd be furious about it. Like Red. But he'd used every bit of his strength to run this operation.

"We have our people inside," Red suggested. "They'll help us."

"We won't get through their security," Aristotle said. "Our sources inside can only do so much without being discovered. I can't ask them to risk more than they already have."

Hopelessness filled Aristotle. So much work. It could all be wasted. He was old; he'd die soon. But the other Shifters were young, and they deserved to live a full life, even it was as tragic as his had been.

"Did you find Camille's father?" he asked.

Red nodded. "Detained in an XCEL detention center in Jersey City."

"Detained? Against his will?" Aristotle asked.

"Yeah. I mean, why else would he be there?"

Detained. And his daughter was working for XCEL. It didn't make sense. Unless . . . unless she didn't have a choice. Unless they were coercing her help. A spark of hope penetrated his defeat. That meant that she didn't *want* to work with XCEL. He was feeling better by the second.

"What about the movements of Camille and Griffin?" he asked.

Red shrugged. "They're investigating our hits. And some of the others."

Aristotle sat up straighter in his chair. "Others? You mean Harding's hits?"

"Yeah, those," Red said and frowned. "That's a little weird. Why would he send them to check those out?"

He wouldn't. He knew Shifters didn't attack those places, and he wouldn't risk being exposed.

Which meant Camille and Mercer already knew of the deception. How much they knew, Aristotle couldn't guess. But he could use that.

"They'll come for us," Aristotle said aloud.

Red laughed. "They'll never find us down here."

"Yes, they will," Aristotle told him. "Because I want to make contact. I want to talk to them."

Red's eyes widened. "What? Why?"

Aristotle didn't feel like explaining his logic. He was too tired. "Keep your enemies closer, Red."

Confusion masked the young man's face. "I don't get it. What if XCEL tracks them to us?"

Aristotle replied, "Sometimes you have to think beyond the obvious. Rarely are things as they seem on the surface."

Red raised his hands. "I can never follow your slow talk."

Wisdom, Aristotle corrected silently.

"How about we test them first?" Red suggested. "Before we open ourselves up."

It was a good option, Aristotle decided. "Yes, that would be wise."

Red grinned. "See? I can be useful."

Aristotle chuckled. "Set up a meeting with them. Somewhere safe for you." Then he remembered that Camille might recognize Red. "On second thought, just Mercer. Talk to him. See what he wants."

Red nodded. "I can do that, but is that enough?"

Yes, perhaps a bigger test was needed. "Assist them in finding more of Harding's hits. Preferably *before* they happen."

Red frowned. "You know how tricky it is to anticipate who they will hit next."

"I have complete faith in you, my boy," Aristotle said with a smile. "You know which ones are the most likely. Put the word out to the informers and the other Shifters. It'll reach them. Then we'll see which side Camille and her XCEL agent choose."

The young man nodded in agreement. He was a good student, a quick learner. Aristotle could only hope that he'd live long enough to take advantage of all these lessons.

"And what about the toxin?" Red asked. "We can't just sit here and do nothing."

Aristotle rubbed his arms. It was getting chilly in his room, even though he knew it wasn't. Hot tea would be nice. Sleep would be better. "I need to think."

Red stood up. "Sure, but don't take too long. We don't have time to spare."

If anyone knew that, it was Aristotle. "Go have fun with your friends."

Red gave him a mock salute. "Okay, boss." Then he left Aristotle alone with the gravity of his situation.

◆◆◆

Shifter suspect number five stood at the door of his apartment in baggy pants and a sweat-stained T-shirt. He was about forty, a little too thin and a little too tall. Behind him, dirty clothes and empty food containers littered the floor. A baby wailed somewhere on the floor below them while Griffin focused on his questioning.

"We just want to talk to you for a minute," he pressed, and flashed his badge one more time.

The Shifter wasn't buying it. "Go away. I ain't done nothing wrong."

Griffin tried to get a few more inches out of the chain link that stretched between them. "This will just take a moment."

Then he felt Cam slide in next to him and let her between them. She gave the man a smile. "You're right, Mr. Trainer. You haven't done anything wrong. We're sorry to have bothered you."

The Shifter frowned at her and glared at Griffin and her in turn before slamming the door and latching a whole lot of locks.

Griffin turned to her. "I'm sure you had a good reason for doing that."

Her eyebrows rose, and she turned on her heel. "He's not our man."

Another wasted afternoon. Griffin shook his head and caught up with Cam on the stairs down to the first floor.

"Did he look like he was part of a highly trained, covert operation to you?" she asked.

"No," he admitted. Although, the Shifter could be changing into a highly trained, covert operative as they spoke. They reached the first floor and pushed through the heavy door to the street. For a while, they stood on the sidewalk and watched the traffic cruise by in a neighborhood that no one should be living in.

Griffin noticed a Shifter standing on the corner waiting for the bus. He'd been there since they went inside. Griffin was pretty sure a bus or two had come since then.

"Does that Shifter look familiar to you?" he asked Cam.

She followed his gaze to the person in question and shook her head. "No. Why?"

Were they being followed? Griffin couldn't be sure, but he was going to start paying more attention. "Probably nothing to worry about."

"Tell me the truth," she said. "Does XCEL have any idea who these guys are?"

Griffin answered truthfully. "I don't think so. They must be well protected."

The Shifter waiting at the bus stop started wandering down the street, away from them. Griffin studied his unique Shifter shadow and filed it away in his memory.

"Or maybe Harding doesn't care if we find them. Maybe it's enough that we identified the sites as Shifter attacks," Cam said. "Maybe it's enough to blame Shifters, whether or not they were responsible for the attacks. Who would care?"

Griffin had thought of that as well, even though he didn't want to. Since the beginning, Griffin had tried to justify every anomaly with this mission, tried to ignore the undercurrent of suspicions.

The hidden trailer.

The lack of any valid Shifter suspects.

The copycat attacks missing from their list.

He and Cam were getting nowhere fast. If they didn't find the Shifters, he was sure that Harding would renege but still use their findings to blame Shifters—

And then he understood what his intuition was trying to tell him. Harding must have planned this all along, set up this whole "legitimate" operation as nothing more than a ploy to make it appear that he was doing something productive. He'd be able to stand in front of any government committee and claim he'd done everything he could to find the Shifters responsible. But he couldn't, and so they'd all be blamed, to what end Griffin didn't know. It was the only scenario that fit. Which meant that Harding didn't need them anymore, or their deals.

"You're right," he said.

Cam's eyes widened as she turned to him. "Seriously?"

He said, "They're going to blame Shifters for all the attacks. And we can't convince anyone otherwise."

"No. No, he can't," Cam said, shaking her head slowly.

"He can and he will," he said. "He won't wait for us to find the Shifters responsible. He'll cut us off."

"But we did what we agreed to," she said.

"We didn't find them," he replied. By the look of fear in her eyes, he knew she understood what that meant. Who knew what would happen to her and her father?

He added, "*Unless* we find the Shifters responsible for the Shifter attacks, and clear them of the copycat attacks."

Cam shook her head, concern on her face. "Whoa, I'm with you up to the whole clearing part. What if you're wrong?"

He eyed her. "What happened to the woman who wanted to save the Shifters?"

"She met Harding," Cam said bitterly. "That's not on my docket, and if Harding finds out—" She stopped and gave a sigh. "I hate myself for saying that. Isn't there anyone else who can clear the Shifters?"

He shook his head. "No one else."

She put her hands on her hips. "We're the only ones who give a damn? Really?"

"Really," he said, and he was pretty sure about that.

She shook her head. "If we can find them and if we can clear them, they'll still be blamed for the attacks that *are* on our list. So what's the difference?"

"The difference is that you and I will finish this mission and get what we want," he said.

They stared at each other for a long moment, both understanding the situation. Griffin could see Cam weighing her options, placing her bets. But he knew she'd always bet on her father.

"Harding isn't going to like you after this," she noted.

He grinned. "He doesn't like me now. You in?"

She sighed. "Let's find them."

Griffin felt a strange wave of relief. He wasn't thinking about his future. Right now, he just wanted to get through this mess. Then he'd figure what he'd do after they surprised Harding with the Shifters.

"They're underground. They have to be," he said as they started walking back to the car. "They're pros. They wouldn't be sloppy enough for XCEL to find them."

Cam made a face. "I hate the underground more than bluffing."

She didn't want to go underground, and he couldn't blame her. The tunnels and infrastructure under New York City had become a haven for Shifters. They'd pretty much cleared out the homeless and squatters. Worse than that, they fought for turf like gangs. Only a lot scarier. Even the gangs didn't go down there anymore.

"So do I." Griffin pulled out his phone and called Ernest. He picked up on the first ring.

"Make it quick, I'm alone," Ernest answered, his voice hushed and strained. Griffin felt a pang of guilt for Ernest's anxiety.

They turned down the street his car was parked on. "We need to go underground. Send me everything you got on that."

"Will do."

"And I need to talk to an informant who's in touch with the underground. You got anyone?"

"I'll see who I can find," Ernest said, a little too abruptly.

"As soon as possible. Cam here is getting bored. She hasn't killed anyone all day."

He caught her grinning. "And if you feel thirsty later tonight, you know where to find us."

"Right." And Ernest hung up quickly.

Cam was watching him intently as he disconnected the call. "Trouble?"

Griffin pocketed the phone. "Is there anything else?"

She was quiet for a millisecond. "You really think that Ernest can hook us up underground? It's a big, bad world under this city."

"No problem," he said, lying through his teeth. He wasn't looking forward to creeping through the city's underbelly, but if that's what it took, that's exactly what he'd do. Somewhere along the line, this had turned into a battle, and Harding was the enemy. Griffin would like nothing better than to beat him at his own game.

TWELVE

The baking chicken smelled wonderful, and Cam found herself watching Mercer's sure movements in the kitchen as he checked dinner. He'd make someone a good husband someday. Not her, but someone.

"I can't believe you don't know how to cook," Mercer said. "What did you eat?"

"Restaurant food, takeout, pizza," she rattled off.

"Every meal?"

"Every meal," she said.

"No wonder you had to cheat casinos," he murmured.

She glared at his back. "So what happened between you and your ex-wife?"

Mercer closed the oven door. "Jesus, Cam. Can you be any more direct?"

"No," she said, leaning on the cool island countertop. "I find that direct works for me."

He gave a short laugh and shook his head. She liked when he laughed. It wasn't often, but it was genuine. He didn't lie to her. He might not tell her everything, but he wouldn't lie.

"So she cheated on you?" Cam asked.

Mercer hesitated as he crossed his arms and leaned back against the stove. "No. Why would you think that?"

"Because *you* aren't the cheating kind," she said.

He seemed surprised by her insight. "Thank you."

Cam smiled. "So?"

Mercer was silent for a moment and then opened the booze cupboard above his head. He pulled out a bottle of scotch and set it on the island between them.

"She couldn't trust me afterward."

"After?" Cam blinked and then realized what he was talking about. "The partner who replaced you. What did he do to her?"

Mercer put ice into two rocks glasses. "I think you know."

"Fuck," Cam said, the realization dawning on her.

"Precisely." Mercer set the glasses on the island and poured scotch into both.

She felt for him, despite being on different sides of an insurmountable gap. No wonder he was angry. Finances was one thing, but family. Family was sacred ground. "I'm sorry. I really am."

He nodded and took a big swig of his drink.

She leaned forward. "You loved her."

He stared into his glass. "I tried. She was safe, normal, not part of XCEL. I could come home and forget everything that happened at work. My partner broke that peace. It could never be the same again."

"Where is she now?" Cam asked.

He shook his head. "I have no idea." Then he raised eyes filled with anger and pain. "Happy you asked that one?"

"No," she said, honestly. "I'm not. I ask a lot of questions, and I expect that I won't always like the answers. But at least I ask them."

Ice cubes clinked in his glass for a minute. "What about you? Any ex-husbands still alive?"

She smiled. He'd asked her a question. "No, just lots of ex-lovers."

He raised an eyebrow. "Lots?"

Cam heard the printer in the living room finally stop spewing pages courtesy of Ernest's hard work and got up to gather them. "You want details?"

"No, I definitely do not," he answered.

She picked up the stack of pages and brought them back to the counter. Ernest had included a private note, and she slowed as she read it. "Good, because I think we have a bigger issue."

She sat on the stool and pushed Ernest's note to Mercer. He scanned it quickly and frowned. "I was afraid of this."

Her sentiments exactly. This was the last set of information he'd be able to send them without prying eyes. Everything he sent after this had to be approved first—by Harding.

"It's almost like they don't trust us," she said.

Mercer nodded, looking disgusted. "Almost."

He pulled up the stool on the same side of the island as hers and sorted through the rest of what Ernest had sent. There were two customer lists—one for the Shifter-targeted sites and one for the copycat sites. Griffin took a few minutes to scan each of them before passing the lists to Cam. Then he shuffled through the last set of pages. They were sections of maps. He cleared the island and started laying out the underground tunnel schematics covering different sections of the city. When he was done, he had three complete maps.

Cam moved next to him, derailing his concentration. Her hair was swept up in a messy ponytail, and she smelled good. Better than dinner.

"The tunnel systems," she observed.

"He sent us three sections. These are our best bets," Griffin added.

She pointed to the areas circled in red. "What are these?"

"Access points."

Ernest had given them places to start based on his analysis. That kid was good. Griffin only hoped they hadn't done any damage to his job or career to get this.

"So again, the question comes up," Cam said, crossing her arms. "How do we do this? Because if you think I'm your magic ticket to Shifter territory, you are sorely mistaken."

Excellent question, and one he'd been pondering for a while. Shifters were naturally nocturnal, so daytime was the best time to sneak around. As if it was that easy. Going underground, into their territory. Asking a lot of questions. That would be anything but easy.

"I figure if we go in there fully armed and ready to kick ass, there's probably a five percent chance of success," he offered.

Cam cocked her head. "I like that one."

"You would," Griffin said. "Or we keep a low profile, use our informants, become part of the community—"

She shook her head. "We don't have that kind of time. Next."

"There's one more. But you aren't going to like it."

Cam tensed up. "Tell me."

He shouldn't have even mentioned it. Now he had no choice but to tell her because she wouldn't give him peace until he did. He sighed. "They know you. They know who you are."

"Yes," she said warily.

"What if we went looking for them to get answers? On their terms. What if we join them?"

He caught her wincing. It was only for a split second, but he saw it. She was remembering the captured Shifter, his accusations against her. Without thinking, he amended, "Forget it. We'll figure out something. I'll connect with a few of XCEL's informants, and we'll go from there."

The oven timer rang, and Griffin went into the kitchen to get the dinner out. He took out a couple plates and served up roasted chicken and baked potatoes, which represented the full extent of his culinary expertise. He turned around to set the plates on the island to find Cam standing in the middle of the living room alone, staring out the window.

"Something wrong?" he asked, and set the plates down.

She didn't answer immediately, and when she did, her voice was thick. "You're right. We should use their knowledge of me to our advantage."

"It was a bad idea. We're not doing that, Cam."

She turned to look at him, and in her eyes was fear. Real fear. The kind that keeps you awake at night. "I have to. I have to save my father. If I don't get him out of there, if I don't find my brother, he'll die."

It took him a moment to absorb what she was saying. Griffin made his way over to face her. "I don't understand. I thought he was just old."

She closed her eyes and tears slid down her face. "He has a

Shifter disease that is slowly eating him away. Sort of like cancer in humans."

Shit. And that explained a whole lot about why Cam was here. "What does he need?" Griffin asked. "How do we treat him?"

Cam smiled a little. "You can't help him. The only treatment is a blood transfusion from several close family members. I'm hoping if I can find Thaniel, the two of us will be enough to save him." More tears fell, and she gave a shudder. "But I don't know for sure. It may already be too late."

And then Griffin felt a stab of guilt. He hadn't done a thing about finding Thaniel, hadn't even told anyone about it. Hell. How was he to know that she needed her brother to save her father's life? And how was he going to tell her that he'd lied?

His thoughts raced. Her father was still alive, so a few more days wouldn't matter. As soon as this was over, he'd find Thaniel himself. He'd make sure of it.

Then her eyes met his. "He's all I have left."

How many times had he said that? After he'd lost his wife, his home, his life. The important things. The things that hurt. Irreplaceable things. He'd seen her fight like a warrior, taking down XCEL agents with ease. But this, this crushed her. Against all better judgment, he reached out and wiped away a tear with the back of his finger. It was warm and real.

"I know," Griffin said. And if Cam found out, he was a dead man.

◆ ◆ ◆

After dinner, Cam retreated to Griffin's bedroom to call her father. He picked up. "Hello?"

Cam smiled and tried to convey that everything was great when it wasn't. "How are you feeling?"

"Oh, you know, the same."

She walked across Mercer's bedroom and peered out the window. "I'm sorry it's taking longer than expected to get you out of there."

"Don't worry about it, Camille. I'm getting plenty of rest, eating well. Probably taking better care of myself than if we were on the road."

That would be true, Cam thought. "Have you seen Ernest lately?"

"Not yesterday or today. He was must be working hard."

A familiar-looking shapeshifter stood on the street corner below—a normally nondescript human male in his thirties reading a newspaper. But his Shifter signature gave him away. "Perhaps."

"Do you think he's in some kind of trouble?" her father asked, sounding worried.

"No," she said quickly. "You're right, he's been busy doing some work for us. I'll have Mercer check on him."

Her father was quiet for a moment. "So, it's still Mercer?"

The Shifter on the corner glanced up at her, and Cam stepped away from the window. It was the same Shifter they'd seen earlier waiting at the bus stop, she was certain. She blinked a few times before answering her father. "What? Well, yes."

"Not Griffin," he elaborated.

She rolled her eyes. "I don't even like him."

"That's too bad."

Cam checked out the window again, and the Shifter was gone. She blew out a long breath. Mercer had her paranoid to no end. "No, it's not bad. We have plans, you and me, and they don't include anyone else."

"Does he disrespect you?"

Cam rubbed her forehead. "No."

"Hurt you?"

"No," she said, more firmly. "And he doesn't kick small dogs either, but that doesn't mean—" She paused, trying to find the right words. "It doesn't mean he's right for me. Why are we talking about this?"

"Because you need someone in your life who cares about you besides me," her father said. "I won't be around forever."

She dropped her hand. "XCEL is looking for Thaniel. And then we'll all have each other."

"You need more than us," he persisted. "You need a true love. A gentleman who loves you for who you are."

Damn, he was one stubborn old bird. Besides, where was she ever going to find a gentleman? "No, really I don't. I'm quite happy with my life."

"And when I'm gone, what will your life be then?" he asked.

She closed her eyes and fought the pain in her chest. "I'll figure that out when the time comes."

"You miss too much, Camille, watching over me."

That made her a little nervous. "I love you. I don't need anything else. And if you go, I'll be very pissed off at you."

He gave a little chuckle. "Be careful out there."

"You be careful in there," she said. "Love you."

"Love you too."

◆◆◆

His informant was supposed to be here twenty minutes ago, and Griffin wasn't liking the wait in the dark. Every sound boomeranged around the Park Place subway tunnels, making it impossible to tell where it was coming from.

He yawned and shook his head to wake up.

When he'd finally connected with an XCEL informant, it was at four A.M. He'd had to sneak out early without waking Cam, because the informant made it very clear that they were to meet alone—period. Apparently, word was out that his partner was a Shifter. No one trusted her. No one trusted him either, but obviously he ranked somewhere above a Shifter in the whole trust matrix.

In truth, that's exactly how he felt about Shifters too. Except for Cam. She didn't deserve to be there. In fact, she didn't deserve any of this mess. Yes, she'd stolen from casinos, but it was only money. This was life or death. Changed everything.

His cell phone rang, and he checked the number. It was his brother, Tommy. He'd only allowed a few numbers through on Ernest's phone. Family was one of them.

"Yeah," he answered. "What's up?"

"What's up?" Tommy said. "Kids are good. Jen says hi. Oh, and Sani told me you have a woman at your place now."

Crap, this was going to be one of *those* calls. "Sani's old and senile."

"You wish," Tommy said, not buying any of it. "So who is she and what are her measurements?"

Griffin scanned the tunnel for his informant. At least then he'd have an excuse to hang up. "It's only temporary."

"What'd you pull, a *Pretty Woman* and hire a hooker for the week?" Tommy said.

"Do I sound like a man who's been laid recently?" he asked.

"No. In fact, you sound pretty pissy. So if you two aren't—"

"Don't," Griffin said.

"Then why is she staying with you?"

He gave up. It was useless. Tommy was like a pit bull. "She's a Shifter, and we're working a case. I need to protect and manage her activities. We'll be done soon." Very soon, if he had anything to say about it.

"Whoa, whoa, whoa. Back up to that first part? She's a Shifter? Are you *crazy*?"

"Yes, I am," he muttered.

"Can you trust her? I mean, Jesus. I just don't want to see you go through the same crap you did with Parker."

His ex-partner's name was almost enough to end the call, but then Griffin saw a man jump onto the tunnel sidewalk a hundred yards down. "I can trust her."

"Man, I hope so."

"I have to go," he told Tommy. "Don't tell Sani about the Shifter part."

Tommy gave a big sigh. "Be careful."

"Always," he said, pocketed the phone, and slid his hand under his jacket for his Glock. A twentysomething kid wearing a gray T-shirt, long cargo shorts, and high-top sneakers walked up to him. His hair was dark, his eyes blue, and he could have been a college student.

Except that he wasn't.

He was a shapeshifter.

And Griffin's informant wasn't supposed to be a shapeshifter.

It wasn't common knowledge that Griffin could see Shifters. Only the higher-ups in XCEL knew. They protected that information, because otherwise he'd be a prime target for Shifters and humans alike and they'd lose a valuable asset.

This Shifter, however, didn't know that.

"Mercer?" he asked as he scanned the quiet alcove beside the subway rail line.

Griffin also realized the informant didn't want Cam coming because she could see him, and that meant he knew a lot more about them than they knew about him. "Yeah. Didn't catch your name."

"Don't give one," the kid said and smiled. Straight, white teeth didn't quite match the predatory look in his eyes. "I understand that you're looking for someone."

"The Shifters blowing up the buildings," Griffin said carefully. He was going to play this out and see where it got him. He was also keeping his gun close.

The informant shrugged. "You and everyone else. They're public enemy number one on the XCEL hit list. Damn good too, if you ask me. No one's getting near them."

He was pro-Shifter, of course, but Griffin sensed something else. Respect? "Can you get in touch with them?"

The kid laughed. "Right. Hey, if I knew that, I'd be a rich man drinking margaritas in Acapulco right now."

Somehow, Griffin didn't believe him. "Let's say that you could get a message to them. Tell them we want to talk to them. Both me *and* my partner. They know her. Tell them we understand what they're doing. We want to know why."

The kid squinted at him. "What do you care about why?"

The noise level in the tunnel increased as a subway train closed in.

"Because there's a cover-up here, and I want to get to the bottom of it," Griffin yelled over the oncoming subway train. It passed nearby, drowning out every other sound and moving still air between them.

The sounds faded into the distance as both men waited, sizing each other up. Griffin hoped his instincts were right. He hoped the kid was more than just an informant. He wouldn't know for sure unless it worked, and he prayed it would. His options were fading fast. There was no way in hell he and Cam had time to check every tunnel underground for their Shifters, even with Ernest's help.

The noise level dropped to normal, and the kid finally said, "Look, I'll see what I can do. Can't promise you anything."

Griffin nodded. "You know how to contact me?"

"Yeah. I'll find you. Later." And then the kid walked away. Griffin watched until he turned a corner, out of sight, knowing without a doubt that the kid was *not* an XCEL informant.

He never asked for his money.

THIRTEEN

Mercer's home phone was on the third ring, and Cam stood next to it and stared at the incoming number. It was his grandfather, and she debated whether or not to pick it up. But then what would she talk to him about? Mercer? That was tempting. She had a few dozen questions about him and his past, but that wouldn't be right. She was direct, not rude.

Another ring and Cam took a step forward. She should pick it up, just to spite Mercer. She wasn't happy about waking up and finding him gone. No note, no nothing. It was enough to make a girl want to do something really stupid.

The final ring before the answering machine turned on. She was still feeling guilty for erasing the last message, and she'd had no right to interfere then, or now. Cam gripped her coffee mug hard as the answering machine played a generic answer message, and then Sani's voice came on.

"Hello, Griffin. This is your grandfather, Sani."

There was a long pause.

"I wish to speak to the Skinwalker."

Cam's mouth dropped open. Impossible. He couldn't know she was here, because Mercer certainly hadn't told him.

He said, "Skinwalker, you walk the desert alone. The sun is hot. The sand burns your feet. You may be lonely. But you are not alone. Others will follow your footsteps. Their feet will not burn as bad as yours. You have made the way safe."

She shook her head and sat on the couch watching the phone like it was alive. *Was he really talking to her?*

"Do not be afraid that you have no trail. Do not fear the dark times. Do not change your path. This is what you are meant for."

Her path? Cam laughed to herself. She had no path.

"These things I know. *Hágoónee.*"

She hugged the coffee mug in both her hands. What if he did know? What if he could see things that she couldn't? Griffin could see Shifters. That had to have come from somewhere. Maybe it *was* hereditary. Maybe he and his people were special, just like the Shifters.

Then Sani said, "You may erase this message now."

Cam blinked at the phone as he hung up.

◆◆◆

Griffin sat in his car a block from his apartment and watched the Shifter in human form watching his place. It was the same Shifter he noticed at the bus stop. It would make sense, given that he just met with another one who was checking them out. He and Cam had definitely made someone nervous. It was nine A.M. now, and the sun was climbing the sky. Cam was probably climbing the walls.

He pulled out his cell phone and called his home number. Cam picked up and snapped, "Where are you, Mercer?"

He grinned. "Waiting outside in the car. We're going to see your father."

"Give me ten minutes," she said quickly, and hung up.

Ten minutes, that would be enough time to find out who their spy was. He got out of the car and made his way to the Shifter. Traffic was light, but a smattering of tourists and walkers kept him hidden from view. The Shifter didn't spot him until he was twenty feet away, but when he did, he took off at a dead run.

Griffin chased him down the street, weaving through people and street vendors. They crossed the street on a green light, and Griffin dodged horn-blowing taxis. The Shifter ducked into a parking garage with Griffin just a few feet behind him.

The Shifter took the ramp down. Griffin knew he needed to catch the Shifter before he shifted. They couldn't shift in daylight, but underground in a parking garage was definitely a possibility. The Shifter was too busy looking back to see where Griffin was to notice the car that careened around the corner right in front of him.

The driver slammed on the brakes, and the Shifter hit the bumper and flipped over the car, landing in a heap behind it. Griffin yelled, "Shapeshifter!" to the driver, and as he expected, the driver peeled rubber to get away. Then he tackled the downed Shifter. They rolled across the pavement until Griffin had the Shifter pinned under him. The Shifter tried to change, but Griffin grabbed his bare arm. Energy surged through his hands, but he forced himself to stop. If he froze the guy, he wouldn't be able to get anything out of him. Then he lost his grip when the Shifter thrashed and kicked and generally made a huge fuss.

"Why are you watching us?" Griffin asked, dodging arms and legs.

The Shifter bucked to shake him. "Let me go."

Griffin grabbed him around the neck and tried to release just a little energy, just enough to slow the guy down. "Who do you work for?"

"Nuuugh," the Shifter said, and then suddenly rolled over, throwing Griffin across the concrete. By the time Griffin tumbled to his feet, the Shifter had shifted and was gone in a puff of black smoke.

Griffin brushed himself off. He didn't bother chasing the guy. He was down in the bowels of the parking garage at this point, probably escaping through a service exit or something.

"Fine, have fun without me."

He turned to find Cam walking down the ramp behind him. She was wearing jeans, sandals, and a soft chambray shirt. She looked good, but then, she always did.

Griffin told her. "He's been watching the apartment."

Cam stopped a few feet away. "I know. I noticed him hanging around this morning. Are you okay?"

His shoulder wound had opened up again and was oozing blood. Cuts, bruises, and abrasions. Par for the course. "Never been better."

"I told you it releases stress—" She stopped, and then she frowned as she stared at him.

He eyed her. "What?"

She moved closer, real close, and he stilled. Her hair was wet from her shower, and her skin was dewy soft in the overhead lights. He could see the curve of her breasts under the shirt.

"Don't move," she said and closed her eyes as she drew within inches of him. She was so close, he could see her long lashes, smell the shampoo she used. Every cell in his body aligned in her direction. He was mesmerized for a moment until he realized she was sniffing him.

She opened her eyes. "That was one of *our* Shifters."

Disappointment surprised him. "I think we're under surveillance."

Cam tilted her head slightly and narrowed her eyes. "Really? I smell more than one Shifter on you."

He headed up the ramp. "About that."

"Uh-huh," she said and stepped up beside him. "Would it have anything to do with your trip to the subway this morning?"

He kept forgetting that she could smell everything. "Maybe."

"The trip I wasn't invited on?" she added.

"I met with one of our informants. A Shifter. He wouldn't meet with me unless I was alone," he said. That was mostly true. He wasn't sure if the guy was working for the Shifters or not, and decided to keep that out for now. "I'll tell you what he said in the car on the way."

That seemed to appease her. "I appreciate you taking me to see my father."

He glanced at her. Actually, he was also going to see how Ernest was holding up, but the look of gratitude in her eyes was worth lying for. "No problem."

❖❖❖

Her father appeared older. Cam calmed the panic in her belly as he handed her a cup of tea and slowly, painfully sat down on the cot next to her.

"They even let me make my own tea now," he said with a wink. "Good behavior."

Cam nodded and stared into her teacup. He didn't have long. Weeks, if she was lucky. She glanced over her shoulder at the expanse of glass behind them. Cameras were recording their every movement, microphones their every word. It was a prison after all. No secrets were to be shared here. At least none that XCEL could decipher.

Her father sipped his tea, hunched over and growing thinner by the day. Cam set her tea on the table next to the cot and slid her hand inside her jacket as she scooted closer to her father. The cameras would see nothing.

Then she took out the small Glock that Mercer had armed her with and laid it in her father's lap. He turned to her in surprise, and she dug back in her memory for an old forgotten language.

"This is for you," she said slowly, searching for the correct translation into their Primary dialect. It was the first language of the shapeshifters, nearly lost from centuries of disuse and acculturation with other worlds.

"Why?" her father replied in Primary.

"Things are getting complicated," she told him, her words falling into place with surprising ease. "We might fail. If that happens . . ." She paused, searching for the words. "You must leave here."

Her father took the Glock and slipped it inside his shirt. Then he took a sip of tea. "I will wait for you."

"No," she said quickly. "No. You leave when you have the chance. I'll see if Ernest can help you."

Her father set down his tea and turned to her. His concern was etched across his leathery skin. "Where will you be?"

"I don't know," she told him truthfully. "I will come for you if I can."

"And if you don't," he asked, "then what can I assume?"

That I'm dead, she thought. Because that would be the only way she wouldn't be here. "I'm out saving Shifters everywhere."

"I hope so." He smiled and put his hand on hers. "You remember the language I taught you."

She gazed at him. "I remember everything you taught me."

"Then my destiny is nearly fulfilled," he said. "Do what I cannot. Carry on for me. That is my final wish."

Reality hurt, more than she'd hurt before. He wouldn't ever be able to fight for what he'd always wanted—to save the Shifters and their culture. "I'll try."

He said, "You are my life's work, my greatest achievement. I am so proud of you."

Emotions flooded over her, and she reached out and hugged him, holding on to his cool, thin body.

He whispered to her, "Save the Shifters. They need you more than I do. I can take care of myself."

She'd seen him do just that in his younger days. Today, she wasn't so sure. But he was setting her free, passing the torch that she knew he'd carried his entire life. She whispered in Primary, "Make sure to shoot Harding first."

Her father's boney shoulders shook with a chuckle, and Cam smiled through her tears.

◆◆◆

Ernest slapped a communications device in Griffin's hand. "This will allow you to talk to me. Forget your cell phones. They won't work underground."

He gave one to Cam as well, and she lifted her gaze to Griffin with some consternation. Agent Roberts, Harding's right-hand minion, watched them from the corner of the armory. Any minute now, Cam was going to kick his sorry ass out.

Griffin wasn't sure what transpired during her talk with her father, but she'd come out of his cell with a whole new killer attitude. He had to admit, he'd kind of missed it. As long as they were on the same side.

Ernest lifted two guns from the wall in the weapons room and held them up. "These are gonna save your butts. New weapon, called a Salt Round. The bullets are designed to crystallize fluids. Basically, sucks the surrounding tissue dry. It won't kill unless you hit a vital organ, but it will sure as hell slow a Shifter down."

Cam frowned. "But they—" She hesitated. "We will still heal."

"Yes, but much more slowly than Shifters normally do," he answered. Then he addressed her pointedly. "Make sure no one uses it on you."

She grinned at him with affection. "I'll make sure."

Griffin watched Ernest give her a goofy smile, and he shook his head. The kid was madly in love with a woman who was too much car for him. "Just how beta is this?"

Ernest put his hands on his hips. "I guess you'll find out if it works when you use it."

"Terrific," Griffin muttered. "Is that it?"

"No," Ernest said and started yanking equipment and armor off the racks in the room. He brought back a pile and dumped it on the table. "Don't know if you'll need all this, but take it just in case."

"Looks like we're going to war," Cam observed.

"You are," Ernest said. "Don't expect a warm welcome down there."

Cam gave him a jaded look. "I don't expect a warm welcome anywhere."

"Anything else?" Griffin asked as he sorted through the gear and loaded it into duffel bags.

Ernest cut a glance at Roberts. "You'll find everything you need in the communications devices."

Griffin made a mental note to take the communications devices apart when he got home. He handed a duffel bag to Cam and hefted the other two. "Talk to you soon."

Roberts escorted them to the door of the detention center and watched as they left. Gray skies threatened rain. Cam was nearly bursting by the time they got out of earshot.

"I hate Roberts almost as much as Harding," she said bitterly. "Do you know he followed me into the ladies' room?"

"Probably the highlight of his day," Griffin said. "We need to check the gear thoroughly before we use it. I don't trust anyone."

Cam scowled. "I hate this."

"So do I," Griffin said. And he did. Because basically, the only people he could trust were Ernest, Lyle, and Cam. "How's your father?"

Her expression turned serious. "The same."

Griffin popped the trunk of his car and felt growing guilt. "Is there anything I can do to make his stay better? Different room? Different place?"

She handed him her bag. "No, but thank you. Thank you for thinking of him."

He got points for asking, but still, he didn't want the old man to suffer. Griffin only hoped he found Thaniel before he got worse.

❖❖❖

Roberts gave Harding his report and left. Mercer and Solomon were going underground to find the Shifters. Ernest appeared to be behaving himself. Everything was going according to plan, but Harding was still not happy. He had a leak somewhere, and Braxton still hadn't located it. And an infiltrator on the loose could ruin everything he'd built for the past year.

He dialed the number on his cell phone. As soon as it picked up, he said, "Did you find him yet?"

"I'm going through all our operatives now. So far, they check out," Braxton replied.

Harding tapped his fingers on his desk. "The final shipments are coming in now. If any of them are stopped, our timeline will be delayed and so will my report to the senate committee."

"I'm doing the best I can to plug the leak. I can't be certain who is responsible—"

"Then don't be," Harding interrupted. "If you even think for a split second that someone is double-crossing us, I want you to get rid of them."

There was a pause. "Sure."

Braxton didn't understand the gravity of the situation. Any delay now would mean that the report would be late, and Harding did not want to miss this opportunity for the president's ear. Especially since Mercer and Solomon were getting closer to the Shifter cell. Harding had to spring this before they found out too much. "You cleaned up any trail back to us?"

"You have nothing to worry about."

"The hell I don't," Harding replied. "I did my part. I got you the protection you needed, the funding, the contacts, the men, even the best scientists. It's your job to make sure that the operation runs undetected. I shouldn't even have to be involved."

"I'm doing my fucking job," his partner said, his voice rising.

"Then find that infiltrator!" Harding said and hung up.

FOURTEEN

Cam sat across from Mercer on his living room floor. Between them lay a pepperoni pizza, miscellaneous weapons, and protective gear. Cam marveled at the trouble XCEL went to to kill her people.

Mercer was carefully taking everything apart that could be taken apart. Cam leaned back against the couch and stretched her legs as she watched him. Bruce Springsteen was playing through the sound system. A football game was on the TV, but the sound was muted. And they were going through their weapons, preparing for battle.

"So, is this a typical evening for you?" she asked.

Mercer lifted his gaze to look at her, a fringe of sleek black hair nearly covering his eyes. "You want to go dancing?"

She laughed, and he smiled.

"Mercer, I don't think you dance. I can't imagine you ever dancing," she said and grabbed another slice of pizza.

"I used to once," he said, and then the shadow of the past

swept over his face. The laughter was gone, replaced with memories. She hated seeing it.

"Maybe we should try dancing sometime," she said, more to see his reaction than anything else.

His eyes focused on her with riveting intensity. Dark eyes watched her every movement, her every breath. The pizza slice was getting cold in her hand, and she didn't care.

"I'm not sure that's a good idea," he said, his voice husky.

The intimate, highly charged moment in the bar came back in a flash. Her body perked up in a hurry, making her feel bold and reckless.

"Why?" she asked. "Are you afraid you might be attracted to a Shifter and ruin everything your world is built on?"

His eyes narrowed as if he was confused by her logic. "I'm not afraid of anything, Cam. I've already lost—" He stopped as if realizing he was heading into dangerous territory.

She set down the slice, suddenly latching onto a significant clue. "You're afraid your life will never be back to normal. Or whatever you consider normal, which I haven't yet figured out."

Mercer gave her a hard look and then went back to disassembling his communications device. "Not in the mood for twenty questions, Cam."

"Okay," she said. "You ask the questions."

For a long minute, he concentrated on removing the front of the comm. Then he said, "Why did your brother leave?"

And she immediately regretted her offer. "Wouldn't you rather know what my favorite color is?"

He shook his head and unsnapped the cover. "Nope."

Cam sighed. Well, she asked for this. "Thaniel and I disagreed on what to do once we crash-landed here on Earth."

Mercer set the cover down on the floor and brought the comm unit closer to study it. "What about your father?"

"He wasn't involved in the discussion."

Mercer seemed to spot something in the comm. "So what did *you* want to do?"

She closed her eyes and tried to get the words out without choking on them. "I just wanted to survive like we did on the last planet."

"You mean take advantage of the situation."

She opened her eyes to glare at him. "It sounds so wrong when you say it that way. I prefer to take advantage of opportunities. Besides, it's not like I chose the spotlight or anything. Think about it, I could have been the president. As it was, I wanted to fly under the radar. I didn't want to become the prime targets in someone's sights. And you see how well *that* worked out."

Mercer smirked. "What did your brother want to do?"

"Thaniel wanted to save Shifters here on Earth. Make a peaceful existence. Be model citizens," she said, feeling the bite of her own words. "It was . . . is . . . was my father's dream."

Mercer used thin pliers to pry something out of the comm. "So you argued and he left?"

She grimaced at the sharp stab of regret in her chest. Thaniel had been right all along. It just took her a few years to figure it out. "Yes."

"And now you need him," Mercer said and pulled out a thin, square piece of plastic.

"Yes," she said with a heavy sigh. "I screwed up."

"We all screw up, Cam. That's life," he said, turning the plastic piece. "SD card."

She scooted across the floor to kneel next to him. "Ernest hid it?"

Mercer slid the card into a slot in the device. "Probably the only way he could get us the info."

The screen on the device loaded. Cam took a seat next to Mercer so they could both look at it. His thigh was hard and warm against hers, and she did her best to keep her attention on the files popping up on the screen.

"Maybe I should print these," he said, his voice sounding rough.

Cam covered a smile. "Afraid of me?"

Mercer opened the first file. "Small print."

Liar, she thought, and she leaned against his shoulder.

"Analysis on the customer lists," he said. "Looks like the human hits are companies that openly support Shifters."

She scanned the report Ernest had written. "Shifter sympathizers."

"That would explain why they were targeted or by who," Mercer said.

Shifter haters heavily outnumbered Shifter supporters. "It would have to be someone who knew to remove those hits from our list, who knew the MO of the Shifter attacks well enough to copycat them."

Mercer nodded. "Could be anyone in XCEL with enough clearance. But why?"

She shrugged. "More wood to add to the Shifter fire? I put my money on Harding," she said. "He's running the show."

He shook his head. "Harding? He's a prick, but he keeps his hands clean. He wouldn't take the chance of losing his position."

She had to agree with that, especially the prick part.

Mercer scanned down the document to the analysis on the customers that the Shifters had hit. "No sympathizers on the list of Shifter attacks. In fact . . ."

Cam put her face inches from his to read the tiny screen. "What?"

He took a deep breath. "Cam."

She turned to look at him, so close she could feel the warmth of his breath. "Problem?"

He stared at her for a few beats and then put his arm around her to draw her closer. She sucked in a breath at the intimate contact. Their eyes were locked on each other.

Mercer spoke, "Some of these companies have been vocal about their position on Shifters."

"Against, I assume," she said, noting the hush in her voice.

"Against," he concurred. "And if you get any closer, you're going to get what you want."

She felt her eyes widen. "And what is it I want?"

Mercer's palm wrapped around the back of her neck and brought her lips to his—a fraction of an inch away. She felt the fire ignite in her belly with anticipation.

"Trouble," he whispered. "And not the kind you're looking for."

That intrigued her. "You want it too."

He peered into her eyes. "No, I don't. I'm already in as deep as I want to get."

"Really?" she said and brushed her lips against his.

"You can't just take whatever you want," he said, but his pulse was getting faster by the second. Maybe he was right and she shouldn't be pushing him. Still, curiosity gnawed at her.

She ran her lips over his and breathed, "Chicken."

He grabbed her arms and pushed her away. His eyes were narrow and hard. And that's when she saw the anger. It was there underneath the façade of civility. She saw the truth. He worked with her because he needed her to get his life back. To get rid of her and her kind. Her people. Regardless of how kind he was toward her or her father, the bottom line was that he was condemning them all.

Somewhere deep inside, the fire that burned with lust twisted and turned, changing into something she hadn't felt before— loyalty. With that loyalty came a surge of pride and protectiveness for her people.

"Fuck you, Mercer," she said, and wrenched herself from his grasp. She moved a few feet away from him. "You'll never understand us."

She grabbed a slice of cold pizza and proceeded to eat it. What had she been thinking? She needed to quit thinking about the fantasy she had about a human male falling madly in lust with her knowing full well what she was. Never happen. Her father was wrong. There would never be a man like that for her.

For the next five minutes, it was silent in the room while Cam fumed and Mercer checked the gear.

"So the human hits are on companies that sympathize, and the Shifter hits are on companies who don't," he said casually as if nothing had just happened between them.

"Maybe it's some kind of secret war, and these are retaliations back and forth," she suggested with a shrug, careful not to look at him if she didn't have to.

Mercer was thoughtful for a moment. "There's something else going on here. Some other reason. I'll get Ernest to look deeper, find the connections between the companies on each list."

"You think he'll be able to with Roberts hanging all over him?" she asked.

"That kid can do anything," Mercer said, and then added, "except find where our missing trailer went."

She did look at him then. "He couldn't find it?"

"Hit a dead end," Mercer said. "I've never seen Ernest hit a dead end, not in the years I've worked with him."

"Then someone buried it," she said. "It had to be XCEL. They were there."

Mercer nodded, albeit reluctantly. "Ernest confirmed that no one at the transportation center called them in."

"XCEL was there all along," she said, licking her fingers.

"Or they were doing the final leg of the delivery," Mercer said.

"To where?" she asked, and she caught him watching her intently as she licked the last finger. And there was a significant bulge in his pants. It finally dawned on her why he was so mad.

He wanted her.

And he hated himself for it.

"That's the big question," he replied and looked away.

◆◆◆

Griffin heard his cell phone ring and fumbled in the darkness to find it on the coffee table beside the couch. He didn't even look at the number. "What is it, Ernest?"

"Not Ernest," a man replied.

Griffin glanced at the incoming number. It read "Unknown." "Who is this?"

"I have a tip for you. Yeager Industries," the man said. He

gave Griffin the location and added, "Make it quick." Then the caller hung up.

Was that a joke or a setup? Griffin debated that for a full minute before getting up and walking to his bedroom door. He stood there for another minute wondering if his life insurance was paid up. Of course it wasn't. He knocked a few times.

"Cam," he said through the door.

"Go to hell, Mercer. You had your chance."

He grimaced. He deserved that. It had been a knee-jerk reaction to a serious hard-on that he'd been trying to distract her from. Because *it* didn't care that she was a Shifter. Or that this was temporary. Or that she would walk away the minute her father was free.

No, all it knew was the way her shadow wafted around him when they were close, teasing him. Taunting him. Reminding him that it had been far too long since he'd held a woman, and even longer since he'd wanted to.

He cleared his throat. "We have a lead to follow."

There was a rustling on the other side of the door, and it cracked open a few inches. Cam was soft, rumpled, and beautiful, and his body reacted way too fast. He stepped to the side a little.

"We have to follow it right now?" she asked, frowning.

"Right now," he said.

She didn't look convinced, and he added, "This could save us a trip underground."

"Fine," she replied and closed the door on him.

◆◆◆

"I hope you didn't wake me for nothing," Cam said testily as Griffin pulled his car along the block near the place. It was 3:30 A.M. and the streets were mostly quiet. "Are you sure it wasn't just a crank caller?"

"Most crank callers don't know how to block their phone number or access a phone that's supposed to be secure," he said. Actually, he didn't know if it was a prank or not, but he wasn't going to tell her that. She'd kill him on the spot.

He parked the car. "Let's go check it out."

She narrowed her eyes at him. "You're a little too chipper this morning. Excited that you get a chance to shoot Shifters?"

Griffin turned to her. "I live for it."

Disappointment settled in her eyes. "I noticed."

They got out of the car and headed down the sidewalk. Streetlights cast a ghostly glow over the roads and buildings as they approached the corner. Sirens wailed in the distance. The city murmured its night sounds, punctuated by car horns.

The building was wedged between two others. It was a typical storefront setup with wide glass windows and a door covered with bars for the night. If he hadn't been given the building number, he never would have noticed it.

When they were about twenty yards away from the door, Cam put her hand out against his chest, stopping him. "There are people inside."

He pulled out his gun and moved them both against the exterior. "How many?"

"I can't tell for sure. At least two," she said, cocking her head as she listened. "Could be workers."

He doubted that. The place was dark inside. "Let's be Good Samaritans and find out."

Her eyes glowed iridescent in the dark. "Good Samaritan is going to be a stretch for you."

"You too," he noted, challenging her. She was in a hell of a mood.

"At least you know where I stand," she stated.

He eyed her. "I think my stance is pretty clear too."

She turned to him, and her shadow with her. It glowed with fire and life. Like a soul. Her soul. It hadn't occurred to him before.

"No," she said, her tone firm. "You want me, but you hate yourself for it. You want your old life back, but you know it wasn't much of a life. You don't know where you fit in, and you're too afraid to find out."

So much for a soul. The woman was heartless. Plus, this was not the conversation he wanted to be having with a gun in his hand. "For someone who routinely uses people for a living, you sure have a lot to say about the way I live my life."

Anger lit in her eyes as she tapped him in the chest with a fingernail. "I know who I am. I know what I want. What do you want, Mercer? What in this whole goddamned, piece-of-shit world makes you happy?"

That did it. She asked what he wanted. He'd show her. He reached out and pulled her to him. She gasped as he kissed her hard. All the pent-up frustration and desire rushed out into that one kiss. He felt her fight him, no doubt still pissed from slinging arrows. And then her tension eased, and she seemed to melt into him.

It was a silent invitation that he couldn't resist. The kiss became his offer to explore all the parts of her that he'd wanted to from the first time he saw her. Her sigh was his passport to her soft belly, her round breasts, the long line of her neck. He groaned when she ran her fingers up his chest to his shoulders.

He felt his erection grow against her pelvis, felt her rock into him. And knew without a doubt that he was in deep trouble. For some reason, that didn't bother him as much as it should. In fact, he felt lighter. At least from the waist up.

The gun tapped against the brick wall, and he remembered where they were. With supreme effort, he broke off the kiss and checked the building they were supposed to be investigating. No action outside.

They were lucky. And he was an idiot.

He stepped away from her and checked his Glock. Now what? How was he going to explain that? Tell her the truth? That he jeopardized their safety and this entire gig by being selfish? She wouldn't believe him. Tell her he was kidding? That was suicide. Tell her he was wrong? That would be wiser. "I shouldn't have done that."

"You need to make up your mind, Mercer. I don't like this game. If you want to take revenge for what your ex-partner did to you, find some other Shifter to play with." Her words were curt and heated.

She moved back against the brick, a ghostly blue in the night. The shadow glowed around her, but all he saw was the confusion and hurt in her face. He'd done that. She was right. He needed to decide one way or another and live with it, no matter how badly it turned out. "We have to get inside."

The glare she gave him worried him a lot. After all, she was supposed to be his partner. She stepped forward and pinned him with a hard look. "You try that one more time, and I'll break every bone in your body."

Then she headed toward the front door of the building and ripped the padlock and chain off with one mighty tug. Mercer realized she wasn't kidding about breaking him in half.

◆◆◆

Cam was beyond pissed and thoroughly humiliated as she broke the handle clean off and pushed open the door. How could she let him get that close again, especially after last night? She'd thrown herself at him then, and he'd pushed her away—literally. And then he'd kissed her and she'd bought it again. She was an idiot.

And goddamnit, she was tired and grumpy from getting no sleep. No coffee, no shower. *Someone* was going to be very sorry he got her out of bed for this.

The smell of gasoline overwhelmed the small front lobby the moment Cam stepped into it. It was strong; she was sure Mercer smelled it too. The place was empty, but there were sounds of movement behind the door that read Employees Only.

Then she realized that something was missing from this entire scenario. "They're not Shifters."

Even as she said it, she knew she shouldn't have. What would he do if it wasn't Shifters? Would he walk away and forget it? There'd be nothing in it for him. After the last few hours, she wasn't sure anymore. Regardless if he left, she'd stay and stop them. The decision surprised her, but she wasn't letting these guys blame this one on the Shifters.

Mercer's expression was unreadable. "We need to get to them before they ignite the gas."

She let out the breath she didn't realize she was holding. "And we should check to see if this company is a Shifter sympathizer."

He nodded agreement. "First things first."

Mercer moved ahead of her and tested the Employees Only door. It was unlocked and swung aside easily as he moved in, gun at the ready.

He led the way down a narrow hallway, passing two offices on either side. He halted her at the end of the corridor that opened to an office space. Men moved between the desks, and Cam concentrated on the voices and sounds.

After a few seconds, Mercer glanced over his shoulder at her. She put up three fingers for the three men, and he nodded. He motioned for her to go right, and he took the left side.

The voices grew louder as she crept across gasoline-soaked carpet and around cubicle partitions.

"Make sure you cover all the computers and servers. We want everything to burn."

"Charges are set with a one-minute delay," someone said.

"I got the keys to the front door. Clear out."

Footsteps came toward them.

Time changed and slowed as she shifted to her Primary form. Everything sharpened; every one of her senses opened up. It was like breathing, like being set free. Powerful and immortal. She eyed the first guy entering her line of sight. She moved, catching him off guard, and backhanded him over a desk.

Then someone gave out a yell and guns fired simultaneously as the other two men dove behind furniture. Cam thinned her structure, ignored the flying bullets, and walked toward the second man. She was a step away when she felt a large projectile rip through and lodge in her belly. Pain radiated deep within as everything around the slug began to harden. She staggered and fought for control of her internal structure, but it wasn't working right.

She clutched her stomach and concentrated on ejecting the object from her form. It took precious time, and her energy was fading fast. *What was inside her?*

She heard Mercer yell as the man in front of her raised his gun to fire again. She couldn't move out of the way, couldn't defend herself. Fear gripped her. Each second ticked by like an hour. Her father's face appeared in her mind.

No. It couldn't end this way.

A gunshot went off, and the man dropped on top of the desk. She doubled over and focused on saving herself from whatever ammunition he'd used on her. Somewhere in the back of her mind, she recalled Ernest saying, "Make sure no one uses it on you." And she knew. She knew she was dead.

Mercer's voice was behind her, yelling, but he was lost in the pounding of blood in her ears and the buzz of the battle waging inside her. Then there was a bright light and a terrible concussion that threw her back against something hard. She smelled fire and felt her skin burn for a brief moment, and then everything went black.

FIFTEEN

Griffin called Lyle as soon as he got her up the stairs and into his bed. His fingers fumbled clumsily with the phone numbers.

"It's five A.M., Griffin. I just got to sleep," Lyle complained when he answered.

"Cam's hurt bad," he said, his voice sounding far away and hollow. The ringing in his ears hadn't stopped since the explosion.

"I'll be right there." Lyle hung up.

Griffin set down the phone and noticed that his hands were bloody and shaking. His clothes were singed, flying debris had sliced his arms, and his lungs burned from smoke inhalation. But he was still in better shape than Cam.

Lying in his bed in her charcoal Shifter form, she moaned as she twisted and flailed in agony. Two bullet holes oozed a thick liquid that he could only assume was her blood. Her thick skin was peeling and ripped in places where the blast had hit her. The giant solid bulge in her belly was what worried him the most. It was like her whole stomach had been turned to stone.

He ran into the bathroom and soaked a couple of towels with hot water. Cam was gasping for air when he got back to her. The stone in her stomach was affecting all her functions. How bad was she? He had no idea.

"Can you hear me?" he asked her, his words echoing in his ears. "Come on, Cam. You can do this. You can heal yourself."

He pressed one of the towels to a bullet hole, and she groaned in pain. Then he laid another one on top of her hard stomach, and she let out loud cry. Griffin held it in place. It had to help. He didn't know how he knew it, but he did.

"Jesus Christ, what happened?" Lyle was standing at the foot of the bed gaping at them both.

Griffin summarized. "We got blown up."

Lyle walked to the side of the bed. "*You* look like you got blown up. What about her?"

"She was shot with something, I don't know. But we need to get it out."

Lyle stepped back in sudden understanding and put his hands up. "Oh, no. No, no, no. I can put in a few stitches, but there is no way I'm operating on her."

"It's killing her," Griffin said, fighting the helpless feeling he'd had since he saw her lying on the floor in the building. His hands weren't shaking from the adrenaline; they were shaking from fear. "So get your kit."

Lyle ran a hand through his hair and swore. Then he turned and ran. He'd be back; at least that's what Griffin hoped. Lyle wouldn't leave her like this either.

"I kissed you because I wanted to," he said. He had no idea

why he was telling her that, but it was the truth. "Not for revenge. Not to play games."

Cam was writhing in pain, and Griffin held her down, feeling a rush of helplessness. What did he have for medical supplies? Maybe Advil and Ace bandages. Nothing to stop her suffering. Then he remembered the tranquilizer in his arsenal. It was a gamble introducing yet something else into her system at this point. On the other hand, he couldn't bear taking bullets out of her without some kind of painkiller.

He made the decision and ducked into the living room to get the tranquilizer cartridge. It was full, which was good. She'd be out for the next few hours. Lyle met him back in the bedroom with a duffel bag.

Griffin held the tranquilizer over her chest and braced himself. In Shifter form, black skin muted her features. But in his mind, he saw her red hair and ivory skin. Then he jabbed her with the tranquilizer, driving the needle deep into her chest. She wailed as the drug emptied into her. Seconds later, all the tension seeped from her body and she sank into the bed.

He put his ear to her chest. She was still breathing, and even better, she wasn't suffering anymore. Griffin sat back, rubbed his eyes, and fought the fatigue that swept over him. His night wasn't over yet.

Lyle set the duffel down and unzipped it. "Are you sure you're ready for this?"

Griffin stared at Cam, dreading the next step. "No. I'm definitely not."

"That makes two of us."

◆◆◆

"Christ almighty, Braxton!" Harding roared as he flung open the door to his partner's office. Braxton was sitting behind his desk, a dark figure against white walls. He looked up at Harding with black eyes and a thick beard that covered up tanned skin. He wore military-grade fatigues and hat.

Harding planted his hands on the front of his desk with a loud thump that he hoped would give Braxton a clue to just how pissed off he was. All the frustration and fury he'd kept in check on the way over here spit out. "How did Mercer know about that attack last night?"

Braxton set his pen down and pushed back in his chair. He laced his fingers behind his head and regarded him with a cool disdain that drove Harding to the brink of futility. "And a good morning to you too."

Harding thrust a finger at him. "Don't get cocky with me. What happened?"

Braxton maintained his typical poker face. "Whatever it was wasn't worth you jeopardizing this operation by coming down here. Your temper is going to be the end of us both."

Harding stood up and clenched his fists to bring himself back under control. Braxton was wrong. A temper got things done, motivated people. Most people. But he'd learned that Braxton would not continue this conversation unless Harding calmed down. He dropped into the chair in front of Braxton's desk. "Report. *Please*."

"Obviously, Mercer got a tip that we were targeting that location," Braxton began. "Both he and his partner proceeded to take out our men. The bombs went off, destroying the place. Mercer carried the woman out immediately afterward. We picked up all our men before the authorities arrived. One was dead, the other two injured."

Harding gripped the arms of the chair and mentally ran through the ramifications of the night's disaster. Mercer and Camille knew that the men weren't Shifters. That would be a problem. "You said he carried her out?"

Braxton laid his elbows on his desk and leaned forward. "My men said they hit her with a Salt Round. She succumbed to it. We may have killed her."

Good, Harding thought. That would save him the trouble. "And Mercer?"

"Minor injuries."

So Mercer would need to be dealt with and soon. Before he could do anything with his newfound information. "Is there any way they can tie the attack back to us?"

"No," Braxton said and smiled. "We're solid."

Harding glared at him. "Really? So you've identified whoever leaked this information?"

That got a twitch out of Braxton. "Not yet, but in a few days it won't matter. The operation is well under way, and nothing can stop us now. We have a few more shipments coming in to complete the large-scale manufacturing line."

They were so close, Harding could taste it. "Make sure those deliveries arrive on time. I won't tolerate any more mistakes."

Braxton's eyes narrowed. "Don't threaten me, Harding. I'm the man keeping your shit together."

It wasn't a threat. Harding had no intention of letting Braxton screw up his plans. It wouldn't be easy, but he could find a replacement for Braxton if he had to. He'd just have to pay him very, very well.

"But it's my neck on the line," Harding replied. "And I will protect it at all costs."

The two men stared each other down. Finally, Braxton picked up his pen and bent over his paperwork. "Go write your report, Harding."

◆◆◆

Cam felt warm and safe. She couldn't tell where she was or what day it was, and she didn't care. The feeling of total love wrapped around her like a soft blanket. There was no pain, no worry, no suffering. She clung to the overwhelming sense of well-being with dogged determination. *I am loved,* she thought.

Then she wrapped her hands around her belly. It was swollen and round. She was pregnant. She didn't remember getting pregnant, but it didn't matter. Happiness flooded over her in great waves. She hugged her child with loving arms, promising it unrequited love and protection. Her world was perfect, and she felt like she would burst with the glory of it all.

And then a gunshot shattered her world. She panicked, grasping at the love and the well-being, trying desperately to hold on to them. They were yanked away into darkness through her fingers. She felt her belly; the child was gone. And in her mind, she howled at the loss.

"It's okay, Cam."

She cried out as pain radiated through her body. Reality returned. *No. Please don't leave. Please.*

"I got you."

Stripped bare, she turned on her side toward the words and the warmth. Strong arms cradled her, and she pressed her face into his shoulder. His scent soothed her grief; his kind caress a balance to the pain.

Griffin. She relaxed against him, knowing that her reality was safe, if only temporarily. The last remnants of her perfect world faded away. Her belly burned, and she checked it with her hand. That's when she realized she was in Primary form. The building, humans, gunshots, bomb blast all came back in a heartbeat.

And now she was with Mercer.

In his bed, in his arms. In her Shifter form.

Panic gripped her, tearing across the wound in her belly as she lurched away from him. She heard his protest and yanked the blanket they shared around herself. His heat lingered on the blanket as she rolled to the far edge of the bed.

"Cam—"

"Don't touch me," she said, ashamed and not knowing why.

His hand cupped her shoulder. "How do you feel?"

She shook off his hand and curled into herself. "Leave me alone, I need to heal."

He didn't move for a long time, and part of her wanted him to stay. The other part, however, was injured and fierce. Angry for feeling shame. Angry for her people. Angry for a perfect world that she would never have.

Then she felt his weight move off the bed behind her. He walked to the door and paused. "If you need anything, I'll be right here."

She closed her eyes and wished she could cry. But Shifters didn't have tears. They simply hurt.

◆◆◆

Lyle sat on the couch across from Griffin and propped his legs up on the coffee table. It was dark out, and Lyle should be tending bar, but he'd brought up a bottle of good Scotch instead. "So, she kicked you out? What did you do to her?"

Griffin watched the ice cubes melt in his fourth scotch. He was feeling no pain. No pleasure either. In fact, pretty much nothing. It was the way he liked it. "No idea."

Lyle chuckled low into his drink. "Right."

"I didn't do a thing," he insisted. Although that wasn't entirely true. He'd held her while she shuddered in his arms. He'd heard her cries. He'd hurt along with her.

"When I checked last, you were in bed with her," Lyle said.

"She was cold, shaking. I thought she needed to be warmer," he said. "Get your mind out of the gutter. Nothing happened."

"But she's still in Shifter form," Lyle noted.

He frowned at his friend. "Yes. So?"

Lyle shrugged. "Wouldn't expect you to touch her in that form. It's some sorta taboo thing with you."

Ah, so that was it. "Don't even go there, Lyle. I'm not in the mood for a lecture on whether or not Shifters belong here."

He laughed. "Not a matter of *if*. They *are* here. It's a matter of *how* they belong." He hesitated and then asked, "Was it that bad? Holding her in her native form?"

Griffin frowned. He needed more booze for this conversation. "No. Happy?"

Lyle shrugged. "It's a start."

"So why did she kick me out?" Griffin asked, half to himself.

"Maybe she's just not that into you," Lyle offered with a big grin.

"If you didn't let me live here for free and bring me good booze, I'd drop you as a friend," Griffin said and grinned back.

Lyle laughed, and Griffin joined him. It felt good to laugh. To forget and float in that semivegetative, relaxed state he'd discovered via booze. When he drank, the past didn't feel as bad. Unfortunately, when he drank, the future didn't look so bright either. Sucked that you couldn't have both.

"Did it ever occur to you that she might not like who she is?" Lyle said when the laughter was done.

Griffin tried to wrap his head around that logic. The alcohol made it a little more challenging. "Why wouldn't she like who she is? She's . . . beautiful."

Lyle eyed him in disbelief. "Are you kiddin' me? You're the one hunting Shifters. You're the one trying to get rid of them."

Mercer frowned. "I'm not trying to get rid of them. I just don't want them around me."

Lyle gave a groan of frustration. "Exactly. They are welcome here as long as they don't bother you or anyone else."

That wasn't even possible, Griffin realized. "No."

"Then what do you want?" Lyle pressed.

Griffin gritted his teeth. "I don't know."

"Then how is she supposed to know where she stands if you don't know?" Lyle said.

Lyle was starting to be a pain in the ass. He was also right. Griffin had played games with Cam, pushing her away and then pulling her back. No wonder she didn't trust him, didn't want him around. He didn't want him around either. That's why he drank scotch.

"I've known you a long time," Lyle said soberly. "We've seen the world hand you some bad times. Seen some good times too. But I've never seen you like this. You gotta decide what you want, what you *really* want in this life. And then you gotta fight for it with everything you got. You have to work and suffer and make it happen, because no one's going to help you."

Lyle's words sunk in slowly, one by one, terrible in their truth. Griffin thought he knew what he wanted—his old life back. The life that was stolen from him. But now he wasn't so sure that life was worth fighting for. He wasn't even sure it was possible. Even worse, he wasn't sure if that was the life he *ever* wanted. He'd spent so much time hunting Shifters and calling them the enemy that he didn't really think about what he was doing or why.

Lyle raised his glass to Griffin. "To life, as it should be."

"Whatever the hell that is," Griffin added, and downed the rest of his scotch.

"I'm cutting myself off," Lyle said. He braced both his hands on the coffee table and stood up, a little wobbly. "Man, I know I'm going to regret this in the morning. I'll blame you then." He gave Griffin a wave and then wandered out the door and closed it behind him.

The apartment returned to its deafening silence, worse than ever before, and he'd felt some pretty crappy silence. He hated it, hated what it represented. He just didn't know how to fix it.

Griffin glanced over and noticed the flashing light on his answering machine. Might as well finish off his day with a bang. He hit the Play button and closed his eyes to listen to the asshole collections agencies try to squeeze money from a stone.

"Hello, this is your grandfather, Sani."

Crap, Griffin thought. He was not in any state of mind to figure out one of Sani's cryptic messages.

"I know you are torn. I feel the struggle in your heart. You are restless. You look for answers."

Griffin frowned at the machine. He understood all of that. He must be drunker than he thought. Maybe that was the key to understanding Sani.

"This is a world of lies. Things are not what they appear. They are not the truth. There is only one place to find the truth."

Griffin sat up in his chair and stared at the machine waiting for the answer.

"Truth can always be found in the heart. The heart sees things for what they are. It feels when it is supposed to. It hurts when it is supposed to. It knows right and wrong. It guides the body and the mind."

Griffin closed his eyes. He didn't want to feel with his heart. He'd done that. It was too hard when everything went to hell.

"The heart loves quickly and heals slowly," Sani continued. "Without this love and pain, life is nothing but endless desert. You can walk the desert from end to end and find the same thing."

Griffin smiled. There was the Sani he knew and loved.

"These things I know," Sani said. *"Hágoónee."*

The machine clicked off. No more messages played. Griffin sat in the silence and thought about what Lyle had said. *Life as it should be.* He had a feeling that was a tall order to fill. He glanced at his closed bedroom and debated checking on Cam. But since he valued his life, or something like it, he stretched out on the couch to sleep off the hangover he deserved.

CHAPTER
SIXTEEN

Cam wandered out into the living room looking for food. What she found was Mercer asleep on the couch, a couple of empty glasses, and half a bottle of Scotch.

Her belly was still tender and the residual pain just a wrong movement away under one of Mercer's T-shirts. But she'd Shifted back to human form, and that was something. It had weakened her, though, and food was high on her priority list.

She paused just long enough to cover Mercer up with a blanket. The day was far too bright as it slipped through the blinds. She walked over and was about to close them when she noticed their Shifter watching the place again.

What the hell was going on? When had they become the hunted? She closed the blinds tightly and went to the kitchen. She opened the refrigerator door and peered inside. Leftover pasta appeared to be the easiest food available. Cam took out the dish and slid it into the microwave.

Five minutes? Fifteen? She had no idea, but she was famished so she opted for five. The microwave hummed to life. She drank four tall glasses of water waiting for it to heat up. The buzzer went off, and she removed the pasta. The bowl was warm. That was a good sign.

"Thought you said you couldn't cook?"

Cam nearly dropped the dish on the counter at Mercer's voice. She set it down carefully and turned to him. "Don't sneak up on me like that. You almost had pasta a la counter."

Then she stopped talking. Mercer leaned against the doorway looking rumpled, sleepy, and really sexy. Rough stubble hugged his face. His jeans were from yesterday, last night. Still covered in blood, probably hers. And he was shirtless. She liked his skin. It was bronze and smooth over hard muscle. Touchable.

But his eyes. His eyes were what shut her up.

"Are you okay?" he asked softly.

She mustered a smile. "Yes. Thank you."

His eyes stayed on her a long time. This kitchen was small; she hadn't realized it until now. "You took the bullets out." Well, duh. They were sitting in a bowl next to the bed. "Hungry?"

"A little," he said.

She avoided those eyes while she retrieved two plates and started piling up pasta on them. It wasn't exactly hot, but there was enough heat in this kitchen to more than make up for it.

She handed him a plate, and they ate pasta for breakfast in silence. Mercer watched her like he was making sure she ate. He needn't worry; she was starving and she didn't care if she was stuffing her face.

He cleaned his plate in the sink and turned around to face her. She had a mouthful of food when she noticed his eyes focused on her with singular intensity and something else. Something that was real. Not a game. Somewhere in the back of her mind, she remembered him talking to her last night. What had he said? *I know what I want?*

He said, "They used the new beta Salt Round on you."

She blinked a few times, because her mind was busy elsewhere. She swallowed her pasta. "I figured that."

"They had access to XCEL weapons."

She put down the fork, still a little foggy and not quite keeping up with him. "You think they stole it?"

Mercer pursed his lips. "I think they were *given* it."

The fog lifted, and she followed the logic, as awful as it was. "Are you saying that hit last night was sponsored by XCEL?"

"I'm saying it's possible," he said.

She should have expected this, should have seen it coming. Should have known that this was all some sick, stupid game that XCEL was playing on them. Her body tightened, and her belly clenched. She grabbed the counter for support. "Crap."

Mercer was around her in a second. "Don't move."

He picked her up in his arms and carried her into the bedroom. She clung to him, not wanting to let go once he deposited her on the bed. She laid her head back on the pillow. "I don't believe this. This is Harding, isn't it?"

Mercer sat down on the edge of the bed. "I don't know. But I smell a rat, and he's the biggest one there is."

"I knew I should have gotten my deal in writing," she said. All this time, she'd held out a thread of hope that Harding would keep his word. What the hell was she thinking, cutting deals with humans? The odds were always stacked against her.

"What do you need?" Mercer asked as she curled up.

A gun for Harding and a cure for her father. Damn, she thought.

Her father. "Don't suppose you'd be in the mood to spring my father from a highly secure detention center?"

Mercer eyed her. "*You* are not in any shape to spring anyone. Harding won't touch your father. We have time. You need rest and sleep. And you should be in Shifter form. You'll heal faster that way."

Who replaced Mercer with someone who cared? "Good thing I gave him my gun."

Mercer's eyebrows rose. "You gave your father your gun? In the detention center?"

"If he wasn't in the detention center, he wouldn't need the gun," she told him.

Mercer started smiling, and then he starting laughing. It was deep and real, and Cam liked it. Then he shook his head with something that resembled admiration. "Something tells me your father will do just fine."

That warmed her heart. Her body, however, was shivering.

"Change back to Shifter form," Mercer said, turning serious as he watched her tremors grow.

"No," she said. She couldn't do it, not in front of him. "I'm good. It's just freezing in here."

"It's over seventy-five degrees in here," he said, frowning deeply. "If I raise it any higher, all the food in the freezer will melt."

Her body was healing quickly, thanks to the food and water. The side effect was the shakes. She was about to tell him that when he stood up, walked around the other side of the bed, and slid under the covers.

Cam stiffened as he wrapped his arms around her and pulled her back against his chest. She felt warmth all down her backside. "What are you doing?"

"Body heat," he said simply. "*Or*, you can shift back to your Primary form."

"Can't do that," she murmured. His ninety-eight degrees seeped into her back, pushing away the cold. Her shivers quieted.

"Why not?" he asked, in her ear.

She closed her eyes, accepting his embrace. "Ugly."

His arms tightened around her a little more. "You're not ugly, Cam. In any form."

She felt cozy and safe. "Liar."

Mercer's voice was sad. "Only when I drink."

It occurred to her that that was true. "I thought you hated Shifters."

He shrugged. "You're okay."

Okay? *Okay?* She was damned hot. "How do I know that you aren't just saying that to get my help?"

Mercer didn't answer for a moment. Then he splayed his hand over her hips very carefully as he pressed her back against his body. She felt the outline of his erection and closed her eyes at the rush of desire that swept over her. He wanted her. And he knew exactly who and what she was. No games this time. She *was* right. He had made up his mind. He was here with her by his choice.

She ground her buttocks against him, and he hissed in her ear. The sound ignited the heat that had been simmering in her body since he slid into bed with her. All those flashes of what it would be like came back with a vengeance.

"Cam," he said softly. "This isn't a good idea."

She wasn't playing around. "Are you in or out, Mercer?"

She ran her hand over his, which was above the covers, holding her, and dragged it up to her breast. His fingers flexed against her through the fabric. She closed her eyes and savored every touch. She'd lied to him. There weren't *that* many ex-lovers.

His breathing got deeper and faster. Heat crackled between them like a flash fire. Still, his restraint was admirable. It wouldn't work, but it was admirable.

"I don't want to hurt you," he whispered against her ear, his breath hot and voice rough.

Part of her knew he was right. The day would come soon when he'd hurt her, but not in the physical sense. She had no delusions about ever fitting into his life or his world. But that was someday.

"Trust me, I'm healing faster by the minute." And she was. The food and water were the extra energy she needed. The pressure in her belly had subsided and moved far, far lower. She lifted her arm and tucked it behind his neck to pull his lips closer. He obliged, kissing her shoulder and neck, his scruff rough along her smooth skin. The tension in his muscles told her he was fast catching up with her on the lust scale.

His hand slipped under the covers and then under her shirt. She felt the heat of his palm skim lightly over her stomach to her breast. Her nipples hardened more, aching for his touch.

She moaned at the firm but tender way his fingers stroked her skin, exploring every inch slowly and methodically. The promise of slow, long, intense lovemaking flooded her mind. Every nerve ending in this body went on high alert.

"Damn," he whispered, and then he was gone, leaving a rush of cool air between them. He lay back on the bed behind her and blew out a long breath. "We can't do this, Cam. You're injured."

Oh no, he wasn't doing this to her. She rolled over and threw her leg over his hips to straddle him. His eyes were so black they were nearly lost in the darkness of the bedroom. His hands wrapped around her thighs and held them in place. "Cam—"

"Shut up, Mercer," she said and leaned over to kiss him. Her hands explored from his abdomen to his shoulders, committing every ridge and valley to memory. Thick muscle, powerful arms, deep chest. His hands slid up her thighs to her hips, and his thumbs worked toward her center. He groaned when he realized she wasn't wearing panties under his T-shirt.

She stopped kissing him and closed her eyes, concentrating on the caress of his thumb on her clitoris. Stroke, circle, pressure—all melding into one wondrous caress. She felt the tension build in her core and stretch across her body like a spring building energy.

Stroke, circle, pressure.

Her breathing turned deep and measured as the climax approached. There was no pain from her wound, only ecstasy that tightened around her insides to the point of breaking. And in a single, powerful moment, recoiled. She welcomed the implosion with a drawn-out, heartfelt groan. Tension flowed out of her body with each pulse.

Her body shuddered with release, and she collapsed on top of Mercer to recover. He stroked her hair, his hands large and strong against her skin. She could have stayed like that forever, savoring the aftermath and the embrace. But they weren't done yet.

She pushed off his chest and looked down at him. His expression was tight and hungry, but he didn't make a move. Looked like she was going to have to take the initiative. Cam lifted off his hips to unzip his jeans.

His hand went around her wrist. "Not a good idea, Cam."

She broke his grip and unzipped the jeans slowly and deliberately. "In or out, Mercer."

A pained look crossed his face as she tugged the jeans down his hips, exposing cotton shorts. Underneath, he was heavy and hard. She smiled. "I think you're in."

"I can't promise to be careful," he said, his voice raw with emotion. His honesty sent shivers down her spine. He wouldn't be careful. The man had self-control in his work, in his life, in every other waking moment. But in love, that's where Mercer would show his true self.

"Good," she said, and pushed the shorts down. His fingers clenched her thighs as she wrapped her fingers around his girth and positioned herself over him. "In or out."

Every muscle in his body was taut, straining. And then he let out a groan and bucked, filling her just partway. He was being as careful as he could, and she sank into him and pushed down all the way. He filled her—body and soul—and she moaned at the longing for more.

His hands held her down. "I'm in."

And then he pulled back and arched into her, his invasion slow and deliberate. There was no pain, only a sense of wholeness as he lifted her up and then filled her again. He drove into her again and again; each long, slow stroke fueling the pressure and the promise. Time spun out, lost in the flood of sensations and ecstasy.

His rhythm became slower and more desperate. Her own need arose, doubling with every thrust. As the spring tightened, she sensed the moment when he lost control, when he became himself, when the weight of the world held no sway. With a great growl, he drove into her one last time. Then her climax overshadowed everything else.

◆◆◆

Griffin was too comfortable to answer his cell phone. It was by the bed where he'd left it last night, too far out of reach. He'd have to let go of Cam, and he wasn't ready to do that just yet.

It went to voice mail, and the tension he felt with it. Cam's body was hot and soft against his. She'd settled half on, half off him while they slept.

The cell phone started ringing again.

Griffin ignored it and turned to Cam. Her Shifter shadow enveloped them both, but he didn't mind. If that's what it took to feel like this, he was good with it.

The cell phone stopped ringing after three rings.

He brushed her hair from her face, felt its silkiness between his fingers. She wouldn't shift to her Primary form because she thought she was ugly. Would rather heal more slowly, suffer more than turn into something she hated in front of him. That was his fault. Well, him and pretty much every other human on the planet. There had been no welcome for Shifters, and that wouldn't happen anytime soon.

The cell phone rang again—twice and hung up.

Griffin sighed. It had to be Ernest. That kid was relentless. Plus, he probably had something important to say. Griffin slipped away from Cam, and she gave a little sigh of protest before settling back onto his bed.

He picked up the phone, walked into the living room, and scanned the incoming calls. All from Ernest. Then he waited. Ten seconds later, the phone rang again.

"This better be good," he answered.

"I gave you a cell phone so you could get my calls," Ernest said, sounding mighty pissed off for Ernest.

"I was busy," Griffin said. "What's wrong?"

"We had a new attack at 5 A.M. this morning."

"On our list or off?"

"Off."

Griffin sensed that there was more. "And?"

"And three people died at this one."

Hell. "You're positive it was a copycat hit?"

"This is *me*," Ernest said, sounding slightly insulted. "They never killed anyone before. In all those other attacks. Why now?"

Good question. They were either getting sloppy, or they were making a statement. There was only one way to find out. "We'll check it out."

"One more thing," Ernest said. "Don't call me at work, just on this cell."

Griffin walked over to the window and checked through the blinds. Their Shifter spy was still there. Man, he didn't learn. "Is it that bad?"

"Yes, I can barely get anything in or out of the office with Roberts on my ass. Oh, and your missing shipment? It never existed."

Griffin stilled. "No record of it?"

"Someone high up had those files erased, permanently. What the hell is going on, Griffin?"

Nothing good, and it was getting worse by the minute. Just how high up did this go? Harding had to be involved. Did the XCEL upper brass know? The senate committee? The president?

Now he was just being paranoid. Regardless, a new line had been crossed, a point of no return. It was time to start cutting losses.

He asked Ernest, "Who would have access to the Salt Rounds you gave us?"

"Just a select few agents. It's not standard equipment yet due to the beta status," Ernest said. "I had to file three separate requests so you could get it. Why?"

"We checked out a different hit in progress last night."

"Wait, how did you find out about it?" Ernest asked.

"Anonymous tip," he said.

"How convenient," Ernest muttered. "Let me guess. Humans?"

"You got it, and they used the round on Cam. Almost killed her."

"No way! Is she okay? Does she need anything?"

Griffin smiled at Ernest's concern. "She's recovered. How did they get the ammo?"

Ernest blew out a breath. "It had to be someone inside."

Definitely, Griffin just didn't know how inside. He did know, however, that this was getting too hot for Ernest to be involved, especially if Harding was behind it. Then he did what he had to. "Ernest, you're fired."

"What? Where did that come from?" he sputtered. "You can't fire me."

"Don't call me again. Don't do any more digging. You're done."

"Griffin, what the hell, man? I want to see this through."

"Trust me when I tell you that you don't," Griffin said. "And I won't answer this phone again." He disconnected, feeling like total shit. But all the signs were pointing to major trouble, and he wouldn't take Ernest down with him. Now he had to tell Cam. That wasn't going to be pleasant either, especially with her father locked away in the detention center.

But sometime during the night Griffin had decided what he wanted. *The truth.*

SEVENTEEN

Cam surveyed the carnage on a bright sunny afternoon. Flashing emergency vehicle lights twinkled red, white, and blue. Beams and walls smoldered from the blast and fire that ravaged the interior and roof of the two-story building. Yellow tape and onlookers lined the perimeter. TV station trucks with satellite dishes mounted on top were lined up like vultures.

Three people died here, it was big news.

It would be bigger news when they blamed it on Shifters.

Except that this wasn't Shifters.

Griffin talked to the law enforcement uniforms protecting the site and then led her through the wreckage. She smelled only human scents and death. Lies and deceit.

"What *was* this?" she asked him.

He shook his head. "I don't know."

"Can't you ask Ernest?"

He turned to her. Their eyes met, and last night sparked between them. "I fired him."

Cam blinked. "Why?"

He took her hand and led her back outside. "What do you think is happening here, Cam?"

"Well, I can tell you that it's not Shifters," she said. But he already knew that, and they both knew what it meant.

He waved to the officers as they left and headed back to his car. "Did you find any other recognizable scents?"

"No," she said. "Sorry."

Griffin slowed as they walked, focused on something down the block. Cam followed his gaze to two men in blue suits. One seemed particularly familiar. Roberts, the agent who had been shadowing Ernest. He watched them as they got into Griffin's car and then used his cell phone.

"Why is he here?" she asked.

Griffin turned on the ignition. "He's following us."

The free-floating anxiety that had started after he told her about the deaths rolled over her in a sickening rush. "Because Harding ordered him to."

He clenched the steering wheel. "Now you know why I fired Ernest."

She waited for his reply in silence, even though she already knew what he was going to say.

"Harding, XCEL, whoever is going to use us and the information we've already reported to pin everything on the Shifters."

Cam closed her eyes, accepting the conclusion she desperately wanted to pretend wasn't possible.

"But until then," Griffin added, "more people are going to die."

"What makes you think that?"

He put on his signal light to pull out. "Because they can't raise the fear and the hatred of Shifters unless they do."

She gaped at him. "They'll kill innocent people to damn Shifters? That doesn't make any sense."

His expression was disgusted but sure. "They've done worse. The question is: What do we do about it?"

"We need to stop them," she said.

He cast her a serious look. "We'll be on Harding's hit list, if we aren't already. And he won't just slap us on the wrists."

Then she realized what he was telling her. She'd have to choose between her father, and human lives and Shifters. There would be no turning back. Once she blew the mission, her father's life would be in jeopardy.

"I can't ask you to work with me on this," he said.

"Are you going to fire me too?" she asked.

A corner of his mouth curled. "If that's what it takes."

To keep her safe. To keep her father safe. She knew he'd made up his mind. She thought it was about the sex. Instead, he'd decided what he wanted. She'd poked and prodded him to do just that. Now it was her turn.

Cam watched the streets passing them by. People milling about, living their lives not knowing the turmoil that was about to be unleashed upon them. A shapeshifter in human form stood on the corner with a grocery bag of food, waiting to cross the street. As they passed by, he smiled at her.

She closed her eyes as anguish radiated through her. Her father would tell her to do what was right, to forsake him. But he was family. He was all she had left in her world that had been pulled out from under her. He and memories were the only things that survived.

Then she remembered their last conversation. He'd known then, and he'd let her go. He'd called it his legacy. Well, he could call it whatever he wanted; she was still breaking him out.

For long moments, she considered her choices. Then she pulled out her phone and called him. He answered, "Hello, Camille."

She turned to Griffin who was watching her. "Your legacy is about to come true."

She heard him let out a sigh of relief and utter a profound, "Thank you."

Tears burned her eyes, rolling one after the other down her face. "I love you."

"I love you too, Daughter. You have made me very proud."

Through her tears, she hung up. "I'm with you, Griffin. Now, how do we get him out?"

❖❖❖

Ernest was waiting for them in the bar. He sat in a back booth with a beer in one hand and a smartphone in the other. Lyle was stocking the bar when Cam and Griffin entered. He hitched his head toward Ernest. "Been here for the last two hours nursing that one beer. Save me, will you?"

Cam smiled. "I love Ernest."

"Don't tell him that, he'll be worthless to me," Griffin warned her.

They went to the back where Ernest was waiting. His eyes were bloodshot, and he looked like he hadn't slept in the past twenty-four hours.

"You can't fire me," Ernest said. "I know where you live."

Griffin walked up to him and smiled. He couldn't help it. Ernest angry was priceless. "Sorry. I just don't want Harding to ruin your life, your career, and your soul."

"I'm a big boy. I know you don't believe that." Ernest pointed his beer at him. "But I can make these decisions myself. Harding is a dip wad."

Cam stood next to Griffin. "He has a point."

Ernest nodded and aimed his beer at her. "See?"

"You come with us, you won't be able to go home," Griffin warned him.

"Already got my stuff in a van," Ernest said.

"And you can't run to your family and friends."

"Don't have either," Ernest countered. "'Cept you."

That took Griffin by surprise. It never occurred to him to ask.

"And you could be on the run forever," Griffin added for good measure. He wanted to make sure that Ernest understood fully what he was getting into.

The kid nodded. "I know all that. I already calculated the odds, and really, you don't want to know them. But for once in my life, I finally get to do something that matters."

Griffin put his hands on his hips and stared at the floor. There was nothing else he could say. "I'm sorry. I should have given you the choice. If you want to ruin your life, you're welcome to hang with us."

"Damn right," Ernest said, and took a big swig of warm beer. He coughed a little and pretended to like it. "What next?"

"I have a very important mission for you," Griffin said. "We have to get Cam's father out of the detention center."

Ernest's eyes widened. "Sweet. Do I get a gun?"

"No," Cam and Griffin said in unison.

"It'll be just me and Cam," Griffin said and then an idea crossed his mind. "Unless . . . you care to join me in some fashion."

He and Ernest smiled at each other and then turned their attention to Cam.

She eyed them warily. "What?"

◆◆◆

The humans had killed three of their own. Aristotle sat at his table and pondered what kind of monsters would do such a thing. But then he'd met many such monsters, so desperate to protect their world that they'd sacrifice their own people. Collateral damage, they called it, to lose a few in order to save the many.

"What do you want to do, boss?" Red asked. "You know they're going to use those killings against us."

The kid was worried and rightly so. Aristotle wished he had words of wisdom to offer or even a suitable retaliation. He had known Harding would ruin property, but to murder innocent people—that had never crossed his mind.

The attacks were escalating, and that meant they were getting ready to launch their final campaign against the Shifters. Time was running out.

"We have to go after Harding," he said.

Red slammed his palm on the table and said, "Finally!"

"Don't get overly excited," Aristotle warned him. "We do that, and we have all of XCEL on our asses. It could make matters much worse."

"At least it'll slow things down," Red pointed out.

"For how long?" Aristotle asked. "There is always another enemy out there."

Red frowned. "It's better than sitting here doing nothing."

That was true, perhaps. But Aristotle feared that it was only a matter of time before his species died. Never in his lifetime did he expect to witness such a thing.

"Anything on Camille or her partner?"

Red shrugged. "They tried to stop the one hit I tipped them on. Camille was badly injured but survived. I think they're ready for us. Except—"

Aristotle glanced at him. "What?"

Red said, "Harding is watching them very closely now. If we make a move on them, we'll have to be careful."

It was a glimmer of hope, although how much of a difference they could make, he didn't know. "Find a safe place to meet."

"Will do. What about Harding?" Red asked.

The old man leaned back in his chair, and it creaked from age. "Watch him for the next few days. We need to know his schedule, where he goes and when. *Before* we try to capture him."

Red asked, "Why?"

"Because if we do it quietly," Aristotle replied patiently, "it may buy us more time."

"And what do we do with Harding once we have him?" Red asked.

That was a good question. "We'll lock him up."

"For how long?"

Aristotle answered, "For as long as this takes."

◆ ◆ ◆

Griffin walked into the detention center for the last time. He had no delusions that this would end his career, and possibly his life.

XCEL gave him one chance to clear himself, and he was about to blow it. There would be no more chances. He probably should feel bad about that, but in truth, it was a relief. He'd served them on this mission, given them exactly what they wanted, and repaid any debts he owed from the mess Parker left behind.

He owed XCEL nothing more. And now, he was going to find out the truth. He and Ernest passed through the security checkpoints with no problems. It was late, so security was light, as expected. The hallways felt colder and even less inviting than normal. And luckily, much quieter.

They made their way to the cell where Cam's father was being held. There was no guard on duty at the door. Apparently, Dewey had proven himself a low-risk Shifter. Ernest swiped his card to unlock the cell door and went inside to get Dewey while Griffin manned the door. Even though most of the regular staff was gone, it didn't mean that getting Dewey out of here unharmed was going to be easy.

Security guards still wandered the building, and cameras monitored the corridors. All the exits were protected by layers of security—automated or manned. An alarm would send the building into automatic lockdown, making it nearly impossible to escape. Griffin hoped it wouldn't come to that, but he anticipated the worst.

Ernest came out with Dewey shackled by his hands for transport. Griffin was surprised by how much the old man had deteriorated while he was here. He'd aged ten years. Ernest gave Griffin a worried look before they headed toward the prisoner transport dock.

They walked in silence, their plan worked out ahead of time. Get Dewey through the exit and to the car waiting outside. A quick getaway with no alarms and no trouble.

Of course, it wouldn't go that way. It never did.

A security guard passed by them and simply nodded. It wasn't unusual for prisoners to be transported into and out of the facility. However, if anyone knew *this* prisoner, they'd already know he was a shapeshifter. And they were never transported without being tranquilized first.

Cam hadn't wanted to risk her father's health by tranquilizing him, and Griffin had to agree with her there, especially after seeing him in person. Dewey didn't look like he could weather the cool night, let alone a drug.

They reached the heavy steel door that led to the transfer room. This is where it would get interesting. Ernest swiped his card, and the door unlocked with a loud click. Once through, they were immediately stopped by two agents.

"Prisoner transfer," Griffin said.

The guards exchanged a quizzical look, and then one of them checked the computer mounted on the wall. Griffin knew they hadn't received any notification of this particular transfer.

"We don't have a record of release for him," he said. The guard came back to them, his rifle at the ready. "Where's your paperwork?"

"Christ almighty," Griffin said to Ernest. "They always screw this up."

"No paperwork, no transfer," the other guard said.

Griffin could see their getaway car pull up outside through the reinforced glass doors. "It's in the car."

Both guards blocked him as he tried to step forward.

"You are not authorized to take this pris—" Griffin didn't wait for him to finish before pushing the rifle to the side and punching him in the face. He absorbed the punch without falling, and

Griffin hit him again. This time, he went down. The other guard raised his gun to shoot, but Ernest wrenched the rifle from his hands with superhuman strength and coldcocked him in the head with the butt.

It was all over in two seconds flat. Griffin held his breath. No alarms. It was a miracle. But they only had a few seconds before the cameras picked them up. "Move!"

Then he turned to find that Ernest had shifted from mild-mannered geek into Cam—her disguise working perfectly. She was helping her father to the outer door that stood between them and freedom. Griffin retrieved both security cards from the guards and gave one to Cam. They swiped the cards in unison on either side of the dock door, and both sides swung open.

Then they hustled Dewey out into the waiting car and the real Ernest sitting in the driver's seat. Once they were in, he gunned the engine and drove out of the compound.

"Any problems?" Ernest asked.

Griffin checked the backseat, where Cam was talking to her father in a low voice and covering him with a blanket. "None. Appears they still like you."

Ernest looked serious in the passing headlights. "Those days are gone now."

CHAPTER
EIGHTEEN

Harding watched the security video in livid disbelief. They'd waltzed into *his* detention center, picked up the old Shifter, and walked out without so much as breaking a sweat. No alarms, no lockdown. Nothing. What the hell was his security for?

"How could this happen?" Harding growled at Roberts.

"We believe that Agent Vincent may have rebooted the security systems during the time they were in the building. Even if an alarm went off, it would have been ignored as a technical malfunction."

The video showed them taking down the last two guards in the transfer room. And then Agent Vincent shifted into Camille Solomon.

"Sonofabitch," he said aloud. He had hoped she was dead. Now he had to worry about both of them. "Where's Vincent now?"

"He left work early yesterday and did not report in this morning," Roberts said.

So Vincent was working with them now. Good, Harding could take them all out at once. He pushed up from his chair in the security center and glared at the security chief on his way out. Roberts followed silently until they reached Harding's office. Then he closed the door behind him as Harding sat behind his desk.

Roberts stood awaiting his orders, and Harding would let him sweat a bit longer. After all, it had been Roberts' job to keep them under surveillance and under control. He'd failed. For that, Roberts could wait.

The next steps would be crucial. Everything needed to be executed with careful precision so as not to raise suspicions now or later. The report to the special senate committee was ready but would need to be revised to include this latest treachery. They had played a better part than he could have ever hoped.

Mercer, Camille, the old man, and Vincent would need to be neutralized, and whatever information or knowledge they'd gained removed from the equation. There really was only one way to ensure that.

The next two attacks on civilians needed to be executed to solidify public opinion against the Shifters. And the completion of the large-scale manufacturing line for the toxin was scheduled for this week.

He weighed each task, adjusting them by priority and logical order. He finally settled on dealing with the traitors, then the two final attacks, followed by his report, and finalizing the large-scale manufacture completion. In a few days, he would have everything he needed to cleanse this country of the scourge that had infected it—once and for all. This time he'd do it right.

He checked his e-mails as he spoke to Roberts. "As of this

moment, Mercer and Agent Vincent are declared enemies of the state. Traitors. I want them captured with all necessary force. Go to their homes, their family. I want them apprehended and brought back here."

"Understood," Roberts replied. "And the two Shifters?"

"A danger to society at large. Destroy them."

Roberts didn't reply, and Harding looked up at him. "Is there a problem with that?"

The man frowned. "If we can capture them alive—"

"Destroy them," Harding repeated.

Roberts blinked. "Yes, sir."

"That's all."

Roberts nodded and left.

Harding stared at the door. Roberts was getting soft on him. There was no room for compassion in the future of this country. Pity. Roberts had served him well up until now, but there were plenty of other agents who could do his job.

Harding hoped Roberts liked paperwork.

◆◆◆

Cam closed the adjoining door between her and Griffin's hotel room, and Ernest and her father's room. It had been a terrifying adventure, springing her father from the detention center, and one she never wanted to do again.

He was far frailer than she remembered, barely able to walk on his own. It hurt even more knowing that she was blowing the chance to find her brother. But to be truthful, she'd blown that chance the day she watched her brother walk away. She could have stopped him then. She could have swallowed her damn stubborn pride and let him win. The sad truth was that she had no one to blame for her father's death but herself.

Griffin was in the shower, and the room seemed even emptier without him in it. She rubbed her arms and walked over to the window. It overlooked a parking lot full of cars and people on vacation or here on business. She'd bet none of *them* were hiding out from XCEL.

She gave a great sigh, releasing the tension and strain of hoping she'd done the right thing. They were all fugitives now, and how that was going to end, she couldn't imagine. It was hour-by-hour, day-by-day survival. Just what she'd always wanted. Freedom to run when she wanted to. No one tying her down, telling her what to do.

Or did she?

Cam stared at her reflection in the glass. She should be used to this life by now—living on the edge. Shifters were the ultimate survivors, and she had the stories and legends to prove it. She had no desire to create her own legend, but maybe there was more than just survival.

She gave a short laugh. Now who didn't know what they wanted?

"What are you thinking about?" Griffin said behind her.

She turned around to find him standing behind her, wearing a towel at his hips. "Survival. You?"

He grinned. "You."

Her belly trembled at the promise in his eyes. Just one look. She was in so much trouble. "Did I do the right thing? I mean, you're going to be a wanted man by XCEL, aside from losing any chance of getting back into their good graces. Same for Ernest. My father and I will be public enemies number one. I'll never find Thaniel now. For what?"

His grin faded as he walked up to her. "First off, Ernest and I are here of our own accord. Our choice."

He slipped his hands around her waist and settled his thumbs along the soft sides of her breasts. A shiver ran up her spine at the intimate touch.

"This is true," she said, wanting more than anything to lose herself in him. To forget everything.

Griffin leaned over and kissed her neck. "Your father wanted you to fulfill his legacy."

Cam lifted her chin and let him nuzzle the tender spots on her throat. "He did."

"And you wanted answers," Griffin said, pulling her close to his chest as he brushed his lips against hers.

"I did," she murmured.

He kissed her deep, and she felt her body give itself over to him. She ran her hands over his skin, marveling at the width and breadth and depth of him. He was so beautiful, so perfect for her. He pulled her toward the bed and laid her down before settling on top. His big body covered her, completing her.

She'd healed fully, but Griffin hadn't touched her since their first time. But today, she didn't want him to hold back. This time, she wanted everything—the hunger, the need, the man.

Cam reached between them and tugged the towel off his hips. His erection filled her hands, and a low groan rumbled through his body. She stroked the full length of him with her fingertips as he pressed against her. His kisses grew harder and more urgent, his body tight with anticipation.

"Are you alright for this?" he rasped against her lips.

"If you stop now, I'll kill you," she replied, her own voice husky.

"Thank God." Then he proceeded to kiss a line down her throat. She arched as he unbuttoned her shirt, one button at a time, kissing every newly exposed patch of skin. When he reached the last one, he lifted off her and spread the shirt open, laying her breasts naked.

For a long time, he took her in, his breathing deepening, his eyes dark. Then he dipped down and flicked one nipple with his tongue. It sent a jolt of electricity down her spine. He sucked and squeezed as he drew it into his mouth over and over again. Then he moved to the other nipple and did the same. His face brushed her sensitive skin with every movement.

She found herself moaning at each little torment. Then he moved down her stomach, kissing, caressing, and stroking with his mouth and hands. Cam closed her eyes tightly and let the sensations sing. Her hands gripped the bedsheets at her sides, clutching them hard with every wave. When he reached her jeans, he paused.

His gaze met hers. He unsnapped the fastener and pulled the zipper down one tooth at a time.

"Faster," she said, wriggling beneath him in need.

He grinned and shook his head. "Not this time. *You're* stressed."

Crap, he *had* been listening. His grin grew as he reached the bottom of the zipper, and Cam held his gaze and lifted her hips so he could remove her jeans. He pulled them off and threw them somewhere on the floor. With her legs free, Cam slid the inside of her thigh along outside of his, opening herself up for him.

He captured her thigh with one hand and leaned down to kiss the soft inner side. Then he closed in on her center and spread her legs. He nipped her gently through the thin fabric of her panties, and she reached for his hands. He pushed her away and sucked her through the fabric.

Cam arched off the bed with a growl that didn't sound quite human. He chuckled. If she wasn't about to have the orgasm of her life, she might hurt him. She felt his thumb slip under the panties and find her.

Fire burned in her belly, setting every nerve ending in flames. The heat was unbearable, setting her on the edge. One more second . . .

Then his fingers left her, and he climbed over her to kiss her face softly. She gripped him with her hips, holding him in place just in case he decided to change positions. Her entire body was in limbo, somewhere between pain and pleasure, and he wasn't going anywhere until she got one or the other.

Her fingernails dug into his back, and she nipped his lips harder than she should.

"Easy," he whispered, and reached down to pull her panties to one side.

"Griffin," she ground out between her teeth. She was out of her mind with anticipation and need. If he ever got done playing around, she was going to make sure he suffered as much as she did.

He braced himself on one elbow while lifting her leg over his shoulder. His fingers slid her panties over, making room for him. She sucked air, fueling the fire that threatened to rip her apart as she felt his swollen head push into her a few inches.

Oh God. Frustration and need ached through every part of her body.

Then he pulled out and pushed her panties farther to the side, holding them there while he entered her again—just a bit deeper.

He pulled out and did it again, each time filling her more until he was deep inside.

Cam tried to force him to move, but he would have none of it. She opened her eyes to find him looking at her, his face etched in pain and struggle. He wanted her as much as she wanted him; she could see the desire in his eyes, feel the way his body struggled. But he was a patient man. She was so screwed.

He withdrew completely, and then he filled her slowly, inch by inch, driving her to the brink of insanity. She couldn't feel anything else but him. After an eternity, he pushed into her core and ground against her. Then as slowly as he'd entered, he slid out, leaving her empty bit by bit.

She groaned and nearly used her Shifter strength to draw him in again. He moved back into her, faster this time and again. His eyes closed as the rhythm consumed him. Cam followed him, stroke for stroke, as his pace picked up.

They rocked together as if they'd done this a thousand times. Cam gripped his arms as the orgasm drew closer with every drive. It hovered in time, building strength, before crashing over her with merciless power.

Griffin growled deep in this throat as she tightened around him. His rhythm broke to a feverish velocity, shaking the bed and sending her back into orgasm. With a great push, he plunged into her and let out a long groan.

Cam held him as he collapsed on her. For a long time, neither of them had the strength to move. When her orgasm silenced, she was left once again with the fear of what she'd done to him. If she hadn't been so selfish about uncovering the truth, he'd have his life back. If she hadn't pushed him to this place, he'd be happy. And where this was going to end, she had no idea. They could find all the answers they wanted, and then still end up being on the run. The tension in her body betrayed her.

"Don't think about it too much," Griffin murmured. "It'll make you crazy."

She closed her eyes. She was already crazy. But this was what she wanted, what she fought him for. To find out what was really going on. Too late to change her mind. "I know."

Griffin raised himself to his elbows and gazed down at her. His eyes were heavy and relaxed. "I can't give you any answers."

"I know that too," she said. It could all break tomorrow, the whole damn thing could spill out into the open. Or it could take weeks. But one thing was clear: Shifters would always be hunted, and he was now one of the hunted.

He leaned down and kissed her again, and she felt him getting harder by the second. She pushed him over onto his back and climbed on top of him. Her breasts brushed his chest as she kissed his face and started to work her way down his body. She reached down and slipped her hand around him. He hissed through his teeth.

She peered up at him and smiled wickedly. "Payback."

NINETEEN

"So I hacked into the XCEL central data warehouse and put a crawler on every index node," Ernest said, hunched over one of three laptops in the hotel room. "Most of them simply coughed up the routine chatter."

Griffin and Cam exchanged an amused look over the coils of cables, servers, and monitors. A geek in his natural habitat.

Ernest raised his finger. "However, I did get a hit when I searched for the location of the last deadly strike. So I followed that, cracked an amateur attempt at a secure algorithm, and located an isolated table that captured the communications stream."

Griffin crossed his arms. "Is there a moral to this story?"

Ernest glanced up at him. "Hey, four hours I worked on this."

"And it's very much appreciated," Cam said, placing her hand on Ernest's shoulder as she narrowed her eyes at Griffin. "Do you know who they are going to hit next?"

Ernest nodded. "Sure do." He brought up a map of Harlem

and zoomed in to a building on the corner of a block. "A free health clinic called Thorp Medical Center. Today at fifteen hundred hours."

"Oh God," Cam said with a gasp. "That's the middle of the afternoon. The place will be packed with patients."

Griffin checked his watch. It was one P.M. now. "That gives us two hours to clear out that building without spooking our bombers. And then stop them."

"And then what?" Ernest asked. "They'll just move onto the next place, and the next. This won't end until they've made their point."

Griffin knew he was right. They'd need to take out the person or people responsible for sending the orders. "Can you tell where the communications are coming from? If they have a headquarters?"

Ernest shook his head. "Not yet, but I'll keep digging."

"Dig in Harding's direction," Cam said.

"Oh, trust me, I have," Ernest said, looking disgusted. "Can't connect him to any of this."

"Then someone else is giving those orders," Griffin noted. He slapped Ernest on the back. "Keep your head down."

Ernest grinned at him. "I'm not the one who's going to get shot at."

Griffin watched Cam go over to her father, who was napping in one of the hotel beds. She sat on the bed next to him and covered him up with the blanket. Concern was etched across her face, and Griffin felt another pang of guilt for not doing more to find her brother. But she'd made up her own mind. Hell, she'd pretty much dragged him into this. Still, he didn't want her to lose her father, and time was not their friend.

He leaned closer to Ernest. "Do you have any micro GPS chips?"

Ernest looked at him like he was nuts. "I have a case of them. How many do you need?"

"I'll take a couple. The range is good?"

"As good as you need," Ernest said. "What are you planning to do with them?"

Griffin glanced at Cam. "Let's just say I'm going to try to speed up our progress a bit."

"That might be a little more difficult than we thought," Ernest said in a tone that Griffin didn't like at all. "Harding has put a contract out on all of us. We're traitors, wanted dead or alive. Personally, I like alive."

It didn't surprise Griffin that Harding would take the first opportunity to get rid of them. "How long are we safe here?"

Ernest shrugged. "Maybe another night or two, but we'll need to move." He leaned into Griffin and added in a whisper, "Dewey needs medical attention."

"I know," Griffin said. Not only that, moving Dewey in his current condition wasn't good for any of them. "No matter what, you stay with him."

Ernest nodded. "Sure. Do I get a gun now?"

"You sure do," he replied.

◆◆◆

Cam and Griffin stood across the street from the clinic and watched patients come and go in the middle of the afternoon. Old folks, children, mothers, babies. Her anger grew with every passing minute. XCEL would let these people die to prove a point. To damn Shifters everywhere.

Over her fucking dead body.

"What happens if they use a Salt Round on you?" Griffin asked.

She scanned the two-story building. "I've adapted a strategy to eject it. It won't work next time."

"Good."

She turned to look at him, and her body temperature jumped a few degrees. He looked especially sexy today. He'd be better naked though. She had to corral her thoughts after a brief detour. "Is the three P.M. time for the explosion or for the mission to begin?"

"Ernest couldn't tell." He led her across the street. "But he said there are apartments upstairs. That has to be their target. Otherwise, someone would notice."

"The second-floor windows are covered with blinds. I can't see inside," she told him.

"Then we'll have to check it out the old-fashioned way."

They walked through the front doors of the clinic. As she feared, the place was wall-to-wall patients. They occupied the chairs that lined the walls and stood where there was no seating available. One beleaguered receptionist sat behind a glass partition.

Griffin walked up to her and discreetly showed his badge. The woman's eyes widened as they talked, their words lost in the noise of the clinic. Then she glanced at Cam and nodded. She pulled a set of keys from her drawer and handed them over. He thanked her, and they headed to the back of the building, past a long row of doorways and busy nurses.

Griffin unlocked a door that opened to a flight of stairs. After Cam closed the door behind her, she said, "What did you tell her?"

"First, I asked her about the apartments. Two are occupied, the one in front is vacant. Then, I asked if anyone unusual had been up here lately."

He pulled out his Glock as they hit the second-floor landing. "And?"

"Three men with the gas company showed up ten minutes ago to work on the vacant apartment, and they're still here."

Three men who knew exactly what they were doing and willing to kill innocent people. Cam was mad enough to handle them all herself. "Did you warn her?"

He nodded. "Told her they were criminals, armed and dangerous, and to clear the clinic as quickly and quietly as possible."

"Good," Cam said. "What about tenants?"

"She didn't know if they were here or not. Not her job."

"Then I guess that makes it our job," Cam said. "Think they'll use the same strategy as last time and set the explosives on a timer?"

"Definitely," Griffin said, moving ahead of her. "No heroes in this bunch. They won't risk getting caught in the blast."

"Well, then today is not going to be their day," she said.

Griffin eyed her. "I don't want to get caught in the blast either."

"It's not like we haven't been blown up before," she murmured.

"Which just means our odds are worse now."

He had a point. They quickly checked the two occupied apartments. There were no sounds or movements, and she didn't hear any signs of people, which was good.

Then they headed toward the front apartment. Old floorboards creaked under their feet, and they had to move more slowly as they neared the apartment door. Cam tuned in to the sounds behind the door.

They moved closer, and Cam harnessed her senses. Three sets

of distinct footsteps. All humans. She smelled gasoline—an accelerant. They wanted to make damn sure the blast would keep burning. Probably made for better TV coverage. The good news was that they were still inside, which meant the bombs hadn't been activated yet.

She whispered, "If we wait them out, it'll be too late."

He nodded agreement. "Ready?"

"Oh yeah," she whispered and shifted into Primary form. She formed her hands into claws. "I'm going first."

Griffin just grinned and then stepped back and kicked the door in. Cam was inside in a flash. Two of the men were huddled over a large box in the center of the room. The other one was the first to shoot at her, and she recognized his face. He was the one who'd hit her with the Salt Round.

Sucked to be him.

She reached one of the men kneeling over the box and kneed him in the head on her way to the man who'd nearly cost her her life. He took a few steps backward, firing as he went. The payload peppered the walls and passed through her harmlessly until she grabbed him by the face. He screamed for all he was worth.

"You, I don't like," she said.

With a mighty growl, she tossed him against the wall, breaking Sheetrock and shaking the apartment windows. He dropped to a still heap on the floor. She took a second to shove a micro GPS unit down his throat before he woke up.

Then she turned around to find that Griffin was grappling with the other agent up against the wall. The man had a gun in his hand that Griffin was trying to shake loose.

"Check the timer," he yelled to her.

As if she knew what a timer looked like. She scanned the steel box and saw a small digital display. It was set for 15:00 and wasn't changing. "It's set but not running."

Then she walked over and ripped the pistol from the agent's hand as he glared at her. Griffin pushed him against the wall with his forearm crushing the man's throat. "Who do you work for?"

The man wasn't talking, and Griffin wasn't happy about that. He pressed the guy's throat harder. "We know you're XCEL."

The man's eyes widened in surprise, but he still wouldn't give it up.

"Want me to try?" she asked Griffin. "I haven't killed anyone all day."

That got a reaction out of the man. He gasped for air, flicked his gaze behind her, and then smiled. "Shifter bitch, die."

Then she felt a bullet hit her in the back. It tried to bury itself in her, but her body reacted, preserving itself and expelling the bullet. She turned to find the guy she'd flung against the wall holding his gun on her. His eyes were the size of saucers. His little toy didn't work this time, and he knew it.

Cam advanced on him as he backed up in terror. Unfortunately, she needed the bastard. On the other hand, that didn't mean she couldn't have some fun first.

She grabbed him around the throat. He dropped the weapon and tried to kick her. "You are really pissing me off," she hissed, and then flung him out the front window. Glass shattered, followed by a distinct thud outside. Fortunately, he was still screaming, so that was a good sign.

Griffin had knocked his man unconscious and was feeding him the GPS when she walked back to him.

He said, "I hope you tagged him before you tossed his ass out the window."

"Hey, I'm a professional." She shifted back to human form.

"I was a little worried for a minute."

She grabbed the third man passed out by the bomb and tagged him with a GPS. "I hope these things work, because otherwise, we wasted a perfectly good opportunity to take these assholes out of commission permanently."

Griffin stood beside her. "I'm going to call in an anonymous tip and have the local law enforcement pick these guys up for trespassing."

She raised an eyebrow. "And what about the big bomb in the middle of the room?"

He said, "The big bomb comes with us."

◆ ◆ ◆

Aristotle smiled as he listened to Red go on about how they'd prevented the attack on the clinic. He'd never seen the boy so excited.

"She threw one of the guys right out the front window," Red said as he continued his animated story. "This is awesome! They stopped the XCEL attack. We didn't even have to provide the location. They know what's going on. What could be better than this?"

If they joined our team, Aristotle thought. But he'd have to be careful. Maybe this was yet another ploy by Harding to locate his operation. One wrong move and everything he'd built would be gone, and along with it, the last gasp for his race.

"And another thing," Red added, his face flushed with renewed hope. "They broke the old man out of the detention center. Right under Harding's nose."

Aristotle leaned back in his chair. That didn't sound like anything Harding would approve of, even as a ploy. Why would he bother to go to such trouble?

"They broke their relationship with XCEL?" Aristotle asked.

"Oh, definitely. There's an XCEL contract out on them," Red said. "Plus they haven't been back to Griffin's apartment in the last twenty-four hours. And one of the other XCEL agents is also MIA."

This was no ploy. XCEL didn't put out contracts they didn't intend to fulfill. And if Mercer and Camille broke off their relationship, they must know that XCEL was involved.

That would make Harding very pissed off. As much as Aristotle enjoyed that thought, he also knew the danger it brought to the only outsiders who might be able to help him.

He pulled his heavy sweater around him. "Did you find a place to meet?"

"Yes."

"Set up a meeting with the two of them, myself, and you."

"I will," Red said quickly. "Aren't you happy about this?"

Aristotle smiled. Disappointment had tempered his enthusiasm long ago. "I am."

"You don't look like it." Then Red frowned. "Are you sick?"

He'd been sick for years. Today was worse than yesterday, and tomorrow would be worse than today. But that was old age. No one to blame, and no sense in being angry about it.

"Set up the meeting."

CHAPTER
TWENTY

Harding was taking out his fury on the phone with his partner. "How could this happen, Braxton? How did they know where the attack was going to be and when? How?"

"Our files must have been hacked," he said, his voice frustratingly calm. "We'll need to double encrypt the orders next time."

"Screw encryption!" Harding yelled, and then glanced up at his office door. He took a deep breath and lowered his voice. "You handle this personally from now on. You deliver the orders, forget technology."

"Well," Braxton said, unhurried, "I suspect that the hacker works for you. The breach is your fault, not mine. *You* handle the orders."

"I can't do that," Harding hissed. "That's why I have you."

"Afraid to get your hands dirty?" Braxton asked.

Harding squeezed the life out of his cell phone. "If I do, then there will be no one on this end to change policy, will there? We made a pact. No matter how bad it got, we would each do our part."

Braxton sighed. "I'll deal with it."

"You better. I want another attack as soon as possible, a successful one." Harding stabbed his desk with one finger. "I want death and destruction. Are we clear?"

"Always a joy working with you." Then Braxton disconnected.

Harding ended the call and set down the cell phone before he broke it. For long moments he sat, fists clenched, working to cool his temper. He'd known there would be problems, but he couldn't allow one rogue agent and a malicious shapeshifter to destroy that. They would win, and he would lose.

Harding stood up to fend off the anger that was edging out his virtuous plan. He was so close, he could taste it. He was the righteous one here. He was the only one who could save humanity.

It was all at risk now because of one dead man walking. He pondered his options and settled on the one with the best outcome. If XCEL couldn't find Mercer, Harding knew exactly who could. He dialed a number he hadn't used in a long time. John Parker picked up on the third ring.

"Well, well. If it isn't my old *buddy*, Director Harding," he said over a lot of background noise.

Harding felt his blood pressure rise just talking to a Shifter. "I have a job for you. How fast can you be in Jersey?"

"When you ask so nicely, how can I refuse?" Parker replied with a distinct slur. He was drinking in a bar with all the other lowlifes.

Harding tamped down his aversion. "We had an agreement, Parker. I get your ass out of trouble, and I own you. Forever."

"Deal with the devil, that was," Parker said with a laugh. "What do you want?"

"Mercer's head on a platter," Harding said. "Yesterday."

The background noise got a lot quieter. "Serious?"

"*Yesterday,*" Harding repeated.

There was a long pause. "I'll be there when I can."

◆ ◆ ◆

"You brought a bomb into our hotel? Are you crazy?" Ernest sputtered.

Griffin shoved the box under his hotel bed. "Would you rather I leave it in your car in the parking garage below us?"

"No! I mean—" Ernest stopped and shook his head. "Never mind. Why am I even arguing? My car, hotel. Doesn't matter. It'll still kill me. Although, I've always wanted to die in my sleep."

"You might get that wish," Griffin said, and walked over to the door between the adjoining rooms. He peered in and saw Cam talking to her father. His skin was a faint shade of blue, his eyes sunken, and his movements few.

"He's worse." Griffin quietly closed the door and turned to Ernest.

"He's dying," Ernest said.

"She has a brother," Griffin said. "He's somewhere in the US. XCEL was supposed to be looking for him as part of her cooperation."

Ernest's expression turned into confusion. "Harding approved that?"

Griffin replied, "I didn't ask Harding. I didn't tell anyone. Except you."

He handed Ernest a thumb drive that contained the information that Cam had given him about Thaniel. Ernest closed his eyes as he took it. "You didn't tell Cam?"

He had his reasons, none of which mattered anymore. Maybe XCEL would have found Thaniel by now, maybe not. Either way, it was probably too late. "No. How long will it take to locate him?"

Ernest pursed his lips. "I don't know. A couple hours, or a couple weeks. Depends on whether or not her brother wants to be found. He's a Shifter, for Christ's sake. He could be anywhere, anyone."

Griffin glanced at the door. "Don't tell her."

Ernest made a face and shook his head. "She deserves to know the truth, Griff."

"You want your life back?" Griffin asked. "Then don't tell her. I'll do it later."

Ernest blew out a long breath as his shoulders hunched. "I hate this."

"Sorry," Griffin said. "You can start looking for her brother, but first priority is stopping the attacks. Do you have a line on the next one?"

Ernest rubbed his eyes. "They're onto us. Moved the files, set up a bunch of dead—"

"Ernest, yes or no," Griffin said, his patience wearing thin.

"Not yet," he said. "Give me an hour."

Griffin's cell phone rang. He checked the incoming number and didn't recognize it. "Hello?"

"We hear you're looking for us," the familiar voice said.

His pulse jumped. "Who is this?"

"Meeting, tomorrow morning at eight A.M. Same place you met your informant."

The Shifter informant. He *was* working for the Shifters. "I'll be there."

"And please bring Camille with you."

Please. That was new. "Absolutely." The call ended.

"What is it?" Ernest asked.

"Our Shifters want to meet," he said.

"And that's good?"

Griffin pocketed his cell phone. "Yes. Unless they plan to kill us."

"Oh," Ernest said, his smile fading. "Right."

"They replaced my informant with one of their own." At exactly the right time, and that was too much of coincidence for Griffin. "How would they do that?"

"No shit," Ernest said, clearly impressed. "I'll see what I can find."

"Find the next attack first," Griffin reminded him.

"Sure." He turned to leave and then stopped. "By the way, your GPS trackers show our three guys are out of jail. I put their signals in your phone."

That was something. Maybe they'd be willing to talk. "Thanks."

Ernest said as he left, "Don't thank me. You might not like what you find out."

That was the truth. Nothing was turning out as he expected.

Griffin stared at the bed where he and Cam had made love last night. He knew he should tell her about her brother, but he needed her for this, especially if they were going underground. Besides, it wasn't his fault that Harding lied to them both. And Ernest was looking for Thaniel now. He was doing everything he could.

Right.

So why did he hate himself for holding out on her?

◆◆◆

"My entire class of people has gone down since I hooked up with you, Mercer," Cam said.

She scanned the manufacturing facility they were hiding in, waiting for someone to show up with a bomb. It was two A.M. and the place was shut down for the night, quiet except for the hum of air-conditioning.

Pallets were stacked four high in the staging area. During peak production, steel presses pumped out product that ran along conveyor belts to packaging and shipping. This company made baby bottles. Bastards, playing the baby card.

She walked between the rows, looking for a box with a bomb. Only one problem. There were thousands of boxes in here. She felt herself give a mighty sigh. All XCEL had to do was set a timer to blow. They could do that anywhere, anyplace, anytime. How could she and Griffin stop them all?

Griffin walked around a stack of wooden crates toward her. The heat of the city continued to bake the metal structure, leaving her hot and bothered.

He said, "What surprises me is how easy it was to break into this place."

She replied, "It helps when you have a geek who can remotely shut off alarm systems and change the security personnel schedules to give them all the night off."

"True."

"And an XCEL agent who can pick a lock or two." She batted her eyelashes at him. "I noticed you didn't have any problem with that."

His dark eyes met hers. "Practice."

She raised an eyebrow. "I like practice."

A slow smile spread across his face as he reached her. She slid against him with ease, fitting to him like they were custom-made. He kissed her deep and slow. Cam moaned and gave in to the potent lust. And that's what it was and would ever be—lust.

He'd lied to her. She'd overheard his conversation with Ernest about Thaniel. All this time, no one searched for him. The lie was only slightly mollified by the fact that he'd been desperate, but so had she. And that's what hurt. Granted, Shifters were accustomed to being used and abused, but this was Griffin. The man who'd managed to gain just enough of her trust to make it mean something.

Did he not think she'd stick this through without something holding her to it? And why wouldn't he? That's exactly what she'd normally do. Make a run for it. Start over, create a new identity. It was so much easier than suffering in one place.

But this time, she wasn't running. She'd realized over the past day that her father would die soon. Very soon. Even if Thaniel was standing right here, even if they gave their father a transfusion, he'd probably still die. Cam wasn't certain when she'd accepted that, or if she really had yet. It didn't change reality. She could hate Griffin for lying to her, but she couldn't blame him for the merciless ticking of time.

So lust it was. Because she'd never be able to trust him with more than that. Besides, it only hurt when she thought about it.

Distant footsteps broke the bittersweet moment and the kiss. She focused on the large overhead doors and the smaller entry doors. Cam stepped away from Griffin and moved toward the staging area where trucks picked up the shipments. Then she stopped. The footsteps were everywhere.

"Something isn't right," she whispered.

She heard Griffin unholster his gun. "Like what?"

Lots of footsteps stopped in various places around the building. "Like, I think we're going to need a bigger boat."

"Can you be a little more specific?"

She turned to him, dread filling her to the bone. "There are at least twenty men outside. We're being systematically surrounded."

"Goddamn," he said, scanning the exits. After a few seconds, he asked, "What about the roof?"

She focused above her. Scrapping sounds, dragging metal, footsteps. "Maybe two."

He grabbed her by the hand and headed for the stairs. "Let's go."

They raced up three flights and through an access door for the flat roof deck to find two men checking their gear. Griffin rammed the first one at a dead run, laying him out cold. Cam shifted and knocked the second one out just as he raised his rifle. She checked for others, but it was clear.

She shifted back to human and checked the man she'd hit. He was dead, and she swallowed the remorse and stole his rifle. Then she turned to Griffin, who was relieving the other man of his weapons and his communications headset.

She moved to the edge of the roof, pressing against the three-foot-tall ledge that ran the perimeter of the roof. The grapple hooks used to scale the three stories were still in place. If she tried to move them, the men below would definitely notice. She peered over the edge to find XCEL agents everywhere. Her long-distance night vision picked up more men gathered a hundred yards away beside a cluster of trucks. Damn, these guys were serious.

"I really hate XCEL," she said.

"They're not XCEL," Griffin said, sidling up next to her.

She turned to him in shock. "Please, you can't still be defending them."

"I'm not. XCEL weapons, XCEL gear, but not XCEL agents."

She shook her head. "How do you know that?"

"XCEL agents don't carry their wallets with them when they go on a mission," he said and showed her a driver's license as proof.

She read the name. "Then who is Jim Whiteman?"

"No idea," he said as he peered over the edge.

Cam couldn't believe how calm he was. How many people were after them? How did these guys know they were coming here? Did someone tip them off? She'd think about that later. Right now, survival was top priority. "Tell me you have a plan."

"Sure don't," he replied. "You?"

It was only three stories; she'd survive jumping from here, but it would be bad for Griffin. "Not unless you can fly."

Then he put his finger to his lips to silence her as he listened to the voice in his headset. He flipped on the comm and said in a gruff voice, "In position," and then turned it off. "We have two minutes."

She watched the agents get into position below them and wondered if she could jump three stories carrying Griffin. She'd never tried that before. As Ernest would say, it'd be a beta jump. Didn't sound like good odds to her.

Griffin had pulled out his phone and was talking on it, but Cam wasn't really paying attention to the conversation. The grapple hooks were an option, but it would take precious time to descend that distance, and they'd be completely exposed. She could do it quickly though and shield both of them. It was their best bet.

He hung up and leaned over the edge of the roof. "Less than a minute left."

She sighed and shifted to her Primary form. Time for Plan Beta. "As soon as they all enter the building, we go over the edge. I'll use the rope to slide down and take you with me. I think I can protect you from any fire we draw, and of course, from splatting all over the concrete."

Griffin turned to her with a look of surprise. "And you'd probably kill yourself in the process."

She shrugged. "I heal."

For a long time, he stared at her, his expression softening. It was becoming a more frequent transformation, and one she had come to crave, which was a real shame.

"Thank you," he said quietly. "But I don't think that'll be necessary."

"What do you mean?"

He grinned. "Wait for it."

She shook her head in confusion, and then all hell broke loose. Alarms rang out in unison everywhere, spotlights came to life, flooding every square inch of the property with white light. Cam heard police sirens screaming toward their location, and men shouting as they retreated in droves.

It finally occurred to her what had happened. *Ernest.*

"Nice one," she said aloud.

"I thought you'd like that."

"And what about *us*?"

"I'm thinking a warm bed would be good."

She smiled and realized she was in Shifter form. He'd suggested sex while she was a shapeshifter. Talk about progress.

"But until then," he added, "we need to get out of here before the good guys show up."

She shifted back to her smaller human form as they headed

down the stairs. The place was empty. They were out the back door and climbing over the fences like common criminals. It felt weird, and yet, strangely comforting.

When they finally got into the car, she broached the bad news. "They set us up with that attack."

He frowned in the dark. "Yeah."

She rubbed her eyes. "How are we going to know if our intel is right anymore?"

"We won't," Griffin said, sounding discouraged as he started the car. He didn't even have to say it. The enemy was closing in around them, and they knew no more about what was going on today than they did yesterday. She wanted to ask him what they should do next, but she was exhausted.

Frankly, a warm bed and a hot man were the only things she wanted to do right now.

◆◆◆

Harding was asleep next to his wife when his cell phone rang. He fumbled in the dark for the phone on the nightstand and got up to take the call in another room.

His wife groaned and rolled over as he padded out of the bedroom and down the hallway to his home office. He answered the call as he shut the door.

"This better be good, Braxton," he growled and dropped into his chair.

"Good? No, I wouldn't call it good. Your little geek is a pain in my ass."

Braxton sounded all fired up for a change. That meant something was seriously wrong. "What happened?"

"I planted a fake attack in our files, figuring they'd bite, which they did. We had them holed up in a manufacturing facility in Queens, when that son of a bitchin' geek set off all alarms and called the cops. You didn't tell me these people had brains. If I'd known, I would have planned better."

Harding closed his eyes. "Did you leave a trail to us?"

"No, didn't even get in the goddamned front door," Braxton said.

That was something, Harding admitted. He'd underestimated Mercer, and now he was paying for that. Obviously, he would need to get rid of him before the plan could move forward. Parker had yet to show up, so he'd need to use the next best thing.

"Forget the attacks for now. I want every available man on them. Find them, and kill them."

"With pleasure," Braxton said and hung up.

◆◆◆

"Are you sure this is where the GPS tracked our guys to?" Cam asked as she surveyed the Hudson River on the way back to the underground. "Because unless they can swim, they're in trouble."

Griffin pointed his phone toward the river. "GPS marks all three of them fifty yards that way."

She followed his line of sight to the other bank of the river, far more than fifty yards away. Then she noticed a long, low trash barge weighted down with twenty feet of garbage being towed by a small tugboat.

"Oh crap," she said, feeling ill. She used her Shifter vision to try to find them, but they'd been buried. No one would ever find them.

Griffin had pocketed the GPS and was frowning at the barge. "They never even made it home. Someone sprung them from the local authorities and dumped them."

She couldn't believe it. "They murdered their own people. Why?"

"So they wouldn't talk," he replied, sounding bitter.

"Someone is going to a lot of trouble to cover their tracks," she noted.

Griffin nodded. "Sure looks that way."

"What now?" Cam asked.

"We talk to the Shifters," he said and turned toward his car.

Cam walked alongside him. "And the fun just keeps on coming."

He smiled a little. "You're a gambler. You should love this."

"Normally, when I gamble, no one is trying to kill me," she pointed out.

"You don't seem to have any trouble with that," he said, rounding his car. "Where'd you learn to fight?"

She couldn't remember ever *not* fighting for her life. On the last planet, in the ship on the way here, here.

"My brother taught me," she told him. "Said I needed to protect myself."

Griffin watched her over the roof of the car. "He was right."

She looked back at him and realized how good it felt to be with him, work with him, sleep with him. So who was going to protect her from the man she was in lust with?

TWENTY-ONE

Everything started out fine. The sun was shining high in the sky, and a warm wind swept over his naked body. Sand stretched as far as Griffin could see, ending at mountains far in the distance. Above him, the sky was bluer than blue, uncluttered by even a single cloud. There was no sound except the wind shaking the shrubs that clung stubbornly to the shifting sand.

That was the thing about sand; it was always moving. Changing. Reinventing itself.

The desert appeared just like it had when he was a kid, except now he was a man and the great expanses seemed less daunting. He'd gotten lost in the desert once when he was eight years old, and Sani had found him. He still didn't understand how Sani knew where to look.

These things I know echoed in his mind. Whenever Sani didn't want to explain something, that's what he would say.

Griffin felt the warmth and love flow over him. His grandfather was a great man, a man of integrity above all else. He'd never disgrace himself or the family name by doing something selfish like Griffin had.

Love and warmth were quickly replaced by regret and shame. He'd left the family and his home to seek adventure and riches in the city. Wanted to leave this antiquated, impoverished world behind him. Prove wrong everyone who thought he'd never amount to much. He'd done just that too, building a life with all the luxuries and things that other people had. Success by any standards.

Except those things were empty. He'd proven nothing except that he didn't know where he belonged. He had paid for that mistake when all those things he'd worked so hard for were taken away, including his very identity. Worse than all that though was the damage he'd done to his reputation and, therefore, the reputation of his family. Now he was branded a traitor to his own country, wanted by XCEL. How was he ever going to fix that?

A movement caught his eye—a sidewinder snake slithered across the windswept mounds thirty feet away. He marveled at the way it traveled, gracefully using groves in the sand to venture sideways. Now there was determination.

He was considering that when a shadow suddenly fell over him, followed by feathers and claws. The Eagle landed on the snake and ripped it with its teeth and claws until it stopped moving. The shock of life and death before his eyes stunned him for a moment.

He felt the injustice of it all. "Why?" he asked the Eagle.

Her blue eyes shone iridescent, piercing the endless sand. Her shadow grew around her, humanlike and black, blocking out the mountains.

In an eerie, detached voice, she said, "I have to survive."

Griffin gasped as he awoke with a sudden jerk. Cool hotel air filled his lungs, and he realized it was only a dream. Or perhaps not. It felt so real. Had it been a vision? That didn't make him feel better. Damn, he didn't want to be like Sani. Visions sucked.

"Are you okay?"

Cam's soft voice soothed his nerves and pushed the sadness and guilt of the vision to the back of his mind. He reached for her and pulled her to his chest. "Bad dream."

"Mmm. I have those too."

He'd never thought about Shifters having dreams. "Do you have good ones too?"

"Yes. Sometimes, I dream about the past."

Griffin kissed her temple. "I thought those were nightmares."

She nestled against him. "My people's past. Back in the beginning, before I was born."

Griffin pulled back to look at her. Her eyes were closed, her expression relaxed. "How is that possible?"

"I don't know," she said. "I never told anyone about them."

He felt a rush of wonder. She'd told *him*. "What was it like?"

She smiled, her eyes staying closed as if she didn't want to lose the moment. "We lived on a world much like this one, but it was only us. Water, sky, land, weather. But different. Everything was fluid and changing. We adapted, learning to change with our environment and climate. We'd have ceremonies for the seasons and for the harvest. Our moons told us what time it was—when to hunt, when to plant. Villages connected to each other in a matrix of paths and waterways. Technology was there, but we didn't use it for every day. Every day was meant to be enjoyed. It was beautiful."

Griffin watched her speak, fascinated by the details she knew and the world her people had come from. "What happened?"

Her voice faltered. "A massive meteor hit one of our moons. It caused a chain reaction of destruction. Some of us were rescued by neighboring planets, some escaped using our own technology. Most stayed and died."

Griffin had known they were refugees, but he'd never known how they became refugees. No one cared to find out. "I'm sorry."

"I'll be the only one left who knows the stories when my father dies," she murmured.

He felt the stab of guilt and decided he couldn't live with it anymore. He had to tell her. "XCEL never searched for your brother. I didn't tell them."

"I know."

Griffin frowned and lifted her chin with his finger. Cam opened her eyes then, and his heart skipped a beat. It wasn't supposed to do that. "How?"

"I heard you talking to Ernest," she said.

Damn, he forgot about her super hearing. "I didn't know it was about your father, I swear."

She answered with a sad smile. "You didn't want to know."

It was true. He didn't ask, didn't check. Just like he didn't ask about her past. He wanted to tell her he was sorry, but his heart was in his throat. She was still here. She hadn't run or tried to leave. He sensed the fatal acceptance in her and hated it.

Then she leaned in and kissed him, and he forgot about his heart.

◆ ◆ ◆

Aristotle climbed the ladders through the maze of tunnels that had become his home. His old legs ached, and his breathing was labored. He reached the top of the ladder, and Red helped him step up to the next level. Aristotle leaned on the boy while he caught his breath.

The young man frowned. "I still don't think it's a good idea that you expose yourself like this. We don't know for certain that they're on our side."

Aristotle started moving toward the next ladder with Red's assistance. "They are."

They stopped in front of the next ladder, and Aristotle eyed it with dread. Maybe it was a bad idea. Maybe he was a fool, but he had to talk to them face-to-face. It was the only right thing to do. A true leader led.

You can do this, Aristotle told himself as he peered up the twenty-foot ladder. "What time is it?"

"Seven thirty-five," Red replied. "You want me to carry you? I can, you know."

That'd be the day. He wasn't that far gone just yet. An old man still held some pride. Not much, but enough to get him up a damn ladder. Aristotle grabbed the rungs and mustered his strength. "Just keep up."

◆ ◆ ◆

The subway tunnel was dark, loud, and stifling hot at 7:50 A.M., and Cam suppressed a yawn. She was tired, and it wasn't all from mind-blowing sex with Griffin. These crazy hours were wreaking havoc with her sleep pattern and her Shifter DNA. She couldn't even remember what day it was as she stood next to Griffin and waited for the Shifters to show themselves.

Even when she did get sleep, she was haunted by dreams filled with uncertainties and doubts. And she guessed that she wasn't alone based on Griffin's nightmare. She would have asked him about it, but she feared it might have something to do with her. She'd already had enough disappointment for one day.

They both stood just inside a service tunnel that opened up to a narrow walkway running between the tunnel wall and three sets of tracks divided by concrete medians. A subway train squeezed by, moving the still air with a heated blast into the service tunnel. The subway slowed and stopped just out of sight at the station platform.

"I can't hear a damn thing in here," she told Griffin in a loud voice. The tunnels echoed relentlessly, making it impossible for her to use her focused hearing.

He aimed his flashlight down the tunnel. "Just watch for any activity."

"So we're going to get answers?" she asked.

Griffin didn't reply, and she turned to him with a bad feeling in her gut. "Griffin?"

A corner of his mouth rose. "You won't like it."

She was going to kill him. "You didn't ask them what this was about?"

He shrugged. "I doubt they'd invite us to a meeting just to kill us."

"Like the setup last night?" she said. "What if this is another ambush?"

"It's not. Remember the informant I met with a few days ago?" Griffin said. "He works with these guys, although I won't be positive until I see his Shifter shadow."

"Ah," she said. "Obviously, he didn't know about your special skills."

Griffin looked away. "Right."

She knew he hated those skills, but he used them to hunt shapeshifters. Like the woman he was sleeping with. Like the Shifters he was about to talk to, and perhaps even join forces with. Thus, the nightmares. "So which came first? The Shifter vision or the XCEL job?" she asked.

"The vision," he said. "I noticed it while I was living in Arizona with Sani. And when XCEL's operations were revealed to the public, I figured it'd be a good way to get the hell out of the desert and find some excitement."

"Well, you did that, alright," she admitted. "What do our Shifter shadows look like to you?"

He glanced at her. "You . . . shimmer different colors. Like a kaleidoscope mirage. Each with a unique pattern."

"Huh," she said, considering that. Shifters just looked like Shifters to each other. "What about in the dark?"

He nodded. "The shimmer stays."

Interesting. "And the freeze ray? When did you discover that?"

"During a takedown," he said. "A Shifter had me by the throat, and I thought I was a goner. But when I grabbed him back—" He hesitated. "It felt like electricity coming through my hands. And then he just stopped moving. Since then I've learned to control it better. Still have no idea where it comes from."

She'd never heard of such a thing, and she bet that XCEL hadn't either. "XCEL doesn't know about that, do they?"

He kept his focus on the tunnels. "The only ones who know are the ones I've used it on."

Including her. She'd almost forgotten about that. "So. Is it still exciting?"

He turned to her then, his gaze intense. "There's only one exciting thing in my life right now."

The way he said it went to her core. The temperature rose another degree or two. "And what about the job?"

His expression turned weary. "It lost its excitement after XCEL threw me in the detention center."

"I still can't believe they did that to you," she said, angry on his behalf. "What the hell is the matter with them?"

"They're scared. Fear changes people."

No kidding. She'd seen that, what? A thousand times?

Then Griffin focused on something at the end of the tunnel. "We have company."

Cam peered around the corner and saw two Shifters approaching. One was young, male, and moved with ease. That would be Griffin's informant. The other was older. Very old, like her father. He walked slowly and deliberately, limping slightly. And he was familiar.

"I know him," she said, stepping out of the service tunnel to greet them.

Griffin moved beside her. "The old man?"

She nodded, staring at him as he drew closer. He was her father's friend, Alli. Relief flowed over her. She smiled at him and he smiled back, knowing she'd recognized him. Cam met him halfway on the platform, with Griffin beside her.

"Alli," she said and took his outstretched hand in hers. "It's wonderful to see you."

He nodded, his white hair chaotic and his eyes bright. "Cala. How is your father?"

Her smile slipped. "Failing, I'm afraid."

"I'm sorry." Then he turned to the young man. "This is Red, my associate."

Griffin shook his hand. "We've met."

Red frowned deeply. "No, we haven't."

"You looked different then," Griffin said and shook the old man's hand. "Griffin Mercer."

"They call me Aristotle here. You are a remarkable human." He appeared impressed.

Cam laughed. "You have no idea. You may as well know that he can see Shifters."

Red stared at Griffin. "But I have a new skin—"

"I know," Griffin said.

"Holy crap," Red replied, his mouth opened in surprise.

"Tell me about it," Cam said. Then she focused on Aristotle. "We have a problem."

"The same problem," Aristotle replied. "A common enemy."

"Or enemies," Cam amended.

"True," Aristotle admitted. "It would appear we need each other."

She smiled. She didn't know why. Maybe it was because of the opportunity to work with "her people." Shifters were nothing if not loners. Few bothered with alliances. It was more like every man for himself.

Aristotle looked at them in turn. "Perhaps we should discuss—"

His words were shattered by a flood of bright lights and a bullhorn saying, "XCEL! You are under arrest. Raise your hands."

XCEL agents poured out of two access shafts across the three sets of tracks. There must have been thirty agents all scrambling for cover, and all carrying heavy weapons and wearing night vision goggles.

They were trapped, a good fifty feet from the nearest tunnel on this side of the tracks. She shifted.

Red dots from laser light targets zipped over them and the walls around them. Griffin had his gun out, Red had shifted, but Aristotle was still in his human form. It occurred to her that he must not be able to shift anymore, much like her father.

Red moved to protect Aristotle, and she moved to cover Griffin. She yelled, "We need to get back to the exit!"

"Put your hands up!" the bullhorn blared.

"Go!" Red said to Aristotle.

A subway train approached, the sound deafening in the enclosed tunnels. The ground shook, and stones danced between the tracks. She heard the first shot ring out over the roar of the oncoming train. Bullets shattered the walls behind them as they ran. Griffin reached around her and fired back. She hardened her molecular structure so bullets, or worse, couldn't penetrate her body or hit him.

Agents moved in, scaling the medians and firing from their left and front. Bullets pelted her hard shell, stinging from velocity. She saw Aristotle fall down ten feet in front of her, and Red immediately dropped to his knees, covering him with his own body.

The subway train entered view, and Cam hoped it would keep XCEL at bay for the brief time they needed to reach the tunnel.

Then she heard Griffin swear. His blood spattered across her skin. He'd been shot in the arm, but he gritted his teeth and kept firing his gun with both hands. One gun against all those agents? It was futile. They were still twenty feet from the relative safety of their exit.

She grabbed the gun from him. "Stay behind me," she shouted to him. The gun felt clumsy in her Shifter hand, but she managed to get off a few shots until the gun was empty.

And now what?

Red had widened his form into a shield to protect Aristotle, and she did the same for Griffin, but XCEL was moving closer, step by step. Soon, they'd be within reach, and then Griffin's protection would be gone.

The train rumbled and squealed by, trapping most of the agents on the other side of it. But half a dozen had managed to beat the train and kept firing, pinning her and Red in place. They weren't going anywhere unless someone drew their fire.

She yelled to Red, "Take Mercer!"

Then she poofed—reappearing in front of two agents and slamming her fist into their faces. Bullets hit her as she reached another agent and took him out with a kick to his gut. In her peripheral vision, she saw Red trying to sidle down the narrow platform with Aristotle and Griffin behind him. Two agents had them trapped, and she poofed right between the two men. The look of surprise on their faces was short-lived as she chopped each of their throats with the edge of her hand.

A split second later, the train cleared, revealing a line of agents that rushed forward.

No, she thought as her heart sunk. *Not enough time.*

Then a banshee yell echoed through the tunnel, and dozens of Shifters streamed out onto the tracks. They swamped the XCEL agents in a wave of claws and teeth. The gunshots ended, replaced by human screams and thuds. Cam jumped up on the platform to help Red. He was lifting Aristotle to his feet. He appeared unharmed.

"*Your* men?" she asked him.

Aristotle nodded. "Mine. And yours now."

And thank God for that. She patted his arm and went to Griffin. He was sitting against the wall, grimacing as he held his bicep. Blood squeezed between his fingers.

Panic shot through her as she dropped in front of him. "How bad is it?"

Pain was heavy in his eyes. "Went through. Missed the artery."

"That's good, right?" she asked, troubled to find her hands shaking. What if he kept bleeding? What if he was wrong and the bullet was still in there?

"My lucky day," he said and laid his head back against the concrete. He nodded behind her. "I like your cavalry better when I'm on your side."

She turned. Every XCEL agent was down, along with two Shifters. Aristotle's men were busy dragging the humans off the tracks and dumping them in a heap in the tunnels.

Cam reached out and put an arm around Griffin to lift him up. "I couldn't help but notice that XCEL is getting pretty damn serious about killing us."

Griffin got to his feet. "Harding's running scared."

"So am I," she said, noting how his head hung in pain. He needed medical attention. She turned to Red and Aristotle, who were talking to a few other Shifters. "Do you have a medic?"

Aristotle walked over to them and checked Griffin's arm. "We should be able to take care of that. You can't go back out there."

He was right about that. "We need a place to stay."

Aristotle nodded. "You can stay with us, if that's what you want."

Cam checked with Griffin. After a moment, he nodded too.

She took a deep breath. "That's what we want."

TWENTY-TWO

Griffin stood alone in the shadow of the cliff. Powerful winds blasted desert sand across his body. Black clouds rolled across the sky, heavy with rain and moving fast. The sun was losing its territory quickly, and danger filled the air.

He watched the Eagle battle the winds to reach her nest high on the cliff face. The oncoming storm buffeted her, knocking her lower to the ground, even as she fought to rise higher. Sharp, craggy rocks threatened, inches away. Feathers tore from her wings, and her head was bowed to the unrelenting gale.

He held his breath, waiting, knowing. His arms and legs tightened with every powerful flap of her wings. He strained, trying to give her the strength to reach safety.

Suddenly, the wind shifted, clutching her in its grip and throwing her against the rock. She bounced hard, folded up, and fell toward him.

Helplessly, he watched her soft body strike ledges and outcrops before tumbling across hard stone and landing at his feet, lifeless. For long moments, he stared at her, hoping against hope that she was still alive. That she would right herself and stretch her wings.

But she didn't. Sand flowed and curled around her, cradling her. Griffin knelt down and cleared her head. She felt soft and still warm to his touch.

And he cried. Tears fell and were instantly stolen by the desert. If he stood here long enough, there wouldn't be any sign that either of them had been here. No one would ever know that he loved her. His heart ached in his chest.

"Griffin?"

He inhaled sharply as he sat upright and into Cam's arms.

She was alive.

"Whoa. Easy, big boy," she whispered.

Griffin noted the cement walls, floor, and ceiling etched with watermarks. A heavy door and the bed he lay in completed the quick inventory. It all came back in a rush—the meeting, the ambush, the gunshot, the Shifters, Cam. He wrapped his arm around her and hissed at the pain, but he didn't care.

"You okay?" he asked, still swiping away the remnants of the nightmare.

She sounded worried as she pushed him back down into the bed and lay down next to him. "Great. I'm a little concerned about you, though."

He held her to his chest. "No worries. Where is everyone?"

"Aristotle's men picked up my father and Ernest. They're a few rooms down from here."

He breathed relief. It was warm and comfortable in the bed, and exhaustion swamped him quickly. "What about the Shifters?"

"Two were injured, but they'll heal. The rest are okay. It's all okay. Go back to sleep."

He could now, because that covered everyone who mattered to him. He drew Cam closer and slept.

◆◆◆

"Don't blame me," Braxton said, arms crossed as he leaned back in his chair in the small window on Harding's cell phone. "*Your* men couldn't even kill them. And that's what they do. So either XCEL sucks, or these two are a little brighter than your average bear."

Harding gritted his teeth and held on to his patience. "I didn't call for you to tell me what I already know. I called for your expert opinion. They've gone underground, all of them. How do I smoke them out?"

He shrugged. "You don't have to now."

"What?"

Braxton smirked. "You got enough for your report?"

"Possibly," Harding replied. He would have liked more, but he could always twist the facts.

"Including the Shifter attack on XCEL agents?"

Harding blinked. He'd been too furious at XCEL's failure to realize that he could use the three deaths and multiple injuries to his advantage.

Braxton raised his hands. "XCEL was trying to apprehend the Shifters who were blowing up our buildings and killing our people, and look what happened? Where does that leave us now?"

The plans were already forming in his head. This was perfect.

He could prove without a doubt that the Shifters were out to kill humans.

"Well?" Braxton asked. "Does that solve your problem?"

It did. He didn't need to worry about Mercer or Camille now that they'd joined the underground. They were part of the problem. "It'll do."

He was about to cut the call when Braxton said, "You should have figured that out yourself."

Harding glared at him. "I was busy."

"No, you lost control of your emotions," Braxton said and pointed a finger at him like a gun. "Told you so."

"Fuck you," Harding said, and hung up.

◆◆◆

It felt good to have her father close by again, even if he did look deathly ill. Cam squeezed his hand on the table, and he gave her a smile.

Aristotle was seated next to him along with Griffin, Red, Ernest, and a few of Aristotle's men. They were hunkered down in a dark, dank room over a makeshift table. It was like a secret society, and in reality, they were exactly that.

"They are developing a biological weapon. We believe it will be lethal to Shifters but not affect humans," Aristotle said.

Cam felt her stomach drop. It shouldn't surprise her, but the simple gall of it all did. "Are you sure?"

He nodded. "We have people inside the facility. They aren't privy to all the information, but they have provided enough of it for us to be certain."

Griffin leaned forward. "If you know where it is, why didn't you just destroy the facility?"

Red piped up. "I know, right?"

Aristotle shook his head. "Harding would just cover it up, or blame it on the Shifters like he did all the other attacks. Then he'd build another facility, this time with all the blessings of a terrified government and society. We'd never be able to come back from that. And if we destroy the evidence, we can't prove anything."

"That's *if* you want to follow the proper channels," Red grumbled.

Aristotle told him, "We do. We need to do this right. If we don't, we are no different than Harding."

"So you tried to impede the development by attacking the distribution line into the facility," Griffin said.

"Exactly. Although, that ended up backfiring on us," Aristotle admitted. "Harding used our strategy to wipe out businesses and people who support us."

Cam tapped her fingers nervously on the table. "How close is the weapon for use?"

Aristotle slid a photo over to her. "Very."

She studied the two dead men—one a human and the other a Shifter—lying on tables. The Shifter's skin was waxy, and his body strangely flat. Like all his insides were mush contained inside his skin. His features were molded together, making him nearly indistinguishable, but she knew who he had been.

She slid it over to Griffin. "It's our captive."

"What the hell?" Griffin said and took the photo to view closer. "What happened to him? He looks melted."

Aristotle nodded. "We think he was. The weapon, probably a gas, dissolves the part of our molecules that allows us to shift. That's why the body looks like it's filled with gelatin. It is. That picture was taken a few days ago."

Ernest leaned over and grimaced at the photo. "Jesus. I thought you guys healed fast."

Aristotle said, "Not fast enough to counter the damage from this toxin."

"Who's the other guy?" Ernest asked, squinting at the photo.

"A human," Aristotle said.

Cam studied the man. He was covered in his own blood. "I thought it wasn't supposed to hurt humans."

"Trust me, by the time they get done with testing, it won't," Aristotle said.

"Which means we have a little time," Griffin said. "Any idea how or when they plan to deploy it?"

Heads shook.

"All we know is that they will. Were you aware that Harding is working on a report to a special senate committee?" Aristotle asked. "It is supposed to outline the findings of our investigation on the Shifter attacks."

"Senate? *Our* senate?" Ernest asked.

Cam ignored Ernest and frowned at Griffin. "I had no idea. Did you know?"

"Yes." Then Griffin cut her a look. "It was just about the attacks."

"By Shifters," she corrected. "So Harding could spring his diabolical scheme on us with full congressional support."

"I had no idea he was plotting anything more," Griffin said, his expression unreadable.

Of course you didn't, she thought. *And you didn't ask.* Just one more thing he neglected to tell her. And why would he? It'd just be a reason to piss her off, and he couldn't risk that if he wanted her cooperation. Would she ever be able to trust him?

"When is the report due?" Aristotle asked Griffin.

"As soon as possible. He may have already sent it in," Griffin said. "He will blame all attacks on you and your men. He will push to use the weapon—"

The door opened, and another one of Aristotle's men came in. He walked over to the old man and handed him a sheet of paper. Aristotle read it silently, frowning.

"Now wait a minute," Ernest said. "Do you really think that our government would go for that?"

"They might now," Aristotle said and passed Ernest the sheet of paper. "A building exploded in South Queens. Killed twelve people, including two children. XCEL is blaming it on Shifters."

Cam's stomach sunk. "Oh God. He's playing to the media. We're dead."

It was quiet around the table for a few long moments while everyone digested the new development. Her father reached for and held her hand. His eyes met hers, full of sorrow. It was happening all over again. Just like it had on the last planet. The memory of her mother's murdered body flickered in her mind. It had been years ago, but it felt like yesterday. Or tomorrow.

"We need to pin this on Harding," Griffin said, breaking the silence. "It's the only way to make this right."

Ernest shook his head. "It ain't gonna happen. If there's one person in the world who knows how to cover his ass, it's Harding."

"There must be something," Griffin said. "Cell phone records, e-mails, something."

"His cell phone is private and secure. I'd need to do some serious digging to access his records," Ernest said. Then he waved the photo. "*But*, I haven't tried to tie him to this facility yet."

"Give Ernest everything you have," Griffin said to Aristotle. "If Harding is pulling the strings, then he has to have some kind of contact with them."

"What about us?" Red asked. "We can't just sit here and let them kill people and blame it on us."

"Agreed," Griffin said. "Ernest—"

"I know, I know. Next target," he said with a sigh. "I'm going to need more bandwidth for this."

"Not a problem," Red said, grinning at Ernest. "What do you think all these cables down here are for?"

"You two figure that out," Griffin said. Then he cut Cam a look and said, "I think we'll do a little surveillance."

She turned to Griffin. "How much time do we have?"

He didn't answer her, but she could see it in his eyes. *Not enough.*

TWENTY-THREE

Griffin used his binoculars to scan the facility. The sign by the front gate read Goodman Research and Development. The facility consisted of several rectangular buildings attached to each other, two tall smoke stacks, and four delivery docks—all surrounded by barbwire-topped chain-link fencing. A guard sat in the entrance—armed, no doubt.

"This place is a lot bigger than I expected," Cam noted.

Griffin lowered the binoculars. "Harding can't run an operation this large by himself without leaving tracks."

"Ernest can't find any connection," Cam said.

"That's because someone else is running it," Griffin noted, and read the information off his phone. "According to Aristotle's inside people, a man named Nick Braxton is in charge. Former military." He scrolled through the pages of notes, and something caught his eye. "Braxton was on the original XCEL committee that was disbanded last year."

Cam asked, "So?"

He couldn't believe it. He knew what the connection was. "Harding was on that committee."

"Oh my God. They're in this together," Cam said quickly.

Griffin sent a note to Ernest. "Let's see what kind of magic Ernest can do with that."

Cam studied the building. "Should we bother to try talking to Braxton?"

"No. If we're wanted by XCEL, he knows it." Griffin glanced up at the formidable facility. "But I wonder how hard it would be to get inside."

Cam wrinkled her nose. "I knew you were going to say that."

"Chickening out on me?"

She cut him a glare. "Please. I was *made* for sneaking around, remember? However, there's also a gas in there that can melt us. Not too excited about that part."

He wasn't either, but there might not be another way.

"You don't need to do this," he said.

Cam turned to him. "If you go in, I go in."

"No."

She raised her eyebrows. "Excuse me?"

He turned to look at her. God, she was beautiful. But she wasn't coming with him. He had nothing left to lose. He'd put himself in this position. She shouldn't even be here.

"This is my idea," he said. "I'll go in alone."

"While I what? Crochet?" she returned. "Do you think you're the only one with a stake here? These are my people."

Her people. He wondered when she'd decided that. He wondered if she even realized it. Whatever that case, he wasn't going to change her mind now.

"So don't even try to stop me, Mercer," she added. "I'm your damned partner. And I don't care how you feel about that."

He'd grown to hate that word—partner. Except when she said it. "I don't like it."

"Good thing no one asked you then," she said. "Besides, we don't have a choice, do we?"

They really didn't. All the answers lay in that building. He lifted the binoculars. "I'll see what Ernest can do about the security systems."

"We pulled that stunt once at the detention center. I don't think they will fall for it again," she said. "Can we use Aristotle's insiders?"

"Perhaps," he said. "Either way, it's going to get messy."

"That works for me," she said and stretched her arms. "Haven't killed anyone all day."

◆◆◆

Dewey looked damned old, Aristotle decided as he sat next to his friend. They'd ducked ammunition together. Fought over women. Done every illegal drug they could find. Ran from trouble more than a time or two. They'd gotten married and started families just months apart. And then they'd lost everything, escaping from a hellish world that was determined to wipe them out.

Where did time go? he wondered. Shifter bodies aged slowly, and they could live to be well over a hundred and twenty-five years. Not so with humans. These bodies weren't made for a hundred years. They were complex and fragile with too few redundant parts. One heart. Who decided on that?

Regardless, Aristotle liked this body. It was better than some he'd worn. He wished he could remember the others, but those memories were lost to the past. There were days when he couldn't conjure up his son's face or remember which tunnel he needed to follow.

Growing old was a crime. He'd rather die in battle than waste away one memory at a time. It was no way for a man to depart his life, and he'd decided long ago that he wouldn't allow it to happen to him. His time, however, was drawing near. The battle cries were getting louder and closer.

Before this week was out, he'd meet the enemy on the field. He'd saved every spare ounce of energy for that moment, and he planned to leave nothing behind.

Dewey opened his eyes slowly and gazed around him without any hint of fear. Aristotle knew why. He was simply too tired to care. His gaze settled on Aristotle, and he smiled.

"You look like hell," Dewey said.

"I'm not the one lying in bed all day," Aristotle said and reached out to shake his friend's hand. "Good to see you."

"You too," Dewey said, giving him a weak handshake. "Didn't think I'd live long enough to run into you again."

"It's a small world," he said. They all were. "How do you feel?"

"Excellent. You?" Dewey was lying through his teeth. He'd been asleep for most of the past day.

"Excellent," Aristotle lied back. Old men and their pride.

"Where are we?"

Aristotle grinned and spread his arms out. "Welcome to my humble abode. Seven levels under the city."

Dewey glanced around. "I like what you've done with the place. Where's Camille?"

Aristotle filled him in on the details. "They'll be back soon."

His old friend closed his eyes. For a moment, Aristotle thought he might have fallen asleep. Then he said, "How bad is it?"

He took a deep breath. "As bad as it gets, old friend."

Dewey opened his eyes. "Can we win?"

"Yes," Aristotle said.

"Is it worth it?"

"Yes."

Dewey met his gaze. "Keep her safe."

Aristotle put his hand on Dewey's. "I'll do my best."

◆ ◆ ◆

Cam felt safer underground again. As they'd come back from the facility, they had run into several demonstrations in the streets. The media had the humans whipped into a frenzy over the Shifter attacks.

Next thing you know, they'd be accusing each other of being witches and burning people at the stake.

She and Griffin were heading to one of many meeting rooms in the underground labyrinth. Aristotle's Shifters had taken over a big chunk of the tunnels that ran under Manhattan. Alcoves had become meeting rooms; corridors fashioned into cubes of living spaces. It was a city beneath a city, guarded by Shifters on a mission.

Red met them at the door.

"Glad you found us okay," he said and ushered them into the small room that Ernest had commandeered for his high-tech geekdom. Metal piping had been opened up and clips taped onto the bundles of wiring. Thick power cords fed a wall of monitors and computers.

"Made yourself at home, I see," Griffin observed. "How's the reception down here?"

Ernest peered at him, happy as a geek could get. "I may move here permanently. See this pipe right here?" He pointed to one of ten pipes. "Lifeline to the best Internet you can buy. And this one." He nodded toward a robust pipe with a slew of clips sticking out of it. "That's the cyber tower to the surface. I can get you anything you want."

"World peace," Cam said.

Ernest rolled his eyes. "Please. Like that's ever going to happen. But, I did manage to call the next attack. Aristotle's men took care of it and left the goons for the media to find too. Hung 'em right out the windows so everyone could see who exactly was trying to blow up the place."

Red crossed his arms. "Until Harding cleaned it up. Told the media it was us."

Griffin cast Cam a quick look. "We need proof."

She was afraid he was going to say that. Despite her bravado, she wasn't looking forward to getting inside the death zone. At least not until she had Harding's throat in her hands.

Griffin asked Ernest, "Did you get the photos I sent you of the exterior of the facility?"

"Got 'em," Ernest said.

"Good. So how do we get inside?" Griffin asked.

Ernest gaped at him. "You know, this isn't as easy as it looks."

"We know," Cam said. "We also know you're the best."

"That's true," Ernest said, turning to his computers. "I'll see what I can come up with. Plus now I have intel from our spies inside."

Griffin asked Red, "How many people do you have inside?"

"Two technicians," he said. "Humans. Both understand what Harding is trying to do."

Cam could only imagine the danger they faced. "How do they check in with you?"

Red held up his smartphone. "I get reports once or twice a week. I downloaded everything to Ernest's computer."

"And I took everything and created an information matrix on the facility," Ernest said, tapping away. "Here we go."

They all leaned over Ernest to view the monitors. Cam noted floor plans, research notes, photos of workers—everything except a way inside.

"Workers have to go through a series of automated gates that use X-rays, human Scouts, and every scanner known to man. Like airport security on steroids," Ernest summarized. "Nothing goes in, nothing comes out that's not supposed to. I'll need to analyze everything to formulate an acceptable plan of attack. Give me a few hours."

"Anything on Harding?" Cam asked.

"Nothing to tie him to any of this," Ernest said. "Oh, and he put out a contract to kill all of us. But you probably already knew that."

Really, she should have killed him.

"When's Harding's next attack?" Griffin asked.

"Tonight. A dance club in Harlem. Aristotle is getting his team together," Ernest said. "Why, you interested in joining them?"

"It could be a setup," Red reminded them.

Yes, it could, but could they chance not following up? she thought. A night attack in a crowded dance club. That would put the nail in the coffin for Shifters everywhere.

Griffin eyed Cam, waiting for her answer.

Oh, what the hell? It was better than hanging around geeks all day. "Time to put on my dancing shoes," she said.

"You might want to bring your running shoes," Ernest said. "These guys are trying to kill us, remember?"

As if she could forget.

◆ ◆ ◆

"I feel a little overdressed," Cam yelled to him.

A group of scantily clad women walked by them wearing strategically placed rhinestones. The *thump-thump-thump* of music piped through speakers, and the noise level was barely tolerable. The joint was jumping.

Griffin glanced at her. She wore a red tank top, jeans, and flat sandals. She looked perfect to him. He leaned toward her and said, "Maybe that's because you're not here to find a man."

Cam slid him a side glance. "Says who?"

He grinned. *Liar.*

"When is Ernest going to call this in?"

Griffin checked his phone. "In exactly eighty-seven seconds."

Then he noticed one of Aristotle's six men across the dance floor. He made eye contact with Griffin and shook his head once. No sign of Harding's minions or a bomb bent on blowing up a whole new demographic for Harding's report. If there was a bomb. Ernest could be wrong.

"We should split up," Cam said, reading his mind.

He leaned close. "Call me if you find anything."

She nodded and made her way around customers gyrating to the music. A brightly lit stage occupied one wall of the bar where a DJ was doing his thing. A light show raced across the dancers and walls. It made the scene feel surreal. Just wait until all hell broke loose.

Unfortunately, there were a lot more people here than he expected. He wasn't looking forward to the stampeding herd when the bomb threat was announced. He tapped his earpiece to activate it and said, "You there?"

"Right here," Ernest replied. "Wow, sounds like a party."

"Are we a go?"

"The call is going in thirty seconds," Ernest said. "Is everyone in place?"

In his earpiece, Aristotle's men and Cam each counted down around the room. Everyone was set for the mayhem.

"You'll have about two minutes to find that bomb. That's the best I can do," Ernest told them. "And then you have to get your collective asses out of there before the cops show up."

Griffin saw Cam by the stage and felt a pang of concern. He shouldn't, he knew that. She could certainly handle herself. She didn't need him. And that was more true than he cared to acknowledge.

"Showtime, boys and girls," Ernest said. "Your two minutes start now."

The sprinklers in the ceiling activated, spraying water everywhere as patrons screamed. Bright white lights overrode the laser show, and the music cut out. A prerecorded voice announced that all occupants were to head to the nearest exits and began listing the locations.

A split second later, everyone panicked and started rushing for the exits. Griffin held his ground, his eyes on the floor.

"Watch for anyone who doesn't run," he told the others.

The manager raced up on the stage, took the microphone

from the DJ, and tried to calm the crowd. But a couple hundred drunk people weren't listening.

Griffin saw one of the Shifters help a woman who was being crushed by the crowd. He was starting to wonder if the fire alarm was worse than the bomb.

"I think I have one," Cam said in his ear.

"Where are you?" he asked, looking over heads. "Where are you?"

"I got him," she said.

"Wait for help," he yelled.

There was a loud *thump* and then a grunt. She didn't wait. "Where are you, Cam?"

"Stage left," she said.

He pushed through the oncoming crowd toward the stage. The place was slowly emptying, and people were interested only in getting out. Which was good. Because that's when the shooting started.

Griffin couldn't tell if it was a panicked partier or one of his or Harding's men, but everyone started screaming and ducking and shoving.

Shapeshifter heads popped up above the people, causing even more chaos as they shifted to Primary form to defend themselves.

"Shit," Griffin said when he saw Cam in her Shifter form take a swing at a man.

"What's happening?" Ernest said in his earpiece.

"The usual." Griffin punched a guy holding a gun in his hand. He dropped to the floor, and Griffin dragged him to the side so he wouldn't get trampled.

"Crap," Ernest said. "You gotta get out of there. A false alarm is one thing. Gunfire? I can't help you."

He was too busy pushing through people to argue. The Shifters were taking out anyone who pulled a gun. In this city, that could be everyone. "Easy, guys. We don't know if any of these people work for Harding."

He reached Cam and found her staring at a black box next to a man lying on the floor in a storage room next to the stage. She said, "He was working this when I found him. Locked it up before I could stop him. What do you think?"

Griffin knelt and checked it over. Could be a bomb. Could be drugs. Or could be a bomb. He said into his comm, "We got what we came for. Everyone clear out *now*."

Cam didn't move, and he noticed that she'd shifted back to human.

"I'm sticking with you," she said.

"No, you're not," he replied. "They know you're Shifters. They'll blame this on you."

"Yes, they will."

Man, she was stubborn. "And we have to take a bomb out of here."

She raised an eyebrow. "I know. I'm sticking with you."

He stopped trying. "Don't blame me when you blow up."

She glanced toward the front of the nearly empty bar. "I hear sirens."

Now or never. Griffin carefully picked up the black box. It didn't go off. Things were looking up.

He followed Cam out through the stage door to the back alley where a small crowd was filing out. A spotlight glowed over the trash cans and boxes.

Griffin was just about to turn toward their escape route when a familiar face caught his attention and stopped him in his tracks. It was dark and utter chaos, but that face—

Parker? It couldn't be. Emotion flooded over him, and he almost dropped the box. People moved, and the face was gone into the night.

"What is it?" Cam asked.

Crazy dreams, visions, and now he was seeing dead people. What next? "Nothing," he said. "Go."

They ran the length of the alley, through a door into the next building and a series of doorways and hatches that linked to the underground. Aristotle's men were waiting at intervals to cover for them. The doors were sealed and locked behind them. Only a Shifter would be able to track them.

Twenty minutes later, they were ushered into an abandoned storefront and met up with a Shifter who was one of Aristotle's contacts and a bomb expert. Griffin was glad to set the box down and hand it over to someone who knew what the hell they were doing.

"Name's Carl," the Shifter said by way of introduction. He wore a T-shirt, jeans, and a Yankees baseball cap. It still amazed Griffin how well they blended in.

Cam said to him, "Tell me we didn't just drag a box of cigars halfway across the city."

Carl bent down and sniffed the box. "Nope, it's a bomb. You sure you want to keep this?"

Griffin answered, "If possible. However, we'd kind of like it to blow when we want it to."

"Okay." The Shifter turned his Yankees cap backward and reached for his tool kit. "You two might want to leave now."

TWENTY-FOUR

Parker followed their scents to the entrance of the underground. If he hadn't seen Griffin with the Shifters outside the nightclub last night with his own eyes, he'd have thought Harding made it all up.

Griffin had switched sides.

Parker never thought he'd see that, especially considering how things ended between them. Griffin had every reason to hate Shifters, and yet, there he was. If Griffin saw him, he didn't bite. He just turned and followed the female Shifter, Camille. Harding was right about that too. Time to see what else Harding had up his sleeve.

Parker called Harding. He answered immediately. "Did you find them?"

"Sure did. What now?"

"Kill him. Kill them both," Harding said. "I thought I made that clear."

He had, but Parker wasn't an idiot. The NYC underground was well known for its unsavory population of Shifters and criminals. He wasn't going down there without a good reason. Harding yelling at him was not doing it.

"It's gonna cost you," he said.

Harding said, "I already saved you once."

"That was then. This is now. He's underground. You can't get to him without me. That's why you called me."

There was a long pause on the other end, and Parker could almost see Harding seethe. Worth every moment.

"What do you want?" Harding finally said.

Parker considered the open invitation. "Let's start with the classic—money. How's a hundred grand sound?"

"What? I can't get that kind of money—"

"Then I can't help you."

Another long pause. Christ, it was priceless.

"You'll have it. But I want the location of the Shifters, *and* Mercer's and Camille's bodies."

What a shame. He was thinking of asking her out on a date. "It's a deal."

Parker disconnected the phone. Time to go kill his ex-partner. Then he checked his weapons and headed underground.

◆ ◆ ◆

Griffin stood in the desert in the relentless sun. It scorched his bare skin, turning it red and raw, but he remained.

The sky was empty.

The Eagle gone forever. She'd never be back here again. At

first, he'd seen her as the enemy. A ravenous creature who took flesh from the earth to sustain herself.

But without her, the world was quieter. Lonelier. Stark.

"You miss her," Sani said.

Griffin turned toward his grandfather. Sani's features were distinctly Native American, proud and strong. The brown skin on his face was weathered but smooth. His long hair flowed white down his back. He was barefooted and wore a white shirt and brown pants. A silver pendant hung around his neck. He was exactly the way that Griffin remembered him the last time they saw each other.

The last time they spoke face-to-face.

The time before the anger and arguments that drove Griffin to the city where he would find his riches.

"I miss her," he said. "Can you bring her back?"

Sani looked over the sand. "I cannot."

Griffin felt the disappointment to his core.

"But you can," Sani continued.

"I have no magic for that," he replied.

"Do you love her?"

Griffin was surprised by his yes.

"Then you will find a way," Sani said.

The wind picked up, and Griffin let the hot air caress him, reminding him of the past and all the good things there. It hadn't all been bad. He'd just been too angry and too impatient. For the injustice of the reservation, for the treatment of his people, for the poverty, the barely livable houses, and too few schools. He'd wanted more.

Now he just wanted the Eagle.

"I miss the desert," Griffin said. "And you."

Sani nodded. "I know. We miss you too."

Griffin smiled at the "we" part. Sani walked barefooted for a reason. He was connected to the earth and the pulse of the land. It was something Griffin had never learned to do. Actually, he'd just never believed in it. Wanting something to be didn't make it happen.

"If you want to bring her back, you must let go of the anger," Sani said. "It will weigh upon you until you do."

The anger. He thought of Parker and what he'd done. How he'd ruined Griffin's marriage and all the rest. Forgiveness was too good for that bastard. The anger would stay.

"Then you have a choice," Sani said. "Anger and love cannot share a home."

Maybe I'm not meant to have a home, Griffin thought.

Sani nodded his head slowly. "If you want a home, you will have to fight for it. Look at the Eagle. She fought the wind. She was battered by the rocks. She didn't give up."

Griffin turned to him. "She also died."

"Are you sure of that?"

Yes, he was. Griffin had watched her die. He saw the Eagle fall to the earth, saw her body still in the sand. She was gone forever.

Then he heard a bird's cry, carried on the wind. He checked the skies but couldn't find her. "Where is she?"

"She waits on the other side for you."

"How do I get there?" Griffin asked.

"You must free your spirit. Let go of these things you think are important."

He didn't like the sound of that. "I've already given everything

I have, Grandfather. My home, my job, my marriage. There's nothing left."

"Have you looked inside?" Sani said.

Griffin felt a pang of apprehension. He didn't want to look inside. "It's empty."

"Is it? Then why are you here?" Sani asked.

Because, he thought, *because of Cam.*

Sani turned to face the wind and smiled.

◆◆◆

"I thought you told me you had these attacks under control, Braxton," Harding said, trying to keep his voice within the confines of his office. "I can't keep fixing your screwups. People are starting to ask questions."

"Well, apparently the computer system *your* people installed here is full of holes," Braxton yelled back. "Don't blame me for that. I can't send a damn text message without it being intercepted."

"The computer system is not the problem," Harding said, stabbing his finger on his desk. "You have a mole. Find him."

Braxton didn't have a response to that, and it gave Harding immense pleasure to know he was right. "The report has gone to the president. I need everything set as soon as possible."

"You think the president has been sitting there waiting for your report? He probably doesn't even remember who you are. I'm pretty sure we have time."

Braxton was really pissing him off, and Harding was about to tell him so when there was a knock on his office door.

"Find your mole and get rid of him," he told Braxton. Then he hung up, pocketed his cell phone, and said, "Come in."

It was Roberts, and he didn't have an appointment, which wasn't like him. He closed the door behind him but didn't come forward.

"Do you have a minute, sir?" he asked.

"Sure, what is it?" Harding said, pretending to be reading the report in front of him.

Roberts took his time before saying, "We have a lot of men on Mercer."

"So? That's what XCEL does."

Roberts nodded. "That is true, but the rest of our cases have been put on hold. And Mercer can hardly be considered a major threat."

Harding lifted his eyes from the report. "Are you questioning my orders?"

"Yes, sir, I am."

Harding stared at his good little soldier. "You have failed in your duty to monitor Agent Vincent, and your remarks are out of line."

The man didn't budge. "I realize that, but this is unusual—"

"You are dismissed from this case," Harding interrupted.

Roberts blinked in shock. He stood for a few moments longer and then turned and left.

Harding leaned back in his chair. He hoped Roberts wouldn't be a problem. If he was, then Harding knew who to blame his untimely death on.

◆◆◆

Aristotle, Griffin, and Cam were huddled over the schematics of the chemical facility in a makeshift armory when one of Aristotle's men came running in, out of breath. "We have a problem."

Aristotle frowned. "What is it?"

"Matt's dead," he said. "Found him lying on the floor. His face is a mess."

"Who's Matt?" Griffin asked.

"One of my perimeter guards," Aristotle answered.

So, it wasn't just a problem, Griffin thought. It was a breach. Someone had followed them. "You need to notify your people."

"I will," Aristotle said. "Warn everyone to keep a look out for anyone who shouldn't be here."

The man nodded.

"How was he killed?" Cam asked him.

"I have no idea." Then he made a ball-like shape with his fingers. "Matt's head is all swollen and hard. Like his DNA solidified."

She gave Griffin a worried look. Apparently, they weren't the only ones who'd gotten the beta version of the Salt Round. It was moving to general release at the speed of light.

He said, "It's a new Shifter weapon. It must be one of Harding's men."

The man shook his head. "No, a Shifter got him. I could smell him. But he's not one of ours."

Griffin stilled as the familiar face in the crowd came back in a flash. "Just one?"

"But he's well armed," he reminded him. Then he studied Griffin. "You know who it is?"

Cam was watching him too. Everyone was watching him. The bad feeling that had haunted him since they left the nightclub lay heavy in his chest. But it couldn't be. Parker was dead. That's what he'd been told.

By Harding.

Griffin could barely think it, he was so furious.

Cam moved closer to him and asked, "Who is he?"

It had been the one consolation he'd had during this entire ordeal, the one bit of revenge he'd ever get. And it had been a lie. Harding had played him to the limit. No more. This ended now. Parker was his.

He turned and grabbed a rifle from the rack behind him. He'd get the rest of the XCEL gear from his room, but he wouldn't be needing the tranquilizers. "Where did you find Matt?"

"Tunnel Twelve B, lower level by the ladder," the man said.

Cam stepped in front of Griffin. "Who is it?"

Even though he had no proof, his gut told him otherwise. "Parker. My ex-partner."

Her eyes widened. "But he's dead."

Griffin pulled on his holster. "If he's not, he will be."

CHAPTER
TWENTY-FIVE

"I don't like it," Cam whispered as she stepped through the couple of inches of water and gross stuff in the sewer. They'd found Matt, and he had definitely been killed with a Salt Round. Now she and Griffin were alone, taking on his ex-partner, who was supposed to be dead, armed with XCEL weapons.

"Which part don't you like? There's a lot to choose from," Griffin said, moving through the waste behind her.

She'd already shifted to Shifter form to make full use of her senses. She slowed to make sure she was still on the ex-partner's trail. "Why is he here now? How does he have access to XCEL weapons? And why don't we have more Shifters to help take him down?"

Griffin said, "To kill us. Harding. And too much noise."

Well, that answered all her questions. It occurred to her that he'd been pretty good about that lately. "I can do quiet."

He made a *humph* sound behind her, and they moved forward

to the ladder that Parker had used. They climbed down a level and into a particularly bad-smelling tunnel. But Parker's scent was growing stronger, and she decided to cut the chatter. He had super hearing too.

How did Harding get hold of Parker to begin with, unless he knew where to look? Which meant that Parker being dead was a lie, and Harding knew it. He'd withheld that information from Griffin all this time. And that meant that Harding had protected Parker all along. No wonder Griffin was loaded for bear. There was murder in his eyes, and his anger was driving him to a dangerous place. A place she understood well. If given the chance to face the people who killed her mother, she'd seek revenge too.

That was never going to happen for her, but she could help Griffin find closure. Maybe then he could move on with his life. A different life. Perhaps even one where he wasn't a Shifter hunter. Sadness filled her. But what if it wasn't enough? What if he couldn't forgive and forget?

Then danger trumped her thoughts as she approached a tunnel intersection. Parker's scent was crisp and strong; he'd spent some time here. Water dripped from the ceilings. Muffled thumps and rattles echoed through the tunnels.

Cam slowed where the tunnels converged, scanning each side as best she could. They were partially blocked by cardboard boxes and plywood sheets where someone had tried to make a home. She silently signaled for Griffin to wait.

She took one step through, and her senses screamed. Suddenly, a body hurtled at her, lifting her off her feet and into the concrete wall with enough force to knock her into next week. The impact stunned her, and she struggled to get up in the slippery slurry on the floor. Gunfire erupted, and she lurched toward the Shifter who was bearing down on Griffin.

He turned at the last second and clubbed her in the face with his fist, throwing her back against the wall again. Griffin was firing at him nonstop, but it didn't even slow him down as he advanced on her. He grabbed her and tossed her headfirst into the opposite side. She twisted to block the impact but heard her shoulder crack. She went down and felt the wet floor on her back while the tunnel faded away.

◆◆◆

Griffin threw everything he had at Parker, and he was still standing. Cam was down though, and that was what made him really mad. Watching it happen, unbearable. He needed to check on her, make sure she was going to be okay. But first, he had to get rid of Parker.

Parker stood in front of him, in full living Shifter glory. The flashlight was ten feet away, facing them and providing minimal illumination. The rifle was in his hands, but so far, it hadn't made a dent in Parker's smug smile.

"Never thought I'd see the day when you joined the Shifters," Parker said in that cocky-ass way Griffin hated. "Didn't believe Harding when he told me."

Griffin threw the useless rifle to the floor. He had something else he knew would work on Parker. "He protected you from XCEL after you betrayed us."

Fearlessly, Parker took a step toward him, bringing them within five feet. "Well, he wasn't going to, but then I convinced him that I'd be worth more alive than dead. And you know what?

I'm thinking the same thing about you." Then he glanced at Cam. "And her."

That sent a rush of adrenaline through Griffin. If Parker so much as touched her, he'd kill him. "Don't even think about it."

Parker grinned knowingly. "Wouldn't be the first time I stole your girl."

His jaw clenched. "Deirdre thought you were me."

"Is that what she told you?" Parker laughed. It echoed through the tunnels and came back twisted and monstrous.

"I got a news flash for you. My affair with her started long before I stepped into your shoes." Parker took another step forward. "She *wanted* me. As me. It was never you."

The kernel of doubt that Griffin had buried firmly in the back of his mind stepped forward, as solid as Parker's words.

Parker said, "*You* were too busy working, trying to make a big name for yourself. She got lonely, Griffin. Simple as that."

Rage flooded over him, turning his mind dark and centered on one realization: Everything in his life had been a lie. "You're going to wish you were dead."

That got a belly laugh out of Parker. "Maybe you aren't seeing the same reality as me. Because you're an unarmed human, and I'm a big bad Shifter. You lose."

Time to show Parker something new. Griffin flexed his hands, inviting the electricity he alone owned. "You'll have to drag me bodily out of here."

Parker smiled and reached for him. "I was hoping you'd say that."

Griffin gripped Parker's wrist and let loose a powerful and reckless surge. Pain coursed through his hand with every pulse. There was no restraint and no reservations; he just let it flow.

Parker donned a look of horror and tried to pull away, but Griffin held him tight.

"Whaaaaa doing?" Parker said in abject desperation.

"Something I wish I'd done a year ago," Griffin said, and watched Parker sway and then drop to his knees. He didn't let go; he wasn't done. "How's it going?"

"Fuuuu—" Parker gasped. His eyes rolled up into his head, and Griffin pushed him onto his back into the sewer. His body started trembling, and color drained from his skin, turning him a ghostly white.

Griffin held on far longer than he ever had before, watching Parker die slowly. Rage gave him strength and conviction. He had the right to do this. Parker had killed innocent people, ruined his life, and needed to be stopped—

Then Cam cried out in pain.

His rage slipped away at the sound as he turned around to look at her. She was covered in slime, fighting to get up.

The last of his anger dissolved. He released Parker, and the Shifter shuddered. He wasn't dead, Griffin knew, but suddenly, he didn't care.

The only thing that mattered was Cam. He left Parker and knelt beside her. He wiped the grime from her Shifter face. She'd slipped back into unconsciousness. He patted her face, but she didn't come to.

This was his fault. He'd put her in this danger, knowing full well they should have had backup. Because he'd wanted so badly to make sure he was the one to kill Parker. To get the revenge he'd earned. Now, she was suffering because of him. He didn't deserve her.

Then he pulled Cam up by her hands and draped her over his

shoulder. He cast one final look at Parker before heading back to the safety of Aristotle's world.

◆◆◆

Cam came to with a pounding head. Her Shifter body had done its thing and healed the broken bones, contusions, and anything else that needed fixing. Except her head.

"How are you feeling?"

Griffin's rough voice surprised her, and she turned to find him sitting on the edge of the bed. He appeared tired but otherwise unharmed. A dim light was on, and she immediately shifted to human form.

His eyes narrowed. "You didn't have to do that."

She didn't even realize she'd done it; it had been an instinctive reaction. "I know how you feel about Shifters."

A slow smile crossed his face. "I'm getting over that."

She smiled back. "I'm so glad. Did you get him?"

Griffin's smile waned. "No. He got away."

Cam pushed to her elbows, ignoring the few extra throbs of her head. This was important to him. He had to find closure. Without it, they—he—wouldn't move on. "Parker is a threat to you, me, and everyone here."

"I know." Griffin gently pushed her back on the bed. "But you broke two walls. I think that's enough for today."

"I'm healed," she protested. And she was. She hated to tell him that slamming into two walls was nothing.

She said, "I know how good you are at your job, and I don't mean to sound unimpressed, but why didn't Parker kill us when he had the chance?"

"Thanks," Griffin said, his eyebrows lifting in amusement. "I think he was planning on using us as hostages against Harding."

"That *asshole*." No wonder Griffin wanted him dead. She remembered being on the ground and listening to them talk, but she couldn't recall what they said.

Griffin leaned forward and checked her head. "How's your skull?"

"Hard as a rock," she replied and waved him away. "What did Parker tell you?"

Griffin's expression turned serious. "Nothing important."

She blinked at him. He was lying to her. Why? Was he cutting her out? It wasn't just her pride that was hurt. And then it occurred to her that whatever they'd talked about might be something he didn't want to face himself. There was a whole lot of history between them. "Are you going to hunt him down now?"

Griffin shrugged. "Probably."

Foreboding loomed. "He'll kill you next time. He won't talk."

Griffin didn't reply, which concerned her even more. "You can't take him down alone. You'll need Shifters."

He looked away from her, and she felt the distance between them grow. He said, "My wife knew it was him, not me."

Oh God. His ex knew it was Parker that she was sleeping with? What next? How much more could Griffin take? She didn't know, but if she didn't do something, it would consume him. Anger would eat him alive and steal any chance of a life. She sat up in the bed. "Then she's an idiot. You can't change that."

"He ran up all my charge cards with her. For her and she knew it," Griffin said. The look of betrayal in his eyes reached all the way to his soul.

She put her hand on his cheek. "You can't change that."

"XCEL locked me up for four months because of him," Griffin said.

"You can't change the past," she said. "You can't live in it either."

He focused on her. "You should hate us all for trying to exterminate you."

His insight startled her. "I do, but it's not like I can kill you *all*. Besides, I don't have a choice. I have nowhere else to go. *We* have nowhere else to live. I'm stuck with you."

For long moments, they sat in silence. She waited. Waited for him to finish whatever it was he didn't want to say.

"Harding was behind protecting him," Griffin said. "That's how he came back from the dead."

"I know," she said, and then smiled. "I don't need to be one hundred percent healed to kill Harding."

Griffin turned and kissed the palm of her hand, sending jolts of excitement through her body. "Aristotle already has Shifters on him." He pressed his lips to the inside of her wrist. "All we have to do is say the word."

She sighed at his sensual pull on her. "Then I'm saying it," she told him. "This has to stop. I'll do it myself."

Griffin pushed her back on the bed and climbed over her slowly. "I appreciate that, but you'd be at the end of a long line. Besides, we need him right where he is."

She accepted Griffin's weight and the line of kisses he planted down her throat. Her hands spread across his shoulders and back, drawing heat with every stroke. "Why?"

His teeth nipped at her earlobe. "I have a plan."

That sounded vaguely promising. She tugged at his shirt. "Does it involve murder and mayhem?"

He pulled his shirt over his head and leaned on his elbows over her. His eyes were dark and focused on her, and only her. His breathing was deep and fast. "Definitely. Are you ready?"

Cam slid her thigh between his legs, reveling in the hard length of him. She was born ready for him. "Try me."

◆◆◆

Braxton had his little moles.

He walked through the corridors of the facility that he called home with a definite spring in his step. The white walls, floors, and ceilings were as sterile looking as they were clean. Every surface gleamed. This was a research facility, after all. He didn't need a degree in chemistry to understand that one mistake, one broken beaker, one slip could mean death to all of them.

He ran this place with military precision. Today, it had paid off. He pushed open the steel doors that marked the outer part of the laboratory. Signs warned of danger everywhere. He donned a mask, gloves, a thin disposable jumpsuit, and booties.

Then he entered the containment cell that puffed air at him until it was sure he was not a threat. The door into the lab opened with a loud hiss, and he marched into the circular room where two beaten and bloodied lab techs were tied to chairs in the center of the room. Braxton addressed the armed guard standing over them. "Did you get anything out of them?"

"Just that they got their orders from someone underground, sir."

Braxton eyed them. "They must have gotten paid somehow."

"Neither of them took any money. We checked their finances. Nothing unusual."

Braxton turned his attention to his two spies. Why the hell would they risk certain death for nothing? Fucking idiots.

"Are either one of them Shifters?" he asked.

"If they are, they didn't try to shift during interrogation."

Braxton nodded. That made it a lot easier. He'd probably gotten everything he was going to get out of them. His men were all well trained. "Kill them and dispose of the bodies."

"Yes, sir."

He left the room feeling mighty good. The moles were neutralized, which would get Harding off his ass and protect his communications. All he needed now was someone to clear him to kill Shifters.

TWENTY-SIX

G riffin sat beside Ernest at the computers as they processed their algorithms or whatever the hell Ernest's computers did.

He was tired. He'd stayed with Cam for hours while she was unconscious, waiting and hoping she'd come back to him. The strain was more than he'd imagined, sitting there helplessly and hating himself for what he'd done to her.

Leaving Parker alive wasn't anywhere near as bad as that. He didn't want Cam to know he let Parker go either. He didn't want her to blame herself, and she would. Besides, there would be another day for him and Parker. In the meantime, he'd left her alone to get some well-deserved sleep while he tried to come up with a plan to get inside the facility. He felt more tired just thinking about it. Even Ernest looked like he'd aged ten years since they came down here a few days ago.

Ernest yawned and said, "I tried, but I haven't found a way in that doesn't include everyone dying."

"We have their bombs," Griffin suggested.

Ernest eyed him. "And if we screw it up, any toxin they've got gets blown into the atmosphere and everyone's turning to jelly."

That was true. The bombs weren't going to do them any good, as much as Griffin was tempted to use them. If for nothing else than the poetic justice of it all.

Ernest stared at the computer screen and shook his head. "There's no underground level that we can access. However, there are guards and guns aplenty. This place is like a fortress."

"We have the security keys from Aristotle's insiders," Griffin said.

"As of today, but the keys change weekly. That leaves us two days to plan and execute an attack."

Griffin frowned. Was he missing something? "Can't you get the new keys next week?"

Ernest rubbed his eyes. "Our two insiders went silent yesterday."

"And you're just telling me this now?" Griffin said.

"Hey, I've been a little busy here," Ernest replied testily. "It's not like I'm sitting here playing solitaire, you know?"

He couldn't blame Ernest. They were all edgy. "Sorry."

Ernest relaxed in his chair. "Naw, I should have told you. Christ, my life is a goddamned mess."

He commiserated. "Sorry about that too."

"It was my choice. Did you ever imagine that you'd be in cahoots with the Shifters?" Ernest asked.

Griffin eyed him. "*Cahoots?* Really?"

Ernest grinned and then laughed. "Cahoots. And fuck you."

Griffin slapped him on the back. "Go get a few hours sleep, bud. Before you fall over."

"Can't, too much to do," Ernest said. "Like figure out a plan of attack."

Griffin studied the monitor. If they couldn't sneak in, maybe they should try something more obvious. "What if we made a special delivery?"

"What'd you have in mind?" Ernest asked.

He smiled at Ernest. "Everyone needs toilet paper."

◆◆◆

Parker had failed.

"You said this would be easy," Harding told him on the phone. "You said you'd have them in one day. What happened?"

"What *happened*?" Parker said, sounding surprisingly shaken. "Griffin happened. Since when does he have the power to take out Shifters single-handed?"

Harding opened the curtains in his home office as dawn etched rooftops in his upscale neighborhood. "What are you talking about?"

"He froze me," Parker said. "He grabbed my arm, and I couldn't move. Couldn't shift, couldn't do anything. Almost killed me."

Harding sat down in his chair and tried to decide if Parker was lying to cover his ass or if he was telling the truth. Working with criminals did have its downside. "You're sure it was *him*? It wasn't some drug he gave you or some weapon—"

"Trust me. One hand," Parker said, and actually stuttered. "He zapped me or something. I don't know where it came from, but it totally incapacitated me. You got any weapons in your arsenal that can do that?"

XCEL had nothing like that. Which meant that Parker was telling the truth, or at least he thought so. Could someone—a human, at that—really have that kind of effect on Shifters? It suddenly all made sense why Mercer was so good at his job. Not only could he see them, he could stop them.

Parker blathered on. "And don't even ask me to go back down there. You can keep your money. I'm out of here."

Harding said, "I protected you—"

"I don't need your protection," Parker snapped.

Harding pursed his lips. They both knew that Parker could disappear at will and no one would ever find him. There was no point in threatening him anymore. "Did you at least find where they operate out of?"

"What's it worth to you?" Parker asked, getting his balls back.

Harding bluffed. "You get the satisfaction of knowing that Mercer will die."

"Deal. I'll text you the location, and that's the end. We're even, and we're done." Then he hung up.

Harding pressed the End Call key, feeling better than he had in days. He could get rid of his last obstacle and move forward with no one standing in his way. He held his breath as the incoming text from Parker downloaded—directions to the location. Parker must really want Mercer dead to actually follow through without money or something equally valuable.

Harding viewed the location and felt a wave of victory. All the trouble had been worth it for this one moment. He logged into the computer on his desk and ran the directions through the underground maps he had. Then he traced a trail to the surface—

streets, buildings, sewers—until he found what he was looking for. Two manholes fed the tunnels that the Shifters were holed up in.

He dialed Braxton's cell phone. The man answered far too awake for five A.M. "I already told you everything was set, Harding."

"Do you ever sleep?" Harding asked.

"No. Now what do you want?"

Harding leaned back, enjoying himself immensely. "It's time. I'm sending you the coordinates for two manholes in Manhattan. Fill them with gas."

There was a long pause. "Are you fucking serious? You know it's not ready. We haven't even tested the last batch. It could kill everyone."

"Make sure our sewer trucks are perfect replicates. We don't want anything that looks suspicious," he continued. "Every detail has to be right."

"Jesus," Braxton said. "There are humans living down there."

Drug addicts and homeless people. "They're already worthless."

That didn't pacify Braxton. "And what if it leaks out? What if Shifters start dropping dead on the street? What if *we* start dropping?"

"If you do it right, you won't have to worry about it. The gas is heavy. It'll find its way to the lowest point and settle. And it can do something we can't—get in the nooks and crannies where they hide."

Braxton gave a loud sigh. "The underground is a big area, Harding. Miles upon miles. We've got about twenty gallons of this formula. It's not like we're cranking this stuff out yet."

That would be enough to wipe out his Shifters, and if he was lucky, Mercer too. "Then it's a good thing you only have two manholes to cover. As soon as possible, Braxton."

"*I'll* say when," Braxton said. "I'm not risking my men so you can get your breaking news story for the press. We'll do it at night. Less traffic, fewer people, even fewer cops, and no headaches for me."

Harding hated waiting, but he'd have to. Braxton was right. No one could know about this. If the senate committee got wind of anything done without their approval, his hands would be tied for months. He wouldn't risk that.

"I want to be online when you do it," he said.

"I know this is your big moment," Braxton said belligerently.

"No," Harding replied. "My big moment will be when they're all dead."

He hung up, feeling powerful and in control.

◆◆◆

"He went into a coma this morning. I'm sorry," Aristotle said to her, but Cam was still reeling from the news. Her father lay in a cot before her, unmoving and barely breathing.

She knew he was sick, and he didn't have long to live. But to actually see it, to watch it happen—that was something she was unprepared for.

"What does a coma mean for a Shifter?" Ernest asked, standing next to her.

"If he was in Shifter form, it'd mean he'd go into a state of stasis. He could survive for quite a while like that," Aristotle answered. "But in human form—"

He didn't finish, and he didn't need to.

"Crap," Ernest said with panic and sympathy in his eyes. "I need more time to find Thaniel. I'm not getting anything on my searches. I need more time."

She put her hand on his arm. "It's okay. Really."

Ernest appeared ready to cry. He gave a mighty sniffle and left the room. She watched him go, tears filling her eyes. There had to be a way. She turned to Aristotle. "I'll give him all my blood."

Aristotle shook his head. "No, Camille."

"Then some of it. It might give Ernest the time he needs," she insisted.

Aristotle replied, "It won't. You know that."

She closed her eyes and felt the tears burn down her face. Her heart ached. She couldn't lose him. "I didn't get to say good-bye."

"He knows," Aristotle said. "Griffin, take her."

She opened her eyes to find Griffin standing with them. His expression was concerned and sad. She could blame him for this, and she was tempted. But he wasn't to blame. No one was. Time was her enemy.

"I'm not leaving," she said, staring down Griffin.

"Aristotle, ask your medic to keep a watch on him," Griffin said as he walked toward her. "If you need any medical supplies, let me know." Then he turned to her and his voice was rough. "I'm sorry, Cam."

She hated them all. She hated the pain. It had happened too many times. To her and to her people. All this time, everything she'd done, she'd done it to save her father. For nothing. It would never change. Nothing she did would ever make it better. She'd die too—either by Harding's gas or some other horrible weapon he came up with. They'd all die. Every Shifter on this planet was doomed.

Cam pushed by him and ran out of the room. The tunnels felt claustrophobic and dark, like a prison cell. And it was. This is where her people had been relegated to. A place for rats and the unwanted fringes of society.

Griffin caught up with her, and she swung at him in an attempt to get away. He ducked and wrapped her up tight in his arms. She let out a shuddering cry and felt her heart rip open and spill out. She sobbed until her chest hurt. Griffin held her and whispered in her ear that it would be okay.

But he didn't know it would be okay. He didn't know what tomorrow would bring, any more than she did. She didn't have any more tricks up her sleeve, no more luck left. She'd played herself out.

Griffin stroked her hair. "I promise you that I will do everything in my power to keep him alive."

She appreciated his attempt to make her feel better, and tears pooled in her eyes. "Wishing doesn't make it so, Griffin. If it did, I'd be with my family."

"I guess we'll have to do for now," he said.

She leaned into him, letting him support her. It felt scary and good at the same time. She wanted to remind him that they were being hunted down, that the odds of any of them surviving were next to nothing. But he felt strong and safe, and for the moment, so did she.

TWENTY-SEVEN

"I am so not ready for this," Ernest said, looking nervous—and, therefore, frighteningly dangerous—holding a rifle in his hands.

Griffin reached over and repositioned Ernest's trigger finger. "Straight along the barrel until you need it, remember?"

"I'm going to kill somebody," he murmured.

Cam said, "As long as you don't aim it toward any of us."

The three of them were huddled together along with six of Aristotle's best men in the back of a delivery truck. Ernest had managed to locate an incoming shipment of supplies, and they'd nabbed the truck along its route. The driver was locked up safe underground.

"Tell me again why I'm here?" Ernest asked.

"Because I need you to access their computer systems," Griffin said. "Just don't get shot, okay?"

Ernest blew out a long breath. "Shot, Jesus."

The truck jerked to a stop at the gate, and Griffin could hear the driver talking to the guard. They idled for what seemed like forever until finally the truck moved forward.

"Masks," Griffin whispered to the Shifters. They donned their masks and then shifted to Primary Shifter form, sealing the masks to their faces. There was no guarantee the masks would work, but it was worth a try. Despite the risks, every Shifter had volunteered for this gig. Griffin was more impressed with them by the hour.

Ernest peered at him through the giant goggles. He was wearing every bit of armor he could find. It was pretty entertaining. "What?"

Griffin tightened his chest armor. "I hate masks."

Cam handed him one. "Don't make me hold you down to put it on."

He grinned slowly. "I don't know, that's pretty tempting."

Her eyes narrowed, but she smiled. "Maybe later."

He could only hope. Right now, he'd be happy to live through the next ten minutes. He took the mask from her and slipped it over his head.

The truck made a left turn around the side of the building, and Griffin motioned everyone into position. His makeshift team was as ready as they were going to be. They formed three lines, tightly stacked together at the rear door. The three biggest Shifters were first in line. They'd clear the way for the others.

Griffin and Ernest were at the end of the line—the cleanup crew. Two more Shifter teams were ready and waiting near each of the other entrances to the building. Griffin's team would get inside, open the doors, and let them in. The plan had been worked out ahead of time, and each person had a job to do. His job was to keep Ernest alive.

Of course, like all his other missions, that carefully crafted plan would survive intact for about thirty seconds. Still, it was a plan, and he was sticking to it.

The truck came to a stop, made a beeping noise, and moved in reverse, backing up to the dock. Griffin cast a quick look at Cam. She focused on the door, unarmed like the rest of the Shifters, and second behind the lead Shifter in her line. He wanted to tell her to be careful, to get out if things went bad. But he knew she wouldn't even if he begged. These were *her* people, and she was risking it all to save them.

He pushed aside the concern and noted that he was risking it all too. Why? In the beginning, it had been personal. Over the past few days, that dream had all but disappeared. To stop Harding? Definitely part of it, although there would be other Hardings.

Then he cut a glance to Cam just as she turned to look at him and smiled. In that quick exchange, he had all the reason he needed.

The truck stopped, and Griffin heard voices on the other side of the door. Everyone in the truck was motionless and silent, and time slowed. There was a loud *thump* at the door handle, and a few seconds later the roller door began to lift up.

As soon as the door was chest high, they exited in a fluid wave. The Shifters moved fast, disappearing in front of him in a puff of smoke. He tracked them with his vision as they took out the four men working the dock in a matter of seconds and used zip-strips to restrain hands and feet. *Damn.* He wished he had these guys working for him all the time.

"Stay behind me," he said to Ernest. He scanned the docking area. So far the layout matched the building schematics. Maybe this once, everything would go smoothly.

Suddenly, one of the doors to the dock burst open and three black-garbed guards came through. Bullets flew, and Shifters scattered. Alarms wailed loudly.

"Down!" he said to Ernest, who dropped to his knees in a flash. Griffin knelt in front of him and peppered the guards with his assault rifle.

Glass windows shattered, and the *pop-pop-pop* of gunfire echoed in the dock staging area. The guards, however well trained, didn't stand a chance against Shifters.

"Go!" Griffin yelled to his team. They split up—Griffin's group moved through the security office positioned between the docking area and the administrative offices. The other two groups took the doors that led into a garage and the main laboratory.

Braxton's men appeared from every corner, it seemed, but the Shifters mowed them down. Griffin let them go ahead and stayed with Ernest, who'd found a wall of computers and monitors in the security office. The monitors showed the Shifters moving through the facility. Red flashing alarm lights created a surreal strobe effect.

"Any sign of the gas?" he asked Ernest.

Ernest shook his head and pulled off his goggles. "Appears clear."

Griffin caught a flash of Cam in one of the monitors, and then she was gone. She'd be okay, he told himself for the hundredth time. But he wasn't with her. He couldn't protect her. He realized that this was his future. Regardless of what she'd said, humans were and would always be her enemy. This place alone confirmed that.

With a pang of sadness and clarity, he realized that she belonged with her own people. They needed her, and she needed them. She was their only storyteller. The only one who could ground them in this unfriendly world. There was no place for him there. And then he realized what Sani was saying. He would have to sacrifice the one thing he wanted more than anything else in order for her to survive.

Then the alarms shut off, and Griffin welcomed the silence. "Thank you."

Ernest nodded, hunkered over the keyboard and mouse, and worked fast. "No problem. Accessing the network now."

Both of the other outside doors had been opened, and the two teams of Shifters rushed in, securing their designated areas. The facility personnel capitulated quickly and were tied up with zip-strips. The whole takedown took less than five minutes.

That had gone far better than he'd imagined, and it worried him. If Harding was so hot to get this gas generated, there should be more people here.

"How many guards did we take out?" he asked aloud.

"I counted eight," Ernest murmured, zoned out in computer land.

That's what he counted too, and that was way too low. "We're missing about ten guards," he told Ernest. "Where are they?"

"I don't know," Ernest said, tapping away. "Give me a sec. Looking for a roster or work schedule now."

Griffin leaned forward and cycled through all the surveillance cameras. Nothing. If there were guards hiding, they were in the bathrooms or they'd snuck out some other way.

Cam came into the security office, back in human form. She was smiling in victory, but her smile faded when she saw him. "What's wrong?"

He hit his comm unit and said to the Shifters, "Check every room, every closet. We're missing ten security staff."

Her eyes widened. "Missing? Do you know that for sure?"

"Should be eighteen or so on a normal schedule," he said, cycling through the monitors again. "This is a skeleton crew."

"Goddamn," Ernest said. "These time tracking records are a frickin' mess. How do these people even get paid?"

Cam moved next to Griffin as he studied each camera view. The answer was here somewhere, he could feel it. Then he stopped on the view of the garage used for the facility's own trucks and other vehicles.

Cam leaned closer. "Where are the trucks?"

That was it. There were oil spots on the floor, but the garage was empty.

"Ernest?" he said.

"On it."

◆ ◆ ◆

Harding paced back and forth in front of the roaring fireplace in his home office with Braxton on his cell phone. He could hear Braxton talking to his men and loud noises. They'd positioned themselves over the two manholes at each corner of the intersection along the route he'd laid out. A protective white tent had been erected over each manhole. Cones and blockades had been set up around the trucks. The hoses were positioned deep underground. So what was taking so damn long?

"Just pump the stuff into the hole," he told Braxton.

There was a rustle, and then Braxton came back into view on his phone. "Why don't you come down here and give this a try? It's not as easy as you think. There are people out on the streets, there's traffic, and it stinks to high heaven."

Minor details, Harding thought. "If you don't start pumping soon, I will come down there myself."

"Right," Braxton said. "Just sit tight. This is my turf. I'm giving the orders here."

There was a *clunk* as Braxton set the phone down, and Harding let out a hiss of frustration. Everything he'd worked for was about to come to fruition, and the anticipation was eating at him.

This city was about to become his again. The gas would flow underground for miles in every direction, killing Shifters for days, even weeks. The others would be forced aboveground where XCEL could catch them. New York City would become a no-fly zone for Shifters.

Once the senate committee announced their findings and pinned the attacks on the Shifters, XCEL would be free to target Shifters everywhere. The thought of it brought a smile to his lips.

"Okay, we're ready. Breathing apparatus, everyone," Braxton was saying.

Harding felt his pulse jump. He stood in front of the fire, feeling the warmth on his face.

"Open the valve."

Harding held his breath.

"Valve open. Gas is releasing."

There was a loud hissing sound through the phone. The gas was flowing. Harding could barely contain his pleasure.

"So far, so good," Braxton said, picking up the phone and pointing it toward the manhole for Harding to see.

A full load was enough to kill hundreds of Shifters. Harding imagined their alien bodies bloating and dying. No one would know what happened to them, even if they did find corpses. No one would know that he was the one responsible for saving this city. He could live with that.

Suddenly, there was a loud bang and flash of light. Braxton's phone toppled to the ground, and someone screamed. Harding heard Braxton yell, "Run! Run!"

"What happened?" he yelled into the phone. "Braxton!"

More loud bangs rang out. People were yelling and coughing. It sounded like Braxton was running. The image in the phone showed a blur of streets and fire. "It exploded!"

Harding felt the rage rise in his throat. "What exploded?"

"Underground!" Braxton started coughing. He peered into the phone, shaking and gasping for breath. "Must have—Must have hit a bad power cable."

Rage turned to dismay. It was something Harding hadn't considered before, but it happened with manholes in the city. Power cables aged and touched. Gases exploded. *His* gas exploded. It was one thing they hadn't tested with their formula. Now his gas would blow out all over the city.

"Harding? What do we do?" Braxton said, looking into the phone. His gas mask was broken, and blood flowed down the side of his head in a steady stream. Behind him was chaos and screams.

"Harding!" Braxton yelled, falling to his knees. Then he went silent and let go of the phone. It rattled a few times before pointing up into the night sky.

Harding pressed the End Call button and tossed his cell phone into the fire. Everything inside him turned cold. The plan had failed. He couldn't allow his anger to overtake the moment. He was still in control, and there was work to be done, files to remove, an airtight case to be maintained around him. Then he sat at his computer and went to work.

◆◆◆

Behind her gas mask, Cam saw the first explosion burst from the manhole, ripping through the tent and throwing flames and people everywhere. The intersection lit up, blinding her momentarily.

Men ran from the truck yelling. A second explosion totaled the truck and blew out the windows of the apartments and storefronts on the corner. Flying shrapnel pelted concrete and flesh.

They were too late.

Griffin and one group of Shifters ran toward the first explosion. She and the rest of the Shifters ran for the second truck. If they could get there in time to turn off the gas . . .

She didn't even get to finish her thought before the second manhole belched forth smoke and fire. Braxton's men stumbled away, clutching their face masks. A large section of hose dropped from the sky right beside her. Thick, green liquid oozed from it as it rolled across the intersection.

Her heart sank. The gas was already in the ground. Her father . . . He'd die for certain. Aristotle and his supporters. And the others, Shifters trying to survive underground.

She yelled into her comm unit to Red, who was holding down the underground fort. "Get everyone out, Red! The gas is in the ground! Get out!"

It was all she could do for them, and she had to push past the fear in her heart. She needed to focus, to make sure everyone knew her people didn't do this, or they'd all be doomed. She wouldn't let that happen again.

People living in the apartments over the businesses on the corner were pouring down the stairs and out into the street. She ran toward them to warn them to flee, but they took one look at her and the other shapeshifters in their native form and screamed in terror. More explosions from underground blew open manholes down the street. Flames shot out from one building. It was like a war zone.

She stood in the middle of the street, feeling helpless in the face of the nightmarish scene.

"Cam! Go!"

She turned to find Griffin waving at her. That's when she noticed that some of Braxton's men were rolling on the ground, coughing. What the hell?

"It's the gas!" Griffin shouted as he ran toward her. "It kills humans too."

Then she realized the downed men's gas masks were compromised. They were dying. That wasn't supposed to happen. It was just the Shifters. Did Harding know that? How could he knowingly do this? It was numbing, inconceivable even for him.

Griffin reached her and dragged her by the hand, but she pulled him to a stop. She pointed to the people pouring out of the apartments. "Those people are going to die."

"Too late, Cam," Griffin said. He wasn't wearing a mask, and he was already coughing. He couldn't stay here, but she could. Her Shifters could. It wasn't too late. They were going to save as many people as they could. This had to stop.

"You get out!" She shoved him away and pointed down the

street. "Go! Call 911. Set up a perimeter. We'll bring them out to you."

Griffin coughed, and she hit him hard in the chest, throwing him back. He stumbled, landing ten feet away.

She didn't wait; she ran into the center of the intersection and started dragging people away from the infernos. The other Shifters followed her lead. One by one, they deposited the unconscious humans half a block away. Each trip, she searched for Griffin but didn't see any sign of him. Hopefully, he'd done what she'd asked and was coordinating a perimeter.

Cam concentrated on her own job, racing through the halls and rooms of the buildings and apartments looking for more people. She lost count of how many people she moved out of harm's way.

Sirens wailed in the distance, bringing with them the risk of discovery, blame, and retaliation for her and the other shapeshifters. But she needed her more powerful Shifter form as she carried people over her shoulders, two at time, and ran with them to relative safety. Every manhole in this city was now a potential bomb. This could turn into a disaster of biblical proportions.

Cam went back five times before she started to feel the effects of the gas despite her protective mask. It burned her lungs and scattered her acute Shifter senses. The last of the people were dragged away, and she told the other Shifters to escape while they still could.

She was about to do the same when she noticed a homeless man curled up in a ball behind a parked car.

"Crap," she whispered and felt the rawness of her throat.

She headed toward him, feeling light-headed, like her feet

weren't touching the ground. The man's eyes were rolled up into his head when she reached him.

"I got you," she said, and pulled him up over her shoulder. Her Shifter knees buckled a little. It was only one small man, she must be tired.

Her vision began to fail as she walked the man away from the intersection. Every step became harder, requiring more concentration just to keep moving. Fog hindered her thoughts. The concrete floated by her. Were her feet even touching the ground? Alarm arose in her mind.

Faster, she thought, *need to go faster.* Then she faltered and felt the sidewalk, solid and unforgiving, beneath her feet. The city swayed around her. She stumbled and fell but managed to protect the man from hitting the concrete. She rolled onto her back, everything spinning. Overhead, the night sky was dark and clear. The city noise faded into the distance.

I want to fly, she thought.

The night sky drew closer as if she were being lifted up.

Take me home.

And then the night swallowed her whole.

TWENTY-EIGHT

t was the morning after. Harding had cleaned out all the files, records, anything else that could possibly or remotely link him to the tragedy playing out across his television. The scenes being reported by TV stations were aglow with flashing lights. Blankets over the dead. Ambulances came and went. Underground explosions were still going off in the streets.

He relaxed with his coffee in a chair by the fire, watching it unfold with deliberate calm. It had occurred to him over the past few hours that he didn't need the report to the senate committee to do what he'd done. He never needed anyone's blessing. His plan had gone through exactly as he'd wanted. Better, even.

They were already blaming the explosions and deaths on the Shifters. There was no one left to argue for them. He'd killed the underground Shifters, Mercer, Camille, Vincent—all the traitors. Braxton and his men were dead. The facility would simply shut down with no one there to run it.

Even if someone discovered the gas, they wouldn't know where it came from. Harding had been right to make sure the final product was known only to a few. The lead scientist would know by now that he was responsible for this and keep his mouth shut. If not, well, Harding had already made sure that the mastermind finger was pointed directly at him.

The doorbell rang. He glanced at the clock. It was nine A.M. in the morning so the visitor was probably one of his wife's friends. She was in the kitchen, and he let her answer it. Voices rang out, his wife protested, and Harding heard the distinct clicking of weapons and heavy footsteps up the stairs to his office.

XCEL agents. It was unusual, but he *was* the director of the local XCEL unit. He'd already been contacted with the details of the attack. They were simply here as protection or had pressing information for him.

He set down his coffee cup and stood to meet them. The first man through his office door was Roberts, followed by three fully armed XCEL agents. Harding was more than a little surprised to see his former right-hand man.

They'd come for him. It was much sooner than he'd expected, but not unexpected either. They could *try* to involve him in this, but they'd fail. Even if they suspected, there was no proof. This was America, after all. He was protected by the most powerful, bureaucratic, and slow-moving justice system in the world. This would be nothing more than a necessary glitch. All he had to do was keep his cool, and when they finally cleared him, it would be over. Except for the dead Shifters.

"What is the meaning of this, Agent Roberts?"

Roberts held up a white piece of paper. "I have a subpoena to search all your properties. Your home, your office, car, everything."

Harding wanted to laugh. "And what are you looking for?"

"Your involvement in the deaths of fourteen humans and shapeshifters," Roberts said firmly. "So far."

Harding pointed to the television. "How could I possibly be involved with something like that? I haven't left my home all night."

Roberts didn't budge, didn't blink. He had a hell of a poker face, Harding admitted. Let them look. Harding asked, "Would you care for some coffee?"

"No," Roberts said. Then he smiled. "How about you, Griffin?"

Harding frowned. It couldn't be. He was dead.

"Not me." Mercer walked into the room and stood next to Roberts. He was filthy from head to toe and grinning. "Thirsty, Cam?"

Harding felt his heart pound in his chest as the shapeshifter took her place next to Mercer. In his own house. *His* home.

"Not for coffee," she said and batted her eyelashes. "But perhaps blood."

He clenched his fists with a fury so strong it hurt. His own people had turned on him. Against their own kind. Didn't they understand what was at stake here? Didn't they realize that the whole human race was going to be diluted by these creatures and that the future of man was in mortal danger?

"It gets better," Mercer said. "We know about the facility."

"And the gas," Camille added. "And the copycat attacks."

He felt his expression falter despite his best efforts to stay cool. "You still have to prove it."

She crossed her arms. "We also have Braxton. He's been more than cooperative."

Harding stared at Cam, feeling the pressure building. "You have no right to be here."

"And yet," she said, "here I am. Taking you into custody. Life's a bitch."

Anger exploded in his head, and he lunged for her throat. He stumbled forward when she vanished in a puff of black smoke. Two men grabbed him by the arms and threw him to the ground, face-first. Mercer was one of them and said, "Don't give me a reason to shoot you, Harding. 'Cause I only need one."

Harding felt a knee to his back and his hands pulled behind his back. He roared in rage.

Then Roberts said, "Director Harding, your services are no longer required. You are under arrest."

◆◆◆

Cam held her father's hand in the sterile laboratory, watching his chest rise and fall. Her brother, Thaniel, sat on the opposite side, holding Dewey's other hand.

And they waited to see if they were able to bring their father back from the dead. The transfusion had been performed. There was nothing else she could do now but hope. He'd opened his eyes once, and then closed them. Still, it was a very good sign.

It had been a grueling few days between recovering from the damage the gas had done to her, reuniting with her brother, fighting off the media, and being grilled by every government agency wanting to get in on the action. She was beyond tired, hadn't slept in days, and yet, she was still thinking clearly.

Something had changed in her body, but she couldn't figure out what. She was tougher now, healed faster, moved quicker. Every Shifter sense had grown stronger and more powerful. It was like she'd been given a booster shot by her own body. Not that she was complaining.

"Never thought I'd see you again," Thaniel said quietly. "I meant to contact you, but I—" He stopped. "I'm sorry."

She lifted her gaze from her father to her brother. He looked handsome with brown hair and blue eyes. He was dressed casually and wore a wedding ring. "No, *I'm* sorry. I didn't listen to you. I didn't want to get involved with the humans."

Even as she said it, her chest tightened at the thought of one particular human. She hadn't seen or spoken to Griffin in the past few days once he'd disappeared into the XCEL fraternity.

"Well, humans aren't as trustworthy as I thought they'd be," he said. "You were right about that."

"But some of them are loyal to the end," she countered, nodding toward his wedding band.

They smiled at each other, and she said, "What a pair we are."

He chuckled, and it was like they'd never been apart. She told him, "Thank you for finding us. You saved him."

Thaniel shook his head. "I didn't save him. You did. All I did was see you on the news and show up. You're the one who never gave up."

"You think I want to get stuck telling all those Shifter stories?" she said.

He laughed. "Me neither." Then he sobered. "It was a great thing you did. For all of us. You could have died."

And she would have if that's what it took. "Someone had to protect our people."

He nodded in quiet understanding. "What do you think is going to happen to us now?"

Cam drew a breath. "I don't know, but we have everyone's attention now. Harding did something truly horrific by any standards in an effort to get rid of us. The government is under a lot of pressure from the American public to make it right."

"You really think they'll give us citizenship?" he asked.

"Perhaps," she said. "Anything's possible."

Cam checked Dewey's vital signs on the monitors again. He was getting stronger, there was no doubt about that, but he was still slow to come around. Perhaps that was a good thing. He could concentrate on healing himself, fighting the unseen battle waging in his DNA.

"I think it's my turn to take care of him," Thaniel said.

She turned and blinked at him. "What? Why?"

He reached across their father and put his hand over hers. "I have a nice place to live. A woman who loves me. A good job. I want to take care of him. I owe him, and you, that much."

Cam didn't know what to say. She'd never considered leaving her father, not unless he left her first. But for some reason, she wasn't afraid of that now. He would be okay, she knew it in her bones.

Thaniel removed his hand and leaned back in his chair with a deliberate smile. "Besides, I saw the way your XCEL agent looked at you."

How did he look at her? She hadn't noticed. It didn't change things though. "He's a Shifter hunter. He'll always be that."

"Didn't he just arrest a bunch of humans too?" her brother asked. "I guess that makes him a bad-guy hunter."

That was true, but he was still working for XCEL. They generally only hunted Shifters, and she doubted they would change, especially now in the midst of this mess. "We're from different worlds."

"Well, duh, aren't we all? You just don't want to get involved," he said. "Still."

Cam sighed. "You're right."

His eyebrows went up. "Wow."

Her eyes narrowed at him. "Don't start."

He raised his hands. "Not a word. You've changed."

"How?" she asked warily.

Thaniel tilted his head as he studied her Shifter form. "I don't know, but you look different."

She nodded. "My body feels different."

"Have you talked to anyone about it?" he asked.

"I talked to Aristotle. He feels great. Stronger, and he can even shift again."

"What about the others?"

"Same thing," she said. "Every Shifter that survived the gas has become more powerful. I think the gas changed us a little. Made us stronger."

Thaniel blew out a long breath. "That's a scary thought. Just don't grow a second head, okay? You'll never get a man if you've got two heads."

It was her turn to laugh. She'd missed her brother so much. "How do you think Harding will react when he finds out he only succeeded in making shapeshifters more powerful?"

"I hope it kills him."

She did too.

"How's the old man doing?" Ernest asked from behind her. She turned to find him looking more rested than he'd been in days. At least he was wearing clean clothes today. He walked over and shook her brother's hand before moving beside her.

"He's getting better with every passing hour," she said and smiled at him. "How about you?"

He grinned. "Same here. This morning, Griffin and I finished up the last of the interrogations and gazillion questions. I got paperwork coming out my ass. I'm just waiting for someone to give me my computers back."

She pressed her lips together. "Where's Griffin now?"

Ernest stared down at his feet. "He left."

Left? "Do you know where he went?"

Ernest made a face. "He didn't tell me. He just said he had something to take care of."

Her mood sank as she absorbed the news. Did he go after Parker? On his own? He said he would. He could have gotten Parker's location from Harding and set out to kill him once and for all. As if that could change the past. She should have known that he couldn't let go of the anger and the injustice.

"However," Ernest continued, rocking on his heels, "I did manage to get a line on his travel plans."

"And?" she asked, almost afraid to. What would she do anyway? Follow him? He didn't want her there.

"He got on a flight to Arizona," Ernest said, grinning from ear to ear.

She shook her head, not getting it. "What's in Arizona?"

"His family," Ernest said.

And then it hit her. *Sani.* Sani was in Arizona. His family, his people. He'd gone home. Her heart swelled, feeling like it was filling her body. He didn't go after Parker. He wasn't seeking revenge.

The tears broke suddenly down her face, and she suddenly felt light as a feather. Free as a bird. Strong as the wind. Complete.

Thaniel looked at her, and then at Ernest, and said, "What the hell did I miss?"

Cam stood up and gave Ernest a hug. Then she looked at her brother. "I love you. Watch Dad. Call me the minute he wakes up."

CHAPTER
TWENTY-NINE

Griffin stood in the desert and marveled at the beauty he'd never noticed before. Sand spread out like a red and ginger blanket between tufts of the mulish sage brush and boulders in Monument Valley. In the distance, he could see the silhouettes of towering variegated buttes against the blue sky. The sun still baked this earth as it had for thousands of years.

He loved it here. Loved the silence and the solitude, and the way the wind felt against his skin. The turmoil of city streets, loud machines, and dead concrete faded away like a ridge in the ever-moving sand. Perhaps one day he would learn to stand still long enough to hear the heartbeat of this timeless place. He'd never realized how incredibly precious it was.

And he couldn't for the life of him figure out why he'd left.

Sani moved beside him, only the shuffle of pants legs giving him away. He stared over the land, blending in perfectly with his brown work pants and tan shirt. His white hair was a little longer.

His face held a few more wrinkles. He looked like the earth itself—weathered and aged but full of wisdom.

They'd ridden the horses out here, and Griffin heard one of them whinny. He didn't know how long he'd been standing there, absorbing the desert into his bones. Minutes, hours—they lost all meaning in this place. But he came here for a reason, and his journey was not over with this stop.

"I'm sorry I disrespected you," he said. "And the land."

Sani nodded slowly. "I know. I have heard your suffering."

Griffin didn't even ask how. But if Sani could hear him, maybe he could help him too. "I have had visions of my own. The Eagle died. I want to bring her back, but I don't know how to save her."

His grandfather kept his gaze on the distant rock formations. "You don't need to save her. Only yourself."

Griffin eyed him. "How will that save *her*?"

Sani smiled. "Does the mouse hate the wind for blocking its tunnels with sand?"

That made no sense at all. "I haven't a clue."

"The wind has a purpose. The sand has a purpose. The mouse has a purpose. None of them are right or wrong. They just are."

Griffin closed his eyes and tried to follow Sani's logic. "So the mouse isn't angry."

"No."

It was the first time Sani had ever answered a direct question with a direct answer. And for the first time, Griffin understood. He heard it deep in his soul, past the place anger and injustice had taken root. There, he found his future waiting for him. It had been all along. He just couldn't see it before.

"Now you can save her," Sani said.

Griffin heard the Eagle cry and opened his eyes. He spun

around in a circle, looking for her. The horses pawed the sand, kicking up a cloud of dust. It was swept away in the wind, and through the dust, a woman walked toward him.

Cam came out of the desert as if from the ancient land itself. The heat of the sun cast her in a mirage that shimmered. But she had changed. Her Shifter shadow was different, the single color mixed with another one.

Was that really her? Was she real? He couldn't tell, but he walked to her anyway. She matched him step for step until they were mere feet away and he could see her face. It was everything he needed.

He reached for her, but she put her arm against his chest, stopping him. Her tone was firm and her expression just as un-yielding as her arm. "That's close enough, Mercer."

So they were back to Mercer, and he remembered that he hadn't exactly said good-bye when he left. Which meant she wasn't pleased at the moment. He had his work cut out for him. Good thing he wasn't going anywhere.

"I came to see Sani," he said, blaming it on Grandfather. Sani would understand.

"Ah," she said, playing surprised. "And where were you plan-ning on going after that?"

"To kill Parker," he said truthfully.

His words had more impact than he'd thought possible, and any playfulness in her retreated in a hurry. Griffin took a deep breath filled with earth and wind into his lungs. When he blew it out, all the anger he'd held on to for so long went with it. "But I decided he wasn't worth it."

Her hand dropped from his chest to her side as she studied him with all seriousness. "What about next week? Will he be worth it then?"

Griffin closed the unbearable space between them and wrapped her beautiful face in his hands so he could look into her eyes. "Not going to change my mind next week. Or the next. It's done."

She pulled a shuddering breath, and he felt her entire body tremble with it. "What about XCEL?"

Griffin was debating whether to start at her neck or just go for the lips. "XCEL can kiss my ass."

She was stock-still, tension holding her like a prisoner. Softly, she asked, "And us?"

He ran his thumb over her smooth cheek, fascinated by everything about her. "I'll go wherever you want. But it's quiet here. We'll be accepted, but not hounded. The climate would be good for your father. And it's a great place to raise kids."

She blinked at him in confusion. "What kids?"

He kissed her lips full on, unable to wait through all her questions. She tasted sweet and soft. He wanted that every day for the rest of his life. He just had to convince her. He broke off the kiss and pressed his forehead to hers. "Our kids."

"But that can't happen," she said. "It's not possible between humans and Shifters."

Griffin watched the second color move in the belly of her Shifter shadow. Happiness flowed over him, pushing everything else aside. "Anything is possible."

When he met her eyes again, they were full of tears. "I know what I want, Cam. I want you."

She smiled through the tears and wrapped her arms around his neck. "I sure hope you're ready for this, because it's not going to be easy."

Nothing worth having ever was. He kissed her to seal the deal.